INVISIBLE SHIELD

INVISIBLE SHIELD

SCARLETT DEAN

FIVE STAR

An imprint of Thomson Gale, a part of The Thomson Corporation

THOMSON
GALE™

Detroit • New York • San Francisco • New Haven, Conn. • Waterville, Maine • London

THOMSON

GALE

LIBRARY OF CONGRESS CATALOGING-IN-PUBLICATION DATA

Dean, Scarlett.
  Invisible shield / Scarlett Dean. — 1st ed.
    p. cm.
    "Published ... in conjunction with Tekno Books and Ed Gorman"—T.p.
verso.
    ISBN-13: 978-1-59414-545-2 (alk. paper)
    ISBN-10: 1-59414-545-8 (alk. paper)
    1. Supernatural—Fiction. 2. Death—Fiction. 3. Future life—Fiction. 4.
Policewomen—Fiction. 5. Homicide investigation—Fiction. I. Title.
PS3604.E1538I58 2007
  813'.6—dc22

                                                            2006035685

First Edition. First Printing: April 2007.

Published in 2007 in conjunction with Tekno Books and Ed Gorman.

Printed in the United States of America on permanent paper
10 9 8 7 6 5 4 3 2 1

For Angella and Christina.

ACKNOWLEDGMENTS

I'd like to thank the following for assisting me in my research:

Retired Assistant Chief of Police (Crown Point, Indiana) William E. Babjak
Deputy Coroner (Lake County, Indiana) Jeffrey R. Wells
The Crown Point, Indiana, Marine Recruitment Center
Charles Ivey, for his extensive weapons knowledge.

A special thank you to David Morrell for soothing my ruffled feathers when I thought I'd crossed the weapons and tactics line.

Muchas gracias to Dan Harris and Clayton Heart for teaching me to swear in Spanish.

My heartfelt appreciation to former First Lieutenant, U.S. Army, Bruce Koziol, for sharing his memories of the Vietnam War.

CHAPTER ONE

God stepped out for a beer on the night I needed him most.

It was *not* dark and stormy. At least not any more. The night was clear and dry after a three-day stretch of rain and I figured I could toss my ark blueprints and get on with life.

The June night remained unusually quiet; looking back, too quiet. No homicides reported, no bodies to view, and my cell phone hadn't chimed the national anthem since I'd pulled out of the precinct lot.

I stuffed my detective shield into my purse hoping I could finally call it a day.

My partner, Gerard Alvarez, rode shotgun in silence as I drove toward his home. The black summer night went on forever and I let the grueling past few weeks slip comfortably into my subconscious.

We'd just wrapped up a brutal case that had taken its physical and emotional toll on the whole department. Little girl, five years old, found six weeks before in a Dumpster. The animal that did it turned out to be a neighbor. Great guy. If tall fences make good neighbors, Anna's parents should have built a fort.

Alvarez leaned back in the seat, closing his eyes. "Glad it's over," he said to the Crown Vic's roof.

"For us and the family." I turned on red. "One less creep on the street."

"Too bad that's all we could do for Anna." He glanced my way.

I knew what he was thinking.

Leaving the station, there'd been no fanfare or reporters salivating for the story, but I knew the child's family was grateful. Closing an investigation doesn't set things right. It can never undo the wrong. But it brings closure and a form of peace to the family and maybe to the victim, too.

I answered my cell phone before "the dawn's early light."

"Frost." I listened carefully to my precinct commander's message. "Gotcha. Thanks for the warning."

"What's going on?" Alvarez sat up.

"Buford Jones has been released."

"When?"

"Today." I checked my rearview mirror. Nothing but a black snake of road lay behind us.

"Did you forget?"

"Not really. Just stuck it too far on the back burner."

"Watch yourself for a couple of days," he warned.

"I'm sure he's forgotten about me by now. His prison time put more pressing issues on his mind. Like survival."

"He's still a snake," Alvarez snarled.

I grinned at his furrowed brow. Alvarez's athletic build is a godsend when chasing down an offender, *and* it provides me with a worthy racquetball opponent. Although he's three years my senior, I've only beaten him twice. The man wears a perpetual frown, even when he smiles. It's a look that serves him well as a detective and can be intimidating, but not to me. Gerard is a pussycat. On the job, he's proven himself loyal to a fault. He's my best friend.

I pulled curbside in front of his bungalow, seeing every light on in the house.

"I'm hurt you didn't invite me to the party," I grinned. His two teenage boys would know better than to pull a stunt like that.

"The kids don't like being alone at night. I get handwritten thank-you cards from the electric company."

"Say hello for me, will you?"

He nodded. "Remember what I said about Buford. Call me when you get home."

I watched him trudge up his walkway to the porch, looking beat.

So was I.

Pulling out, my thoughts of home and a cold beer were interrupted by Alvarez's warning. Buford Jones. The name brought back a shitload of memories from the drawn-out trial five years ago. Buford had a history of slipping through the cracks, but when I'd made the arrest, I'd done everything by the book, and then thrown it at him. Luckily it stuck.

He'd threatened to kill his attorney, Marie Yates, and me, after a guilty verdict involving a drug bust that put him away. For the past couple of weeks, I'd been vaguely aware of his upcoming release, but dealing with Anna had taken every waking moment and most of my mental energy. Now that her case was closed, I hoped my life would get back to its routine. I hit Interstate 65 heading toward my Southfield Heights home.

Working murder investigations outside the larger cities like nearby Chicago has its advantages, like fewer homicides. But Indiana is plagued by its own set of problems that sets the tone for working in violent crimes. For the most part, Indiana is known for its corn crop, and I can live with that, but thanks to a few authors with vivid imaginations, and several prominent ghost-tracking groups, we've been labeled "haunted Indiana."

As a detective, my job involves finding clues and securing hard evidence to prove theories. Professional training has molded my basic school of thought, resulting in one simple rule: if my five senses can't make it real, then it doesn't exist. Don't get me wrong, I've seen plenty of evil in my time, but it has nothing to do with the boogeyman or demons. Unfortunately, mankind is responsible for crimes treacherous enough to make Satan ashamed he didn't think of them.

What I didn't realize was that my disbelief in all things paranormal was about to change.

I pressed the accelerator.

Our division may not get much media attention, and no one has yet offered to write a cop show about us, but we certainly get our share of the action. One of our neighboring towns has joined the ranks of various cities dubbed a "murder capital." All that and I get to drive past cornfields and grazing cows at the end of the day. It's a trade-off, I guess, a little balance on the crazy high wire of life.

Tonight was no different, and I'll admit my guard was down, dwelling on more pleasant activities as I drove. A tall beer, a hot shower, and eight hours of solid sleep stood fifteen minutes away. The deserted streets and black velvet sky invited mental wandering and I compiled a to-do list that would never get done. Laundry, shopping, and an oil change wouldn't stand a chance against sleeping in, dining out, and sex. Not necessarily in that order. Two of the three were a given; the sex might prove challenging.

Hitting the off ramp, my thoughts drifted to my fiancé, George Anderson, and the possible reasons he'd distanced himself lately. It seemed he'd rather spend more time in the basement with his wine collection, caressing his Pinot Grigio. I reviewed our past few months together as an engaged couple for possible clues. Nothing came to mind. Sex had never been better, when we got around to it, and he spent more time at my place than his after trading house keys. I was totally committed, ready to share my bathroom, cook an occasional meal, and legally trade Frost for Anderson.

I'd learned from watching other detectives' lives and marriages fall apart that too much time spent with the dead could be murder on the living, and I'd been careful not to neglect George. Aside from my gym time three days a week, I spend most of my off hours with him. George refuses to go to the gym with me, relying on golf to satisfy his exercise requirement. Chasing a little ball around on a golf cart isn't my idea of exercise. I need something more physical that only a bottle of Gatorade and a hot shower will cure. At thirty-two, I'm a typical woman battling unwanted bulges and the dreaded arm wattles, and I have to keep in shape because in my line of work you never know when you'll have to cut and run in order to catch a criminal, or save your own ass.

A pair of dim headlights inched its way toward my bumper. I sped up. He followed. I'd grown a tail. Cold sweat erupted under my sleeveless blouse, sending chills up my arms. I couldn't see the driver in the darkness.

The car continued to gain while I fished the Glock from my shoulder holster for quick access. Buford might not be *smart* to come after me, but insanity has no IQ.

The asshole hit his bright lights as he inched up to my bumper. I adjusted the mirror to reflect the glare back and sped up. Adrenaline revved through me.

Suddenly the car tore around the side, edging up fast beside me.

I slowed down and so did he.

Then he leaned over and raised his right arm. I grabbed my gun.

He shook his middle finger at me then sped off like a true coward, leaving me shaken from the realization that I'd almost shot a man for flipping me off. I hit cruise and let my nerves recuperate in the right lane.

Turning up the radio, I decided to force my thoughts onto something else and considered a variety of creative ideas to get my relationship with George back on track. The track came to a dead end when I pulled into my driveway.

I returned a wave to the teenage boy across the street who was taking out Mrs. Jenkins' garbage, thinking the poor kid must be bored out his mind, being forced to skateboard and take pictures of Grandma's flower garden while his parents vacationed in Barbados. Perhaps George and I would plan a honeymoon there, that is, if they have golf courses.

The garage door slid closed behind me with a gentle thud. My eyes adjusted to the dim bulb above, as I scanned the garage interior. The sight of the mower in the corner added one more item to my never-to-do list and I considered hiring a lawn service. Although the shower and beer called to my tired, stressed-out body, I remained in the car, watching for an extra minute.

Fear of the dark has never been a problem, but something made my arm hairs salute when I entered my unlit kitchen from the garage entrance. Police work trains your senses, and after a while, a good cop can smell trouble. Something stunk.

I slid the Glock from my shoulder holster and slowly headed past the kitchen. Distance, shielding, and movement came to mind from my academy days. It reminded cops to keep their distance from a criminal, shield themselves, or become a moving target. Those three words had saved my ass on countless occasions, so I cautioned myself to use them now.

Height has always played a part in my ability to stand my ground in a male-dominated career, not to mention intimidate the shorter criminals. When I look up to someone, it's usually in reference to his or her abilities on a professional level. At five-foot-nine—that's six foot in heels—I'm probably braver than I should be. But moving through my home, I had the advantage in the dark.

I took stock of my home's normal sounds and detected nothing out of the ordinary. A flashing red light on the living room answering machine signaled a message. The refrigerator hummed against the tic-tock of the grandfather clock, a familiar white noise I'd grown comfortable with in my cozy bungalow. In silence, I waited.

As the minutes passed, I felt foolish. I searched the entire house with ninja stealth and came up empty. There was no one in the house, as George was out of town on business. I thought about calling him, but my stomach grumbled loud enough to tell me George *and* my shower could wait. Strange how solving a crime always signals a healthy appetite. The bright kitchen light brought a sense of reality to the situation, and I grabbed a beer and the fixings for a ham sandwich from the frig with Alvarez's warning repeating in my head.

I glanced at my gun on the counter, and skewered a pickle. Buford Jones ranked as a low man on the drug totem pole. The chance of him showing up at my door was remote. Besides, I'd been threatened before, by much bigger fish in the crime sea, and decided his release would not imprison me. I sliced and diced calories galore, all the while picturing Buford's murderous expression in the courtroom that day as he called out a warning for his attorney to watch her back. When he'd turned his promises of revenge on me, I'd left before he got to the really good parts. They'd been the run-of-the-mill threats that I'd heard a hundred times before and I'd deleted them from my mental hard drive before I left the courthouse parking lot.

Draining the beer, I grabbed another. It never tasted so good and after a long draw, I relaxed enough to let George take center stage in my mind again. My sister, Kate, calls him "Mr. Excitement," convinced that the most daring thing he's ever done is fart in church. But they do say that opposites attract, and maybe tranquility is good for a violent crimes detective. Someone to keep me grounded in this crazy world.

I headed to the living room with the sandwich, beer, and a late-night movie calling to me, and dropped into the recliner ready to cable surf. I'd earned this time alone. I rested my head back, closing my eyes.

A fiery jolt hit my neck, sending my plate crashing against the coffee table. Suddenly I was on the floor. The room went briefly dim and I saw a tall shadow overhead. I grabbed for his legs, trying to knock him off balance, crying out at the sharp pain of crunching bone when a boot pinned my hand. Cold steel shocked my chest, throwing me back against the carpet. The sound of my heart pounding out of control filled my ears. Fire exploded in my lungs. I couldn't breathe . . .

My father always told me that my stubborn nature would get me killed one day. He turned out to be wrong. I believe it was my stubborn nature that kept me from reaching the end of the tunnel and saying adios forever.

The whole incident happened in less than ten minutes. That was all the time it took to end my life. Thirty-two years—not a long engagement on the stage of life. When the lights went out, there was no ovation, no call for an encore. But one thing I *do* know; I haven't left the building—not by a long shot.

Chapter Two

I viewed the crime scene from the bathroom doorway, wondering why the techs hadn't asked me to move when they passed by. I couldn't recall how I'd gotten here or why. It was time for Starbucks.

A body lay inside my old-fashioned four-footed bathtub, with knees draped over the edge, spread-eagle style. What a humiliating way to go. The victim's head lay partially submerged, preventing me from seeing the face. I guessed female by the length of blonde hair. Who the hell drowned in my tub?

Sidestepping tech equipment, I tried to position myself for a better view. Lenny from the crime lab crawled on his hands and knees behind the tub, his gloved hands bagging what looked like a razor blade. I prayed he didn't find anything more revealing, like a lost thong.

Before I could get close enough to see, my sister, Kate, pushed her way inside the crowded john, abruptly stopped by Alvarez. She was dressed in her police uniform; I figured she'd probably heard the call from the patrol car.

Four years younger, Kate had followed in my footsteps and become a cop. We've always had an unspoken competition between us, sometimes bordering on rivalry, so it didn't surprise me when she entered police training. Frankly, I never thought she'd last, given her designer tastes and affinity for long lunches with friends after a tarot card reading with her psychic. Kate in a navy uniform wearing gun residue instead of Halston didn't fit the sister I knew. She fooled me by ranking among the top ten in her class and, I have to admit, her academy graduation remains one of the proudest moments of my life.

"Kate. Don't." Alvarez grabbed her shoulders.

"Get out of my way . . ." She pushed past him.

The crime techs froze. Had it been anyone but Kate stepping onto their turf, they would have been all over her, but after four years on the force, she knew how to maneuver in a crime scene without disturbing evidence.

Her vivid blue eyes blazed as Alvarez laid a hand on her arm, and I knew he'd better remove it if he didn't want to lose it. Kate had a temper when it suited her. He backed off.

"No!" Kate yelled when she peered into the tub.

I started forward, but Alvarez held her around the waist.

The last time I saw Kate looking this vulnerable, she'd been twelve years old and had discovered her pet cat, Boots, dead in the backyard. She wore that same expression now, and I found myself helpless to comfort her, as helpless as I'd been with Boots.

"C'mon." Alvarez led her out, walking right through me.

That's when I knew. Oh God. That's why no one spoke to me. That's why I felt so numb. I tried to force myself to wake up.

I moved over the glossy tiles, past my overflowing clothes hamper, up to the tub. Can't say I walked; it was more like gliding. My feet never met the floor.

Wake up, Lindsay.

No one said a word to me. No one yelled for me to stop, or asked any questions. I knew why, but hoped I was wrong. The shower curtain had been pulled all the way back, and I saw more of the body, still partially submerged in the pink water. Forcing myself to look inside, I felt the familiar stomach twinge I get when viewing a corpse.

During my four years in homicide, I'd seen my share of victims. It takes some getting used to, but once you make up your mind that the victim needs you there to find justice, it gets easier to keep a clear head. But nothing could have prepared me for this. *I* was the victim.

The first thing that caught my attention was the 9mm Beretta still strapped to my ankle. I'd been stripped of everything, including my dignity, except for the gun. My blonde tresses lay limp in the water like spaghetti in sauce, and my face wore an unbecoming purple tint. No more pouty lips and crystal blue eyes. I knew my muscular build would stiffen for several hours then grow hopelessly flaccid, turning my perky breasts into deflated balloons. So much for all my gym time.

One of the techs mentioned suicide to Lenny, shaking his head.

They were on the wrong track.

I carefully analyzed the scene, realizing their conclusions seemed justified based on the situation, but I also determined it had been staged. Someone wanted me to look bad and had succeeded. There was no way I'd let this go down as a suicide. I needed to process the scene quickly, before they cleaned up pertinent evidence that might disprove their theory.

Without a physical presence, I figured I wouldn't disturb the crime scene, so I stuck my hand into the pink bath water. Unfortunately, I couldn't feel the water temperature. If it had been hot or warm when my body went in, the process of rigor would have been sped up, making me look as though I'd been deceased longer than I had. Time of death remained an important key to finding possible suspects and leads but the water temperature could throw that off. I wondered if that had been intentional on the killer's part.

The look on the crime team's faces remained grim and I knew what must be on all their minds. I wanted to call out for the crime techs to stop, for everybody to just stop. The situation wasn't what it seemed. The fact that Alvarez had shown up with a crime team made it clear he thought the same thing.

My parted lips looked ready to whisper final words of wisdom to those left behind, although I really couldn't think of anything profound at the moment. Seeing your own corpse will do that. I forced myself to stare hard and drive the fact home. It didn't seem real. Shock and horror don't even begin to describe what I felt. I'd literally stepped into two worlds simultaneously. As the victim all I could think was, why hadn't someone covered me up? As a detective, I knew they had to work the crime scene as is to secure key evidence.

I regretted not shaving my legs that morning and realized the hideous monstrosity known as the Frost Freckle lay exposed on my inner thigh for the attending officers to see. When I was a teen, my poor mother tried to convince me the *beauty mark* was something to be proud of. Beauty mark my ass. I've seen prettier warts.

The scene moved in slow motion as I watched the techs doing their jobs efficiently and a little too quietly. Cameras and video documented the crime scene as they moved carefully about the bathroom seeking clues. They all seemed as shocked as I to find Detective Lindsay Frost in a bloody bathtub with slashed wrists.

It might have been instinct, or perhaps a desperate attempt to hold on to my sanity, but the detective inside took over and I started working the crime. In my mind, it had just become a murder investigation; the biggest case of my life—or death, I suppose.

Distancing myself from the *victim* came easier than I thought, and I focused on the facts. The dry walls and floor indicated I hadn't fought much going into the tub, probably because I'd been unconscious. That told me whoever did this had to be strong enough to carry my body and place me inside. I'm five-nine, a hundred and forty-five pounds—okay, make that one forty-eight, and add another couple of pounds for clothing. I recalled the crushing boot on my hand just before I passed out and tried to picture its owner. It remained a blur.

My guess is the guy used a Taser or some sort of quick-acting sedative to knock me out. The place on my neck where I'd been hit lay hidden under the murky water, and I longed for a better look. I made a mental note to try and sit in on the autopsy and get a look at the toxicology report, wondering how I'd manage that. The playing field had changed, and I was the new kid. I didn't know the rules or if there were any. If I planned to work this investigation I'd be limited physically and I had no partner, no backup. In short, I was screwed, but that had never stopped me before.

I tried to think back to my last moments and visualize the slayer. It had all happened so fast. I replayed my moves from the moment I'd entered the garage to the last memory. No clues jumped out at me. I'd been caught completely off guard, which told me the guy knew my routine.

Who wanted me dead, besides Buford Jones, and who wanted to leave a permanent smudge on my good name? I immediately crossed ol' Buford off my list. He couldn't have planned this—he wasn't smart enough. That left just about everyone I'd ever put behind bars, or pissed off. I should have been dead years ago.

At this point, I was only sure of one fact—this had been personal.

I noticed my legs had been positioned, which meant the murderer had a message. I would have blushed if I'd had skin. My spread legs exposed the most personal equipment I owned, causing me great humiliation. I examined the positioning and wondered if it was sexual in nature or if it sent a different message. *Here's to life. Kiss my . . .*

It seemed someone had gone out of his or her way to make me look bad. Whoever did this knew my co-workers would see me at my absolute worst, and I would forever be remembered as the detective who offed herself.

I paced back and forth, getting the bearings on my new body—which wasn't a body at all, simply a form. It looked like my sister had been right about the paranormal world. We'd had some serious disagreements in the past over Kate's belief in otherworldly forces. As a kid, she was the Ouija board queen, adorning herself with regal crystals and a tarot card court of her crazy friends. She called it open-minded. I'd labeled her nuts.

I'll never live this down. I hate it when she's right.

I noticed I still wore a facsimile of the clothes I'd been wearing in the living room. At least I wouldn't have to go through eternity naked. The thought struck me hard. Eternity. Could I be in hell? I hadn't had a trial. Not even a brief meeting in God's chambers!

Think, Lindsay. There'll be plenty of time for that later. Eternity.

One of the crime techs, Ted Burns, examined the razor blade through the baggie.

I moved close enough to see the sweat on his neck. I blew softly over his skin. He didn't flinch. Not even a goose bump.

Examining the weapon, I realized I didn't own a straight razor. My tastes run to safer modes of shaving, like those sickening pink shavers you buy at the five-and-dime or the stinky foam products. George opts for total safety by using an electric razor. Someone had certainly come prepared.

The ME, Thomas Stern, turned to Alvarez, who'd returned from the other room. "You found the body?" he asked my partner.

"Right. When she didn't call me, I came by to check."

Stern let out a subtle belch and nodded. "I'd put the TOD

around four hours ago," he said, hoisting his squat body from the tub's side.

"Cause?" Alvarez clenched his jaw.

"Don't know. A couple of things I have to check out first." He signaled to the techs to lift my body up and pointed to my exposed chest. "Those red marks are odd, and there isn't enough blood to prove she bled out. It *looks* like suicide," Thomas glanced over my body, "but that doesn't make it so."

"I agree. Lindsay had everything to live for. I'm her partner, I would have known if things weren't right."

Thomas mopped his shiny forehead with a hanky. "Don't blame yourself. No one really knows anyone."

"I do," Alvarez said. "And I don't accept the initial findings."

Thomas nodded, returning the limp rag to his pocket. "Any note or insurance policy laid out close by?"

Alvarez shook his head.

"They don't always leave one," Thomas said.

"You're on the wrong track." Alvarez started to go. "I'll need your findings ASAP."

I watched Alvarez walk away—thinking, that used to be *my* line.

Chapter Three

"Mission accomplished," a harsh voice whispered. Dark eyes peered through the wooden fence slats in the yard across the street from Detective Frost's home, watching emergency vehicle lights spiral red, white, and blue against the night.

"I don't understand why we're here," came the woman's frightened response.

"You will," the commander said.

"But I didn't want to come here tonight. You made me do it."

"Shut up before we're caught. Our work was perfection. Quite professional. Textbook."

Her toes squirmed inside the oversized boots. They felt like lead weights on her feet. She watched the strobing lights, trying to push the evening's event from her mind. "I'm going to throw up," she declared.

"You're weak, like I used to be. But you'll soon toughen up and come around. Then you'll be thanking me."

"I doubt that." She felt a spark of anger. "But I intend to see that you make good on your promise."

"Oh, really? You're growing bolder already. Just don't overstep your bounds, or I'll have to put you in your place."

"You don't own me," the woman said, grabbing the gate's latch. "How would you like to be on the ten o'clock news?"

A searing pain clutched the side of her head, shutting down

her sight. She feared she'd been blinded, when slowly her vision returned.

"What have you learned?" the commander demanded. "Tell me!"

"Respect, duty, and honor," she said, repeating the memorized mantra.

"And which one is first?"

"Respect."

"Don't make me remind you again."

The coroner van's back doors slammed closed and the crowd began to disperse.

As the woman watched emergency personnel leave the scene, she felt consumed by a sense of overwhelming dread. This was only the beginning.

"Mission accomplished. For tonight anyway," the commander chuckled.

"I just want this nightmare to be over," the woman replied.

"The road to victory is long and dirty. Like that poem says, I have promises to keep, and we have miles to go before *we* sleep."

CHAPTER FOUR

Kate Frost slammed a fist into her sister's kitchen pantry door. Hot tears burned her face. Nothing made sense. Suicide was out of the question. She hoped Alvarez and the rest of the team could see beyond that. Lindsay would have come to her if something had been wrong. They'd had their differences, but Lindsay wouldn't have left her completely out. It just wasn't her way. The burning truth left her fighting to catch a full breath. Her sister had been murdered.

Who did it? Why? How much torture would they be able to withstand when she caught them?

She watched fellow officers and crime team workers wandering in and out of her sister's bathroom, through the house, in and out. This looked like any number of crime scenes that she'd witnessed, except her mind couldn't stay on the job at hand. By now she should be following protocol, most likely starting to canvas the neighborhood for witnesses.

Frozen beside the kitchen counter, flashes of her last time with Lindsay raced through her mind. It had been last Saturday at their parents' house, and she recalled now that Lindsay had seemed distracted, but that hadn't seemed unusual at the time. That was always the way with Lindsay when she worked a tough investigation. The detective in her never took time off until it was solved.

Kate fast-forwarded to their lunch date the other day, replaying every word of their heart-to-heart over salad, diet drinks, and a double-fudge brownie. The only problem in Lindsay's life outside of work was her rocky relationship with George Anderson. Lindsay felt they'd fallen into a rut and had prodded Kate for inventive ideas to spark their love life.

The idea nearly caused Kate to gag. In her eyes, George was a manipulative, high-maintenance jerk who probably hadn't been breast-fed long enough. She never understood the attraction and had openly said so. But Lindsay had come to his defense, telling Kate they proved a good combination because he was her complete opposite. Yeah, like a turd in a rose garden.

Now her sister was on her way to the morgue and Kate closed her eyes trying to wash the crime scene from her mind. How could such a vibrant, dedicated, tough woman be a victim? Someone had known she'd be alone. George came to mind, although she couldn't imagine the pansy risking a bloodstain on his Izod shirt.

Her mind spiraled in multiple directions, panning the vast array of possible criminal suspects who might want revenge on Lindsay. The list stretched as long as God's beard.

"Kate?" Alvarez said.

She palm-swiped her cheeks and faced him. Technically, he outranked her, even if she was the victim's sister. "Yes?" She forced herself to remain calm.

"You okay?" His dark eyes pinned her.

"No." She fought another round of tears when she spied Lindsay's gun on the counter. "Jesus, she didn't have a chance."

"I'll have one of the officers give you a ride home. You're entitled to bereavement time. I suggest you start immediately."

"I'm not going anywhere. She didn't kill herself."

He motioned to one of the officers across the room, telling Kate, "I can't let you stay."

"You're all heart." She turned away.

"Kate. Stop. You know Lindsay meant a lot to me, but right

now I need to think with a clear head. I can't do that with you here. You're family."

"Right." She brushed past him.

It wasn't fair. She needed to stay and do something so she could stop feeling helpless. Going home meant having to deal with the truth. Having to call her parents. Her throat tightened around a fresh wave of grief. Alvarez was right; she was too close.

In doing the job he excelled at, he couldn't afford any distractions. She turned to thank him, but he'd gone.

A half hour later, Kate tossed her keys onto the kitchen table and headed into her bedroom. It felt good to get out of uniform and lie on the bed thinking. The evening breeze fanned across her bare skin from the open window as she watched the ceiling fan twirl. She couldn't get the bathroom image out of her mind.

A framed snapshot of the two of them together at the beach smiled back at her from the nightstand. Girls' day out with plenty of sun, gossip, and the umbrella drinks they'd snuck inside a cooler. Kate's plan had been simple. Sit Lindsay on the beach with tanned, half-dressed, gorgeous men roving about, get her drunk, and make her forget George's last name. The plan had failed miserably, with Lindsay talking nonstop about the boring accountant. Still, it had been a beautiful day, one that she knew she'd treasure now more than ever.

Staring at the picture, she smiled. They could have passed for twins, with long blonde hair, blue eyes, and similar height. Now she felt alone. A piece of her soul had been savagely ripped away, leaving it vulnerable and bleeding. The pain couldn't have been more real. The anger burned through her grief as she thought about the animal that killed her sister.

Something about the scene in the bathroom nagged her but she couldn't pin it. Lindsay had been slain, leaving her to figure it out.

The phone jarred her thoughts like a cold slap of water. She let the machine take the call, as she hugged a pillow and sobbed at her mother's voice.

"Kate. It's Mom. Just wondering what to do about Lindsay's birthday. Got any ideas? Call me."

Kate ran to the bathroom and threw up in the toilet. Her stomach convulsed to the point of dry heaves. Finally, she slid against the wall to the floor, sweaty and panting, and pulled herself up to the sink, catching her tired reflection. "Get a grip. Lindsay would kick your ass if she saw you like this."

Kate started the shower and let the steaming water slide down her body, mingling with her tears. Within the hour, she'd be driving to her parent's home to break the unbelievable, unforgiving news. Fighting the urge to retch, she concentrated on the scene of the crime still fresh in her mind.

She hated the fact that everyone had witnessed her crying, especially Alvarez. He could be tough as nails, sometimes too tough, and she didn't understand how Lindsay put up with him.

"Alvarez is a good guy. He's always there for me. You have to respect the people you work with. You'll never make detective with a bad attitude," she'd told Kate with a playful shoulder punch.

Kate shook her head. "I may never make detective, but I am going to find who did this to you, Sis. There's no way I'll ever believe you killed yourself." Kate closed her eyes and let the water wash over her. Soap stung her eyes, and she blindly fumbled for a towel, spraying water everywhere. After the burning stopped, she shut off the water, laid the towel on the floor to soak up the mess, and stopped.

Kate stared as her hair dripped water onto the tiles in large drops. She let it splatter and pool around her feet. She had her first solid clue.

Wrapping up in the towel, she hurried to the bedroom and phoned Alvarez. She might not like him, but right now, she needed him. The wait seemed eternal, and she almost hung up and redialed, when he came on the line.

"Alvarez."

"It's Kate."

"Are you all right?" He sounded alarmed.

"I'm home. But there's something you should know about the scene."

"What's that?"

"Something wasn't right, but I didn't figure it out till now."

"Kate, I told you to leave it alone—"

"The bathroom floor wasn't wet."

"I don't understand."

"Listen, I'm convinced the whole thing was staged—"

"I agree. I'm treating this like a homicide investigation, unofficially."

"Unofficially? What the hell does *that* mean?"

"It means until we get more proof, the medical examiner will call it based on the evidence."

"That's bullshit!"

"I don't like it anymore than you do, Kate, but until I can prove otherwise—"

"So prove it! There was no water on the floor. I stepped carefully around that tub so I wouldn't disturb anything, and there wasn't one drop of water. Doesn't that strike you as strange?"

"Not if Lindsay got in the tub on her own."

"But her feet were draped over the foot of the tub. Why wasn't there water on the floor?"

His silence gave her confidence. She knew she'd struck a nerve.

"That means someone cleaned up, and *that* someone was in the house with Lindsay when she died."

"There were no signs of forced entry."

"So, maybe it was someone she knew and she let them in. Maybe it was George. All I know is something doesn't add up and I think you feel it too."

"Kate, let me handle this. If you go stirring the pot before we have all the facts, it could hinder the investigation. Promise me you'll stay out of this."

"Stay out of it? How can I do that?"

"Because I'm telling you to. You're too close."

"That's exactly the reason I need to work on this."

"I disagree."

"Naturally." Kate fought to contain her anger. "I'm a street cop, right?"

"That's not it. You're family."

"I'm a family member who happens to be in law enforcement. I *need* to do more than pass out tissue boxes."

"Sorry, Kate. It's out of the question."

"My sister always defended your actions, for reasons I just can't see."

"Don't say things you'll regret, Kate."

"I'm not. I mean every word." She disconnected, more determined than ever to find the truth.

CHAPTER FIVE

You know the old adage, *I'll sleep when I'm dead?*

Don't be fooled. I work harder now than I ever did in the flesh.

As to the question, *do the deceased sleep?*, unfortunately, I can answer from experience. Yes and no.

After my sister left the scene, it seemed I blended into the walls for a while. My hands felt for anything solid, meeting a complete void without sound or light. No panic, no struggle on my part to hold on—after all, I'd already experienced death and had nothing left to fear. I shut down like a computer. Everything just melted into gray. I couldn't say it was actual sleep, but then again I'd had worse nights tossing and turning in my bed.

Guess I must have stayed in *the zone* for a while, because when I came out of it, sunlight surrounded me. I found myself in a brightly lit office watching a Katie Couric look-alike handling a multitude of phone calls like Xena taking down a hydra.

"I told you, Mr. Paulson, you'll get your copy when I get my money." The woman pushed the next lit button on her phone.

"Mr. Who? Yes. No. I don't care." She disconnected and took the next call. "This is Marie Yates."

She tapped a manicured nail against the desk. "I see. Well, I'll be in court all afternoon. No, I'm not leaving town . . ."

Marie swiveled in her high-back leather chair when someone knocked on the door. "Come in." Her harsh expression melted when the door opened.

She shut a side desk drawer and came around to greet the visitor. Her smile widened when Alvarez came in wearing a tailored blue suit and the tie I gave him last Christmas. The man sure knows how to charm 'em.

"Sorry to intrude, but your receptionist seems to be out and I saw your door partially open," he apologized.

The phone rang again and she disconnected the call without answering. "Can't seem to find good help. They're too young, too flirtatious, or too stupid. Not much to choose from."

Marie Yates had been the criminal attorney who'd helped get Buford Jones five years in the big house downstate. With his record she thought she'd done him a favor. He hadn't seen it that way. Yates was a well-known Taylor County lawyer, who'd fight for her client like a pit bull, but Buford's trial had been a fluke and a nasty surprise to her ego. She figured he'd get off with minimal time and some probation; instead, the prosecuting attorney pulled a witness out of his hat, sending Marie into therapy and Buford to his new home.

Alvarez had given her the heads up yesterday about Buford's release, a warning she'd apparently heeded, unlike a certain *lieutenant*. What can I say, I like my independence.

Marie motioned Alvarez in while she cut off the last few callers. I could see he had her full attention, as she straightened inside her wonder bra to give her fifty-something posture a lift.

"Detective Alvarez. What can I do for you?"

Can you believe she had the nerve to blush?

His stone expression cracked a brief, nearly noticeable smile. "Just checking on you, Marie."

"Can I get you some coffee?" She stood to pour.

"Thanks. Just half," he nodded.

She handed him the coffee and placed a coaster before him on the desk. Her eyes held him a moment, and then, "I'm sorry about your partner, Gerard."

That's it? "Your partner"? I don't even rate a name? The bitch.

I'd gone to high school with Marie's daughter, Chandler, although I never knew her too well. She'd come off shy, kind of quiet, too quiet for my boisterous personality and I'd never had the urge to buddy up with her.

Whenever I'd gone out for anything in school, whether track, cheerleading, or even a cute guy, it seemed she was always there. As backwards as she seemed, at times she turned into another person entirely, talking and laughing like she was the prom queen. I never saw her after graduation, until our ten-year class reunion four years ago. Shortly afterward, I heard she'd killed herself. Turned out she suffered from bipolar disease. Marie never recovered.

Alvarez winced. He'd caught the slight. "Lindsay's death has devastated the whole department." He stared her down.

"I'm sure she'll be greatly missed. Now, what can I do for you?"

You can get down on all fours and bark like a fox . . . I hate fakes.

"I'm investigating the findings and want to be sure I can count on your help if I need it."

"Investigating? I thought she killed herself." Marie took a sip of her coffee and wiped her lipstick smudge from the cup.

"That's what it *looks* like, so I'm working on damage control here. If the press gets a hold of this before we can prove otherwise, it will tarnish Lindsay's name forever."

"I see. And what about Buford Jones? Has anyone found him?" She held her pen like a dagger over her paperwork.

"We're looking. He shouldn't be too hard to find. Meantime, I'd appreciate it if you keep your ears open. Please don't hesitate to call me."

"I'll do that, Gerard. Thanks for caring."

I watched Alvarez excuse himself and leave, probably before

he puked all over his suit.

After he'd gone, I reevaluated my feelings about Marie when I saw her bury her head in her hands and begin to sob. Maybe I had her all wrong.

Before I could give it much thought, I saw her office blur and found myself fast-forwarding between what looked like two gray walls. I've never been one for carnival rides; believe it or not I have a weak stomach. I'm fine with mutilated corpses, but you can forget theTilt-a-whirl. Without the physical equipment, however, I felt no ill effects when the movement finally slowed.

Overcome by panic, I thought this might be my one-way ride to either heaven or hell, and this brief respite between worlds had only been the waiting room. Meeting my maker or shaking hands with St. Peter didn't concern me. I worried more that I'd never get to solve this crime. It's the curse of the anal-retentive. We like all things tidy; loose ends tied up.

I can only describe what I saw next as beyond bizarre, and I wondered if I hadn't lost my mind along the road to eternity. A vacant parking lot lay before me, housing a newer-looking brown brick building. The sign on the front read: Tri-City Labs. I'd heard the name before, but couldn't place it.

A sharp voice sliced the silence. "Can I help you?"

I turned to find a twenty-something Caucasian woman hold-ing a dilapidated teddy bear. Black frizzy hair stuck out of a loosely tied ponytail, draping over one eye. At about five-three, around thirty pounds too heavy, she appeared stuffed into her salmon-colored scrubs. At first, I thought *medical personnel,* until I saw the uniform's pristine condition, which screamed *reception-ist.* All the lab techs and nurses I know wear white. For some reason, office personnel get to wear all the fun colors. But the teddy bear had me stumped.

She moved toward me, clutching the stuffed animal, and repeated her question. "I said, can I help you?"

Her exposed eyebrow lay thick enough to see from several feet away. Would I be rude to recommend waxing?

When she came close enough, I realized she was a spirit. What skin remained on her bare arms looked melted, around limbs of charred bone. It didn't take a coroner to label this one a fire victim.

Admittedly, it felt good to meet a kindred spirit, so to speak. I'd begun to fear I was the only person in this strange limbo. Her brow crept dangerously close to her eyelid and I feared she'd hand me a clipboard overstuffed with insurance forms to fill out if I didn't answer her. I decided to go on the offensive.

"I'm Detective Lindsay Frost with the Southfield Heights PD. Can I ask you a few questions?"

Clearly intimidated, she shot back, "No. Now can I help you?"

"Is that the only line you know?"

Seeing that I wasn't easily intimidated either, she ran a deformed hand through her hair, revealing a pair of too-large brown eyes that stared at me for several seconds before she answered.

"I'm Sally O' Shannon. I work at the burp-and-spit lab over there. Or at least I used to. Sorry about the attitude. It's survival as a receptionist. Get 'em in, get 'em out."

"Excuse me? Burp and spit?"

"It's a sperm bank."

I had to ask. Might as well go for broke and ask my next loaded question. "What's with the teddy bear?"

"It's my death tag." She hugged it tight.

"Will I regret asking what that means?"

"You have one too. All of us do, or we wouldn't be here."

"A tag? You mean like a toe tag?"

"No. Like the personal item you brought with you when you crossed over. I believe it's tucked under your shirt." She nodded toward the badge hanging around my neck.

"This is my detective badge."

"Right. You'll hold onto that until you work out your issue and then you'll be able to move on to the next level."

"What level? What issue?" I started to panic.

"My problem has to do with loneliness. I've always been an outsider, never made friends easily. As a kid I always grabbed my teddy bear for comfort and so it has become my death tag. It's something I need to work out."

I stared, utterly confused.

"Don't sweat it. I was the same way when I first got here. I take it you're a newbie?"

"If you mean at being dead, yes. Can you please explain what you mean by level?"

"Well, after you work out your remaining concern, you'll be able to leave your tag behind and move on to the next level to be reborn."

"You mean reincarnation?" Kate would love this.

"I guess. But you can't get there if you're still holding onto problems from your most recent life. That's what death is for. It's just a stop along the way of our eternal path. It's not the end like most people think."

I fingered my badge. Unfortunately, what Sally said made sense. My shield had everything to do with the one unresolved problem in my life. Except I had no intention of giving it up.

CHAPTER SIX

Kate unlocked Lindsay's front door while the uniformed officer waited beside her. Carl Withers had proven to be one of the best cops she'd ever known. Lucky for her, he was also a softy.

"You don't have to stay with me, Carl. I'm a big girl now," she winked.

"I know, Kate. But Alvarez will kill me if he finds out I left you alone." His blue eyes pleaded with her.

"Look. I know you're both doing what you think is best for me, but I need some time alone in the house. You know. She was my sister, and I'm trying for closure. You understand." She laid her hand on his arm.

He sighed, glancing up and down the street. "Compromise. I'll park a few houses down and wait. If you're not out in fifteen minutes, I'm coming back. Got it?"

She reached up and kissed his clean-shaven cheek. "I owe you, Carl."

Kate stalled in Lindsay's foyer, looking and listening. The crime scene tape had been removed and it looked as though her sister could race in at any moment. Except Kate knew Linz would never run late again. She moved through the living room, taking in the elements of a life cut short, viewing the photos that lined the mantle.

She spotted her favorite, of Lindsay with their parents at Disney World. Kate tried to shut off the memory of her parent's reactions the night before upon hearing the news.

Perry Frost's six-foot frame had withered before her eyes. She'd rushed to his side, helping him to the couch, where her mother stared into space.

"Lindsay, gone?" Carla Frost repeated softly.

Kate sat next to her dad, wrapping her arms around his waist. They'd all cried together for what seemed to be hours, finally falling asleep with their clothes on.

This morning, her mother made coffee and they'd discussed funeral arrangements. It seemed to Kate her parents had aged ten years overnight. They'd all died a little, along with Linz, and nothing would ever heal their wounds. Of course, not one of them believed she'd killed herself. It was the only reason Kate had been able to get on with the day—she had a butcher to find.

Her first order of business had been an early call to Alvarez.

"Alvarez," he slurred.

She knew she'd awakened him. "Lieutenant. This is Kate Frost. I need to bring burial clothing to the mortician. Has the crime scene been released yet?"

"Kate, you have time. The autopsy is today. Wait until they release her to the funeral home."

"Look, I have two grieving parents to care for, and a funeral to plan. The least you can do is let us have her clothes."

His exhausted sigh filled her ear, and she pictured him counting to ten.

"Well?" she pressed.

"I'll have an officer there to let you in later today."

"I have a key," she said impatiently.

"I don't want you there alone."

"Fine. Tell him I'll be there in an hour." She hung up.

This was her chance to revisit the scene. So far, she'd been able to glean bits and pieces from other officers who wanted to help, and had learned they were still searching for her sister's fiancé George Anderson. He'd mysteriously disappeared.

Six months ago, when Lindsay had announced her engagement to the stuffy, self-absorbed accountant, Kate couldn't believe it. She knew, in her heart, that her sister wanted to settle down, and George seemed like a good man. He was smart, stable, and great company. If you enjoy golf and reading. But Lindsay's outgoing, fun-loving nature wouldn't allow her to keep still for long and Kate figured her sister hadn't chosen to settle down, she'd simply decided to *settle*.

She moved through Lindsay's house in a daze. Who killed her sister? She'd learned from Officer Withers that they'd picked up Buford Jones for questioning, but so far no arrest. Her finger hovered over Alvarez's preset on her cell phone, itching to call, until she shoved the damn thing into her purse, vowing she'd eat rusty nails before begging him for information. Time grew short and Kate's impatience soared by the minute. Every hour the guy roamed free pushed their chances of finding him further away.

Pacing in front of the coffee table, Kate realized she was putting off the inevitable return to the bathtub. The scene replayed vivid in her mind. Alvarez had been right about one thing—she was too close. It ranked as one of the most painful things she'd ever had to do.

Her hand grazed the picture frames on the mantle, telling the brief story of Lindsay's life and loves. One of her greatest pleasures had been time spent with the Special Olympics. It was a cause close to Lindsay's heart and she'd grown attached to a twelve-year-old mentally challenged boy named Richard.

Each year, Richard tried his hardest, but never quite achieved his goal of scoring a run for his team in the softball event. Kate's heart broke every year when she'd listen to Lindsay tell how hard he'd tried, going to bat time after time wearing a great big smile.

He would say, "This one's for you, Yinsay."

Her throat tightened when she realized that this year Richard would have to try for someone else.

Kate went over every inch of Lindsay's bathroom on her hands and knees, looking for clues the crime team might have missed. She knew it was a waste of time. The only real clue they'd found had been the razor blade containing Lindsay's prints.

Her knees burned against the floor tiles and she took a break, going to the bedroom closet. Lindsay's wardrobe reflected her personality, bright and sassy, with a touch of designer here and there. With its garden of color, nothing in the closet seemed appropriate for burial. Kate studied several dresses, and hung them back up. Maybe she should buy something.

Someone grabbed her around the waist from behind, yanking her close. Kate struggled to break free, but the grip tightened. A hand groped her left breast, while hot lips trailed her neck. She shoved an elbow into the attacker's gut, followed by a quick uppercut to his jaw. He fell backwards, landing close to the bed.

Kate frowned at the sight of George Anderson rubbing his chin, looking like a guilty child.

"Hold it!" Carl moved inside, gun drawn.

Kate stepped between them. "It's okay. I know him."

The officer lowered his weapon. "You okay?"

She nodded. "Can I have a minute, Carl?"

The officer shook his head and left the room.

Kate turned to her sister's fiancé. "Jesus, George! What are you doing?" Kate offered a hand.

"I thought you were Lindsay." He waved her away. "Any idea where she's hiding?"

"She's dead." Kate watched his response.

"Is that the only way you can think of to get rid of me?" He shook off the punch.

"Lindsay *told* you what I think?"

"She didn't have to. Now where is she?"

"I told you."

His eyes narrowed. "What are you talking about?"

"Lindsay died last night, George."

He paled and dropped onto the bed. "How?"

The words caught in Kate's throat. They weren't true, but she had to make him think they all believed it. "Suicide."

His eyes grew wide, eyebrows raised. "No way."

"That's the ruling. She slit her wrists in the tub." Kate swallowed hard at the memory.

George paced before the dresser. He rubbed both hands over his face as if to awaken himself from the nightmare. Kate noticed his designer suit showed telltale travel wrinkles.

"Where have you been, George?"

He stopped, brushing a hand through his dark curls. "Away on business. Why?"

"You're a person of interest."

"Call my boss, he can verify my whereabouts."

"Alvarez will handle that."

"Alvarez? Why is he involved? You said she killed herself."

"Standard procedure," Kate lied. "When a detective dies of unnatural causes it's routine to make sure there's no foul play."

"So why are they looking for me?"

"Like I said, Alvarez has to be sure."

"Then they aren't sure what happened?"

"Don't get your pants in a twist. It's procedure." Kate turned back to the closet and counted to ten. She didn't want to hit him again, although he deserved it. Disappointment filled her when she realized poor dumb George wasn't their guy.

She jumped when a manicured hand rested on her shoulder. George's breath tickled her ear.

"Kate, I'm sorry about your sister. You must be heartbroken." He leaned close.

"Like you *should* be, but somehow, I'm not getting that vibe from you."

He smiled easily, and shook his head. "Lindsay and I were having some problems. I think we both knew the engagement was a mistake, but neither one of us had the heart to officially break it off. That's partly why I jumped at the chance to go out of town for a few days. I needed to clear my head and think things through. Actually, I'd already made the decision to end our relationship."

"Then why the come-on when you thought I was Linz?"

"You can't blame a guy for trying. One last time, you know?"

"You lying bastard." Kate shoved him away.

"What?" He followed her. "You think I killed her?"

She stared him down.

"I don't believe this. If I killed her, why would I tell you my plans? I could have just let it go and played the heartbroken fiancé."

"So why *are* you telling me this, George? What's the point?"

He trailed a finger along her forearm. "I thought maybe . . ."

Kate saw red. Her fist connected with his eye and he went down like a prizefighter in the last round. He landed hard enough for his head to bounce against the carpet.

Kate bent beside him, yanking his head up by the hair. "You just jumped to the top of my suspect list."

After overseeing the removal of George's things, she gained satisfaction watching Officer Withers escort him from Lindsay's home, hoping next time it would be to prison if he turned out to be the perpetrator. His out-of-town excuse had become a standard alibi for all white-collar criminals, one she'd be sure to verify.

"Wait!" she called out as they reached the drive.

George reached into his pants pocket before Kate's outstretched hand.

She palmed the house key with a warning glare. "*Now* you're through."

Making her way back inside, she glanced down the street in time to see the squad turn the corner, and only then did she slip the small vinyl booklet from her pocket. George's daily planner seemed overbooked with golf dates; phone numbers and several entries penned *business lunch* marked by a star. He'd described most of the entries in great detail, giving client names, first and last, as well as times, and complete address locations. All except the notations marked by a star. Apparently, George had a secret. Kate checked each page, noting the rest of his world seemed even less interesting than the man himself. Why would a grown man need a manicure?

Paging through, she noted that all of the starred weekly lunch dates were at a Chicago restaurant called Hugo's. She'd been there one time on a date that she'd chosen to forget, but knew the place catered to a higher-tax-bracket clientele.

Additional notations near the bottom of each date raised her suspicions about goody-goody George.

See B. T. Back booth.

Her imagination conjured a large mafioso type named Big Tony, wearing a dark glare over a spaghetti bib. With George's office located only one town over from Southfield Heights, his client base lay no more than twenty minutes away. She wondered what kind of *business* George could have an hour away in Chicago?

Pocketing the book, she decided B.T. might be important enough to research.

Chapter Seven

I found my new situation strange. It occurred to me I didn't *feel* deceased, because I didn't feel much of anything. Many of my concerns had fallen to the wayside, making me wonder why they had been important in the first place. Who cared that my checkbook hadn't been balanced in six months? Was it really important that I hadn't cleaned out the hall closet since I'd moved in several years before? Now it would be someone else's problem.

I no longer worried about dieting, or looking fat. I had no desire to check my look in a mirror, although it probably would have been pointless.

Unfortunately, I still had to battle emotions, with anger placing number one in the top ten. I wanted the jerk that killed me—bad—but in order to find him, I had to learn to work with my second raging emotion, guilt. Instead of calling the ME for toxicology results, or going to the computer for information, I eavesdropped and peeked over shoulders to get the details I needed. That's not my style. I believe in being upfront and I like calling the shots. I felt like a voyeur in my own investigation.

I watched Alvarez in his office working later than usual, his dark eyes narrowed and tired. It seemed surreal to be standing beside him with no acknowledgment. By now, we should be arguing over the best course of action, coming to a compromise, then stepping out to get the job done. He hunched over a mountain of paperwork, checking and rechecking the details.

I'd never seen him look so frustrated and alone, and knew he'd hit a dead end. My case had grown cold.

"Alvarez," I said, trying to make him hear me.

He didn't flinch.

"Hey!" I shrieked into his ear.

I rushed the desk, sliding my palms across the mountain of paperwork, hoping to cause a reaction and draw attention to myself, but instead I fell through the desk, landing on all fours. His phone rang, interrupting my carefully selected curses, and I eavesdropped like the stealthy little spy that I am.

"Alvarez," he mumbled.

Gerard's face lit up and I knew it must be one of his sons.

"Hey, *mijo. Qué pasa?*"

He listened a moment, smiling.

"Honor roll? That's great," he said. "Tell your brother to hold off nuking the TV dinners. I'm bringing home a pizza to celebrate."

Suddenly I felt left out.

During Gerard's divorce a year ago, I'd watched him go through hell. As time went on, he started sharing his dilemmas in his new life with the boys. You could fit what I know about raising teenage boys into a shell casing, and have plenty of room to spare. It didn't matter to Alvarez, though; he needed the sounding board, and so I obliged.

He has joint custody of John, seventeen, and Paul, fifteen. Not easy ages under quiet circumstances, but throw a hostile divorce into the mix and you have the makings for a volatile situation. So far, I think Gerard has done all right. It seems everyone has adjusted, including me. I got used to hearing the teen-tales, both humorous and otherwise. It made me feel like I was a part of the family. Now I'd been shut out.

Alvarez laughed into the phone and leaned back in his chair. It felt good to see him ease up a bit and get back into life. I felt partly to blame for his recent stress, yet I knew I remained helpless without a body. We weren't partners any longer.

From the information on his desk, I saw that the evidence supported the ME's preliminary conclusion. No signs of forced entry, no fibers or hairs, no unusual prints at the scene or on my body. No evidence of rape, or that I'd even fought. But I knew that.

I tried to ignore the graphic photos, with that damn freckle showing up in most of them, and reviewed the evidence so far. My memory would be forever tainted in the hearts and minds of my co-workers if I didn't find the truth. I realized being deceased doesn't bring closure to anything. I have more loose ends to deal with than ever.

Both suspects had fallen through. After interrogating Buford Jones for several hours, they'd determined he was otherwise occupied with a hooker on the night of my demise. Thankfully, George was no longer a person of interest, having a solid alibi. His convenient trip to Ohio had saved him, although I doubted he had plans to kill me. According to Alvarez's notes, my fiancé had shown shock and remorse at the news. I felt bad about that. I didn't get to say goodbye or tell him where I'd put his latest issue of *Golf Digest*.

The only other pertinent fact had been discovered on the neighborhood canvas. My neighbor across the street, Mrs. Jenkins, told an officer she'd seen a dark sedan parked two doors down from her house for a couple of hours that night, and the next morning, she'd discovered muddy footprints on the walkway behind her fence gate. The gaper photos from the crowd outside my house that night lay beside the report. I studied them carefully, picking out each of my neighbors, staring blankly against the flashing emergency lights, wondering what happened. No one stood out as unusual; in fact, I knew all of them.

Based on Mrs. Jenkins' report, I knew the killer had found a safe place to hide—behind her fence—while he watched the chaos he'd caused. So far, the only thing the size-ten boot prints had proven was that eighty-year-old Mrs. Jenkins wasn't a suspect.

Then I read something scribbled in the corner of the report about my sister.

Kate noted lack of water on bathroom floor. Suggested the killer is female. Pertinent?

I thought so. It was the only solid clue that hinted I might have been slain. How had I missed that?

Kate's insight told me she didn't buy the original theory either, but it didn't change the fact that we'd hit a dead end. If I was going to solve this, I needed an extra pair of hands, preferably solid hands. Kate seemed my only hope.

"Okay, *mijo*," Alvarez said. "I'm leaving now. Be home soon."

He disconnected and stood, stretching his muscular arms overhead and popping his neck, a habit I detested in life and still do. I watched him grab his jacket and head out.

Fine, leave me alone, I wanted to shout, but of course that would have been a wasted breath if I had one. He had a job to do both here and at home, but so did I. And right now, part of it included finding a new partner.

Ask any cop and they'll confirm that starting with a new partner can be awkward. I've only had to do it once before, after my first partner had been killed by a murderous asshole. During my first year as a detective, Joe Sumner fell in the line of duty. Working practically side by side for forty-plus hours a week, stretched out over a year, gives you a good insight about the person you work with. Joe took all the awards when it came to dedication, intelligence, and most importantly, street smarts. That day, however, he'd needed jungle savvy. It wasn't a gangland punk who ended his life, but a sadistic, military wannabe named Tanner Jean Hoyt, who took him down like the Vietcong. He never saw it coming. Unfortunately I did, only too late.

Hoyt gained notoriety as a military fanatic who brought her own style of justice to the streets of our fair county. Dressed in camouflage, she blushed in grease paint, wearing a Marine buzz cut. She sported a muscular body, complete with a Marine bulldog tattooed on her left arm, complementing her impressive arsenal that included an AR15 pistol that resembled a smaller version of the M16. Seriously twisted had been my best guess, and I nicknamed her GI Jane.

She was responsible for at least eight slayings, mostly gangbangers, and the local cops wanted to send her a thank-you card, until she killed a judge. Granted, the guy had been taking bribes and sending gang members free while his wife drove a new Caddy, but murder is murder. Judge Carter had been missing a week when we found his naked body dumped on the courthouse steps, gavel in hand. His blackened genitals had been burned, along with his face and hands, and the autopsy revealed he had finally succumbed to a six-inch dowel tapped through an ear into his brain.

We worked nearly around the clock for a week before catching a break, or so we thought. An anonymous tip came in she'd been spotted inside her vacant childhood home on the edge of town. Flags went up in my mind when I saw the front door standing wide open. Joe and I were the first ones inside, as the rest of the team surrounded the house.

To my left the living room looked like a hospital ward, complete with IV pole, portable commode, and boxes of latex gloves. It was all that remained of Tanner's mother Jean's battle with cancer. Tanner had cared for her mom until the end with the help of home health services.

We moved cautiously down a narrow hallway, against overwhelming silence, weapons raised and ready. Joe moved past a closed door hugging the wall on the right, with me on the left.

"Tanner Jean Hoyt! Come out with your hands up," I called.

Nothing.

Joe's nod meant he'd go in on three, with me covering. Our standard had always been to go in low and fast.

He pushed open the door, his gun sweeping.

"Jesus Christ!" He started inside. "You've got to see this Linz."

I heard a dull thud to my left as a twenty-inch crossbow bolt impaled the hallway wall through Joe's eye. He fell back, dropping his gun, his sunken socket oozing blood.

At first, it didn't register, then I heard myself shouting, "Officer down," into my shoulder radio. My gaze traveled inside the first-floor bedroom and downward to a loose trip wire on the floor. I followed it to a crossbow mounted above the bed with pulleys. Tanner had lured *us*.

Several officers came to assist as I stepped inside the room. I jerked back when a bright green viper with yellow eyes hissed at me. About five feet long, the snake dangled from the ceiling held by a rope. It had provided the diversion Tanner sought in order to spread her evil. I wanted to shred its body with bullets, but the sound of shattering glass at the rear of the house prompted me to think about finding the sick bastard that killed Joe. I knew she was in the house waiting.

Suddenly I heard shouts from the second floor as officers broke down a bedroom door. The all clear sounded in my radio but I suspected Tanner had more in store.

My eyes never strayed from the open door at the end of the hall as I maneuvered ahead. I figured it must lead to the basement and I carefully anticipated more surprises. Staying beside the door, I gave it a shove and waited for fireworks. Nothing but silent darkness. I started down, with two officers following.

A partial wall running along the stair handrail provided adequate cover, and I scanned the dimly lit basement with my gun, settling on a dark shadow in the corner.

"Drop it, Tanner. It's over."

Something grated the bottom of my shoe. A sudden blinding light and deafening explosion threw me onto my ass.

Several rounds fired, chipping the wooden handrail and sending me scampering back up the steps, blindly returning fire into the shadows.

The brief silence that followed made me think I'd hit her and I peered around the wall to see her snaking closer. Light from a window well allowed me to see she had two assault rifle magazines taped together at opposite ends. She dropped down to reload behind a waist-high wall of cinder blocks. I had less than two seconds to gain a clear shot as she flipped the empty mag and inserted the other end.

I set it up.

"Drop it!" I shot out a chunk of concrete wall behind her.

She bolted over the wall, firing as she came.

I fired back.

Her body jerked in mid-air, then met the cement floor with the sound of cracking bone.

Officers surrounded her with weapons drawn. I nudged her body over with my foot to see that a single dark hole marked the center of her forehead like a third eye. The hate froze on her face and I wondered if she would join Judge Carter at Satan's dinner table. That's one feast I'd pay to see.

Time hasn't erased the memory of Joe's mutilated face, or the gut wrenching emotional pain that followed. At his funeral, it had been Joe's wife, Kathy who'd comforted me, saying, "Joe died doing what he loved. He died a hero." I looked at his two children, ages eight and ten, and wondered if they felt the same. Ask any kid and they'll tell you they'd rather have a living dad than a deceased hero.

I don't care what my shrink says, some scars never fade, and the healing process is as fickle as a teenage boy. In my opinion it's certainly cause to reconsider the partnering up idea. However, I no longer had the choice.

Honestly, I don't mind working alone. I'm a self-starter, *and* finisher when need be, and I'd told the chief that, after losing Joe. I admit part of it stemmed from the idea that it seemed a good way to prove myself, but frankly I didn't want to go through losing another partner. Since the department prefers us to work in pairs, they decided Alvarez and I should join forces.

It took me weeks to break through enough to make him crack a smile. After all of my futile attempts at jokes and quirky comebacks, it was an accidental slip in a pile of dog crap, landing me on my rump, that finally sent him into an actual gut laugh. That smelly mound melted the ice between us and earned me the nickname of Detective Doo-Doo.

Right now it looked like I was about to gain a new partner— one I never would have chosen otherwise, not because I didn't trust or believe in Kate's capabilities, but because we had an ongoing competition that overshadowed just about everything we did. I always looked at it as a healthy rivalry, but knew it would never work outside the scope of our personal lives. Now, I had to rethink that theory.

I knew the word *challenge* wouldn't begin to describe working with my sibling. Combine that with the added pleasure in knowing my bullheaded, strong-minded sister would be butting heads with Alvarez. As long as I can remember they'd never seen eye-to-eye, always at odds on everything from procedure to picante sauce. It made for interesting off-duty get-togethers. The only thing keeping Kate from verbally pummeling him so far had been their difference in rank. The day she makes detective is the day Alvarez will question his scope of English slang.

My last attempt at communication with the living had failed, but I had to try. As I saw it, Kate remained my last hope as the only one I could trust with the truth. Kate was the most dependable, levelheaded person I knew.

CHAPTER EIGHT

Kate let out an unexpected belch. "Oh, scuze me. I think I'm drunk," she said to a nearby patron. Signaling the bartender, "Nother round if ya don't mind."

The stocky bearded man frowned and poured her another shot and a beer. "It's time to call it a day, Kate."

She propped an elbow on the faded wood of the bar and offered a lopsided grin. "Yeah. I know, Joe."

O'Brien's Pub thrived just off the town square, tucked neatly between a barbershop and a small bridal boutique. Over the years, it had become the favorite watering hole for local law enforcement, providing an occasional Friday night band.

"How about I call you a cab?" Joe O'Brien said, wiping down a glass.

"Why not? I've been called everything else."

The man shook his head and turned away.

Kate turned her attention to the man beside her. "You come here often?"

"Is this a pick up?" He blew his nose with a yellowed hanky then returned it to his back pocket and smiled a toothless grin.

"I don't think so," Kate slurred. "I was supposed to meet someone, but he never showed."

"Boyfriend?"

Kate had to think about it a moment. She'd met Boden a few months ago at a party, wildly attracted to the buff build and bronze tan that gave him the California surfer look. After getting to know him, though, she realized her skyrocket attraction had dwindled to a sputtering fizz due to his lack of interest in anything but bodybuilding. She first spotted trouble when he showed up at her door wearing a healthy sweat and asking for a protein drink.

"No boyfriend," she told the guy.

"I'm kind of a regular around here, but I haven't seen you before."

"Rough week." Kate felt her eyes cross and squeezed them shut.

"I can tell."

"Why is that?"

"You don't seem like the typical drinker. I drink cause I like it. You seem to be trying to forget something."

"What are you, psychic?" She drained her beer.

"Just observant." He turned away.

Kate closed her eyes to the painful truth. She was officially smashed enough to turn off a drunk. George's pocket planner lay on the bar beside her beer and empty shot glass. So much for her investigation of B.T. and company. Braving the Dan Ryan Expressway, at risk of limb and sanity, she'd made lunch reservations at Hugo's in hopes of learning the mysterious identity behind the two letters. It had proven a lesson in humility.

This afternoon, she'd returned from Hugo's convinced she'd lost her mind somewhere between Michigan Avenue and Lake Shore Drive. Her pride stood badly bruised and her feet throbbed from the high-heel pumps she'd worn with her new designer suit. Now the shoes landed with a thud under the bar stool as she tried to unwind and forget.

Hugo's had been everything she remembered and more. A buttery glow melted over the foyer chandelier as patrons adjusted their windblown hair in the mirrored walls. Classical music complemented the relaxing elegance as enticing entrée aromas teased the senses.

The maitre d' showed Kate to a table near the back, passing several couples seated at window tables. She checked the back booths for any signs of Big Tony, disappointed to find them empty.

She ordered a light meal and ate slowly, watching the lunch crowd thin. The clientele at this hour consisted of men and women dressed in business attire, drinking martinis and speaking in hushed whispers. *Business lunch.* The booths remained untaken, and she stalled for time, ordering dessert. Finally, when the bill came and the server stopped offering coffee, she figured she'd wasted her time and hard-earned overtime check.

A reed-thin man wearing an Armani suit and a bad toupee passed her table carrying a leather briefcase. Her eyes caught the case's gold engraved initials—B.T.—as he made his way to the back booth. When he ordered coffee and nothing more, she bit her lip, wondering if her next move should be flat-out confrontation or the old you-look-like-my-uncle guise.

George saved her the trouble. She caught his reflection in the mirrored wall in time to lean over and retrieve a conveniently dropped fork. When he'd slid into B.T.'s high-backed booth with his back to her, she relaxed and watched both men. The clatter of silverware and conversation prevented her from hearing them and she dug inside her purse for her wallet.

A moment later, she called over the server. "Excuse me." She flashed her half-hidden badge, careful not to let the woman get much of a look. "I need to move to a booth near the back without drawing attention."

With no more than a small white lie, Kate had secured the booth behind George.

"I cannot let it go for that," B.T. was saying.

George's tone grew dark. "We've discussed this several times and this is my very last offer. Take it or leave it."

After a momentary silence, the man said, "In all my years as a private collector, I've never been in this position. I suppose you leave me no choice. I'll take it to the auction house, where a rare Bordeaux will receive the price and respect it deserves." He started to collect his briefcase.

"What!" George's outburst drew several stares across the crowded dining room. "You can't do that."

"I just did. As of now, my offer for the Château Margaux is off the table."

Kate felt her cheeks warm. The mysterious meetings had been over a bottle of wine.

The door to O'Brien's Pub opened, spilling afternoon light across the sticky floor tiles. Kate squinted to see Officer Jake Tucker coming toward her.

"Shit," she said and nearly fell getting off the barstool.

"That your friend?" the guy asked her.

"That's right," Jake said, catching her by the arm. "C'mon, Cinderella, party's over."

"What party? Did I miss something?"

"You're missing the point, Kate. Time for bed." Jake grinned and waved at the bartender on their way out.

On the way home, Kate felt herself sobering up. Jake brushed her repeated apologies off like annoying flies.

"I told you, Kate. Forget it."

Now she could add *ass* to her list of nicknames.

"Hey, Jake. What's the word in the department about Lindsay?"

"We're all devastated, Kate. Why do you ask?"

"Are they buying the truth, that she was murdered, or are they convinced it's a suicide?"

He stopped for a red light. "No one wants to believe she killed herself. We all knew her and it doesn't fit."

"But?"

"No 'but.' She's earned the respect of the entire department and we'd all like to find the guy who did this."

Kate let the subject drop, feeling her head begin to spin again. Maybe Jake had been right, and Lindsay's memory wasn't as tainted as she thought. She wanted to believe that, as much as she wanted to find her sister's slayer. With the guy behind bars, they could all find closure and clear Lindsay's name once and for all.

At home, she watched the squad car pull away from the curb and then tumbled onto the couch. The telltale hangover signs had begun, making her head feel twice its size. She leaned back, closing her eyes.

"I always *could* out-drink you," Lindsay said.

"Shut up—" Kate stopped.

When she opened her eyes, she saw her sister on the recliner, wearing her usual cocky grin. Kate closed her eyes again.

"Great. Now I'm hallucinating."

"No, you're not," Lindsay said. "You're not that drunk or you'd be puking. Remember that night when you were fifteen, and I caught you sneaking in through the bedroom window? I covered your ass, *and* mopped up your mess. Mom and Dad never did find out. You owe me."

Kate kept her eyes closed as the room spun. "I see you're still keeping score. Go away, you're dead."

"Yes, I am. But I'm not going anywhere. We have a case to solve."

Now Kate sat up. "I can't deal with hallucinations right now, I'm grieving."

When she opened her eyes, she saw that Lindsay was still sitting across from her, apparently waiting for her to say something. She was alive!

"Jesus, Lindsay! How did you pull it off?" Kate felt her heart jump to triple time.

"Pull what off?"

"Faking your death." Kate stumbled to the window and closed the shades. "Are you on special assignment?"

"Kate, stop. I didn't fake anything. What you saw in my tub was real. My funeral is tomorrow, and nothing will change that."

"But . . ."

"Sit down, Kate. We need to talk."

Kate obliged when she felt her knees melt. Ghosts and booze didn't mix. "I've really overdone it this time. No more shots for me."

"That stuff will cook your liver. You shouldn't be drinking anyway. Now get a grip. I need your full, *lucid,* attention."

Kate stared hard, trying to make sense of the situation. "You look faded, Linz."

"Of course I do. I'm a spirit. I'm not playing a trick, or working with the feds, or anything like that. So listen up. We both know I didn't kill myself."

"Okay, I'll go along with the hallucination. It looks like it has to run its course. What do you want from me?"

"I was victimized and I need your help to find whoever did it. I can't do it without you."

"I should have known you'd turn this into another competition."

"How do you figure that?"

"Look, Lindsay, I know you didn't kill yourself. Alvarez doesn't believe it, either. But this is something I want to do by myself. It will be the last thing I'll ever do for you, because its something you can't do for yourself. *Now* you're trying to take that away from me."

"And Alvarez is giving you his full cooperation, right?" Lindsay raised an eyebrow.

Kate squirmed.

"That's what I figured." Lindsay paced. "He's not going to let you near this because you're family. Don't take it personally. Given the circumstances, I would do the same thing. Remember when you were nine and we visited Aunt Etna on her farm?"

Kate cringed. No amount of liquor would ever erase that memory.

"You begged her to let you feed the geese by yourself. She tried to convince you that you were too young and inexperienced. She even offered to have me go with you, but you refused. Finally after an hour of your incessant whining, she gave in."

"Linz, you don't need to go on, I remember. Besides, I'm not feeling that well."

"Mom and I stayed in the house because we couldn't bear to watch. We all knew what was coming. It wasn't until I heard you bawling like a baby out in the yard that I peeked out the window. I saw you there in all your glory, surrounded by about twenty-five geese."

"More like thirty," Kate corrected.

"What a sight. Covered with bite marks as they pecked at the empty bucket in your arms. I've never seen so much goose shit in my life."

Kate suppressed a gag.

"The point is, you aren't ready to take this on yet. You're a great cop, but you can't do this by yourself."

Kate started to get up but didn't. Her head exploded with pain. "You're wrong," she managed through gritted teeth. "I need to do this for closure. If I don't, no one will ever have peace, not Mom and Dad, not me, not even you."

She heard Lindsay's familiar sigh, the one that signaled truce.

"All right. I get it. But you won't get anywhere without my help. I know how to run an investigation, and it's not about competition; this time it's about experience. Face it, Kate, you need me. And *I* need you to be my physical presence, to get to the information. So how about this; I promise we'll work as equal partners, no competition this time."

Kate eyed her warily, waiting for the catch. Lindsay's expression held no signs of an ulterior motive. Finally, she nodded. "Deal. Now let me get some sleep before I crash and burn."

As she drifted off, she figured this would all be a distant memory in the morning.

CHAPTER NINE

I watched Sally cuddle her teddy bear beside me on the park bench across from Smith's Funeral Home. The sun washed over her form, making it more transparent than normal. Still, I saw clearly enough to recognize her.

"I went to my funeral." She gazed toward the beige bricked building. "Wasn't much to see. A few close friends and neighbors, several co-workers. I actually counted the amount of Kleenex they went through. Ten."

"Ten boxes?"

"Ten tissues. That's it."

I'd been counting cars. Maybe tissue boxes were the real grief gauge. "Sally," I said, "can you tell me why no one greeted me when I crossed over?"

"You mean like they show in the movies? All that sappy crap about deceased relatives welcoming you with open arms?"

"Right."

"That's bullshit. You have a lot to learn." Her overly large brown eyes lit up. "Maybe I could teach you. You know, kind of like a tutor? Yeah. I like that.

"Anyway, the reason no one showed up to give you the grand tour is because everyone has their own path to walk and they're on different levels, depending on how long they've been here."

I chewed on that a bit as cars began spilling onto the street in search of parking spaces. Sally didn't seem to notice. "Can I ask you something else?"

"Sure." She seemed eager to help.

"The other day I tried to make contact with a close friend and he didn't respond, but later, my sister did. Why is that?"

"Oh that's simple navigation. You need to work on your skills. It takes practice."

"Navigation?"

"Yeah. You see the reason your friend didn't respond is because he's probably not open to it. Some people just aren't good with the whole beyond thing. But I guess your sister is more willing to hear from you. Now as navigation skills go, all it takes is some serious concentration on your part."

"What do you mean?"

"Well, if you want to make contact with someone, you have to focus on reaching into their mind. And if they're open, they'll hear you."

"How do you know all of this? Is there a course I can take, Great Beyond 101?"

"When you've been here as long as I have, you just learn things."

"How long ago did you pass?"

"Five years."

Now I recalled why Tri-City Labs seemed familiar. It had been about five years ago when a group of overzealous do-gooders torched the lab for freezing sperm, calling it an affront to the creator. In a warped sense of heroics, they burned the place to the ground, not realizing a receptionist had come in on her day off to catch up on some filing. That woman had been Sally.

"Five long years," she repeated.

"And you're still . . . here?"

"Guess I'll never resolve the loose ends of my life." She looked away. "I just never fit in. Never got close to anyone. Why else would a twenty-two-year-old woman be filing charts on her

Sunday off? I had nothing better to do."

I watched her squirm on the bench as cars started parking right in front of us.

"Looks like a good turnout. You must have a lot of friends." She rested her chin on the stuffed bear.

"There's always room for one more, Sally."

She smiled then, easing her grip on the bear just a little.

I'm not going to lie. Gazing at my corpse in the casket unnerved me. Kate had done a great job picking out my clothes; she has impeccable taste for someone who spends most of her time in a navy uniform and dark shoes. I made a mental note to thank her later for not burying me in my uniform, although as a member of the police department I'd earned the right. But that wasn't my style and Kate knew that. Instead, she'd chosen a baby blue suit jacket, matching skirt, and a cream-colored blouse. It looked professional for a detective, yet feminine enough to please the older generation of aunts and neighbors who'd known me growing up. My blonde hair stayed put for a change, fanning over my shoulders like silk. The rest of the mortician work seemed lacking, but then to me it always does. Call me a pessimist, but no amount of makeup can pull off the illusion that the deceased are simply sleeping. I've seen too much on the job. Still, it was a nice attempt.

I realized the importance of attending my own wake and forced myself past cosmetics. This might be a good opportunity to snoop around for clues, and see who turned out to be the loyal ones in my life. I've made many friends over the years in the department, but many more enemies. Police work can be quite political. Since I couldn't do much of anything else, I decided to kick back and watch the who's who passing down the receiving line.

When I felt a shiver, I realized my fiancé, George, had literally walked right through me on his way to the front of the room where my casket rested. A twinge of guilt ripped the fragile veneer I thought I'd sufficiently hung in place to guard against my own sorrow. Can't explain it, but I felt guilty having left everyone behind, especially George. He looked so lonely, so lost. I wanted to comfort him and tell him he'd be fine without me. I watched helplessly as he tenderly took my grieving mother into his arms and buried his head against my father's shoulder as they all wept together. I turned away, unable to wrestle the demon of self-control into its cage—it had me on my proverbial knees.

Then I saw Kate marching toward the group, a look of fiery determination on her face. No one was more surprised than I to see her grab George by the elbow and lead him away from my parents. Kate has a way of taking charge without taking over. No one seemed to be the wiser, including Mom and Dad, when the two made a hasty exit to the funeral parlor foyer.

I couldn't pass this up, so I followed close behind.

Kate's teeth gritted. "You have a lot of nerve." She turned him to face her.

A charcoal suit reflected his dark mood. He kept his tone low as anger simmered beneath the surface of a forced smile. "What's your problem, Kate? Is this upstaging necessary? Can't you let Lindsay have her last get-together without some sibling competition?"

I bit my lip—well, attempted to anyway. My new form would take some getting used to.

Something had happened between them; I could see my sister fighting to keep her fist at her side.

"You have no business here," Kate fumed.

"I'm the grieving fiancé. Do you want Lindsay to look bad? What would people say if I didn't show up? Regardless of what you think of me, I have morals and I did have feelings for her."

Did? Wait. What *did?*

"You said yourself it was over. If she hadn't been killed, I'd be introducing her to someone new this afternoon. Get over yourself, George, and while you're at it, get out."

What was she talking about? George and I had our problems, but as far as being over . . .

"I'm not going anywhere." George held firm.

"Yes, you are." Two uniformed officers towered over his six-foot frame on either side.

"Do you need an escort?" one of the officers asked.

Kate called out as he left, "And don't leave town."

I followed her to the ladies' room. Seeing no one else inside, I navigated myself into Kate's mind. Her sudden gasp told me it'd worked.

"Linz?" she whispered. "It's really you?"

"I told you before I'm not going anywhere yet."

"Jesus. Are you trying to kill me?" She took a deep breath and closed her eyes.

"Nope. I need you here, remember?"

She pinched the bridge of her nose as if warding off the tension. "I thought . . . hoped, that our last contact had been a case of too much booze on my part. But you're really here, aren't you?"

"Mostly," I nodded. "Well? Aren't you going to say it?"

Her blue eyes washed with tears. "Say what?" her voice quivered.

" 'I told you so.' Go on, you've proven me wrong."

"What are you talking about?"

"Remember when you dragged me to that awful séance when we were twelve?"

I saw recognition flash in her expression. "Right. Julie Baker's house. You were such a skeptic."

"And you thought you'd done it when that creepy whisper

came from behind the couch."

Kate laughed. "That's right. Julie had paid her kid brother to play the part of the ghost. Man did we hightail it out of there! You should have seen the look on your—"

"*Me!* Who hit the john at the speed of sound when we got home that night? You almost didn't make it!"

Kate stifled a giggle, wiping tears from her cheeks. "Okay, okay. But now I get the last laugh big sister, because I was right." Her smile faded gradually as she looked at me. "You're really gone, aren't you?"

" 'Fraid so." I let the moment hang between us, then changed the subject. "So, George planned to end it, huh?"

She paled in the mirror. "You heard?"

"It's a good thing for him I'm dead, and not because it gets him off the hook."

"Let me take care of that little weasel. He's still on my suspect list, even if he does have an alibi."

"How could I let this happen, Kate? I didn't see it coming."

"George or your demise?" She touched up her lipstick.

"Very funny. Both, I guess."

"You didn't see George's intentions because you didn't *want* to. I think you knew all along he was wrong for you, but you're stubborn and wouldn't admit it, even to yourself. As for your current situation, I'd say it's one of life's sucker punches that no one anticipates.

"Hey, by the way, why would George feel compelled to hide his wine-buying activities? What's the big deal about Bordeaux?"

"Big dollars. Why?"

Kate told me about George's *secret* meeting with B.T.

"George recently started collecting wine, but I wasn't into it. I went with him to a wine-tasting session in Chicago and couldn't believe the exorbitant prices people will pay for a rare vintage. Since I'd opened a savings account for our wedding, he probably figured I'd kick about the money and wanted to hide it from me."

"I like him even less, if that's possible." Kate snapped her purse shut. Changing the subject, she asked, "So, what do you think? Nice turnout for your wake."

"Mom and Dad look drained. I've never seen Dad so quiet. How are they holding up?" I knew the answer before Kate opened her mouth.

"They're devastated, of course. We all are. I suppose closure would bring about a certain amount of peace. But the scuttlebutt I'm hearing around the station is that the investigation is cold. Whoever did this put a lot of forethought into it. It wasn't just a random act. Which leaves a lot of your old enemies out."

"Why is that?"

"Most of them aren't intelligent enough to put a hit like this together."

"A hit?" The truth sounded so cold.

"What else would you call a planned, calloused act like this? It reeks of vendetta. We just need to figure out who."

I smiled.

"What are you grinning about?" Kate turned to leave.

"You said 'we.' Does that mean you've agreed to partner up?"

"Even during our most heated competitions, we've always been on the same team. Let's get this bastard."

I allowed Kate some privacy with the visitors and made my way around the spacious room lined with floral arrangements. I bent to sniff the roses from my parents, but to my disappointment, they had no scent. Come to think of it, I hadn't smelled anything since I'd crossed over. Another question for Sally. Working as a paranormal detective, I needed to know my *physical* limitations.

Reading some of the cards touched my heart while making

me melancholy. I wanted to shout, "I'm right here, everyone! No need to grieve. Let's step out for a couple of brews!"

I scanned the crowd, noting small clusters of people who knew one another through me, staying close together, speaking in low tones. Kate worked the room like a pro, relieving my parents from the task. I owed her big time.

My attention zeroed in on a strange man making his way about the room without speaking to anyone. At first, I thought he might be at the wrong wake as he wandered through the crowd looking lost. He seemed to be about five-foot-seven, and was dressed in a faded red-and-green flannel shirt and dirty green trousers, with too-long cuffs covering most of his worn sneakers. His faded gray eyes darted back and forth over a large hooked nose. I wondered how long it had been since his ruddy cheeks had felt a razor. How did I know him?

When he moved toward the casket, I followed close behind. Something felt wrong about him, but I couldn't place it. I glanced around for Kate but she'd been commandeered by Aunt Minnie, going on in great detail about her passel of cats. She'd be busy for quite some time.

The man stopped before my casket, making no movement or sound. To my horror, I saw him raise a whiskey bottle in a mock toast. No one seemed to notice this street-type derelict at my wake and I hoped people didn't assume he was an old friend or lover. Of course, at this point, I realized he might have been a better choice than George. Then it hit me. The odd visitor was a spirit.

I came up behind him, wondering if it would be polite, or even possible, to tap him on the shoulder. Finally, I settled for, "Excuse me. Are you looking for someone?"

He turned with his rheumy eyes wide.

Then I realized where I'd seen him before.

"Abner? Is that you?" I said.

His expression broke into a broad grin. "Yup. I knew I'd prob'ly find you here."

Abner Taute had been one of the department's best snitches. He was a walking encyclopedia of street activity and not afraid to share it for a price. Everyone knew him and felt sorry for the old buzzard. As a homeless alky, he'd been slain a few months ago for a pack of cigarettes. Guess it's true that smoking can kill you.

I led him toward the back, away from my supine corpse. "So what are you doing here?"

"Oh, just thought I'd pay my respects. And I hoped to see you, too."

"Why is that?"

He looked around as if he might be overheard. Some habits die hard. "I have some information . . . kind of a freebie now that we're both on the same side." He chuckled at his own joke, then continued, "You're in danger, Detective Frost. Gotta watch your back."

I sighed. Some things never change. "Look Abner, if you're still out for favors, it's a little late. I don't have any connections on this side, and if you're trying to scare me, there isn't too much to fear at this point."

"Oh, I wouldn't be so sure. *Your* troubles have just begun, Detective Frost."

CHAPTER TEN

Several days after the funeral, Kate's squad fishtailed answering a call, her adrenaline pumping. Her car raced toward the familiar warehouse district known for gang and drug activity.

Responding to a call at an abandoned building in the heart of gangland territory, her senses grew razor sharp. The suspected rapist was armed, and holding a female child hostage.

She jumped when Lindsay suddenly appeared in the passenger seat. "Can't you give me some sort of signal before you appear?"

Lindsay frowned. "Why are you back at work so soon after my funeral? Surely you've got more time coming than just a few days."

"I have to keep busy. I'm better off at work."

"What's the call?"

"Rape suspect with a hostage."

"Shit. Better call for backup."

"Who's runnin' this call?" Kate felt the old annoyance resurface. "I can handle it."

"Don't go in alone."

"I'll do what I have to do. He's got a little girl with him."

"I'll go in ahead of you."

"Don't try to pull rank on me, Linz. When I agreed we'd work together, I didn't say you'd be in charge." She parked and got out of the squad.

Kate spoke into her shoulder radio, "12–22. I need another car."

She headed toward the graffiti-coated side door standing half open. To her annoyance, Linz followed.

A child's cry inside prompted her to draw her gun.

"12–22. Victim in distress. I'm going in."

The radio screeched a static response and she snaked her way along the wall, stopping when her shoe crunched broken glass. She strained to see across the vacant warehouse in the dim light.

"I'll go check it out. You wait here." Linz took off across the room.

"Stop," she whispered after her.

"Why? He can't see me, but I can find him. You'll be on him before he can fire."

A piercing scream sounded from the second floor and Kate took off for the stairs. "12–22. Where's my backup?"

"Let me go first," Linz pleaded. "Take the advantage."

Kate knew that if another officer had been able to offer this kind of assistance, she wouldn't have hesitated. There was no way to lose and she had to think of the victim's life. She'd tripped over her pride before but this time a child could die.

She nodded, allowing Lindsay to go up ahead of her.

After a moment, she heard Lindsay's instructions.

"He's in the southwest corner with his gun at her head. You've got a clear shot at his back."

Kate went in blind, trusting her sister. What choice did she have?

She rounded the stairs, gun pointed. "Let her go or die," she commanded.

"He's going to fire. Get down!" Lindsay shouted.

Kate dropped behind a row of wooden crates as gunfire erupted from the corner.

"Now!" Lindsay yelled.

Kate fired twice, then heard a muted grunt as the man fell. The girl screamed, backpedaling against the wall.

"It's okay, honey. You're safe now," Kate assured her, running toward the child.

"He's not moving," Linz told her. "But he's still breathing."

Kate moved close enough to kick his gun across the room, keeping her weapon aimed. She leaned down and found a pulse.

"12–22. Offender secured, needs medical attention."

Flashing lights penetrated the dingy warehouse windows as backup arrived.

She dropped down beside the crying child to cradle her. "Everything's okay. It's over. You get to go home now."

She caught Lindsay's proud look and knew they'd crossed the line that had kept them at odds for most of their lives. Although there would always be that level of competitiveness between them, today proved they made a good team. They'd saved a life and got the bad guy. Maybe Lindsay's idea to partner up would work after all.

In the squad, Kate looked over at her sister's faded form, still trying to put it all into perspective. How could Linz be gone? She wasn't gone, yet she knew she couldn't tell her grieving parents about Lindsay's not so eternal rest. It didn't seem fair that they had to continue to suffer, while Lindsay rode shotgun on police calls. Life isn't fair, she reminded herself, and apparently, neither was death.

Her eyes widened when she spotted Lindsay's detective badge hanging around her neck. Lindsay caught her expression.

"What's wrong? What are you staring at?"

"Your badge. How come you're still wearing it?"

"I'm still a detective."

"You don't get it. No one ever found your badge. Alvarez is

convinced the murderer took it as a trophy. He thinks it's a clue."

"Oh shit."

"Yeah. How can I tell him *you* have it?"

"You can't. Forget it."

"I guess you *can* take it with you, huh? Dad will be glad to hear that." Kate shook her head.

"It's a death tag. As I understand it, I have to work out my last issue before I can move on to the next level. Until then, I'm stuck with the thing."

"Do you want to move on?" Kate bit her lip.

"Hell no. I'm having way too much fun annoying you. Speaking of annoying, how's that clown you're dating . . . what's his name, Bobo?"

"It's Boden, and he's *not* my boyfriend." Kate frowned.

"That's not what I heard. Prove it."

Kate felt their old camaraderie resurface and easily slipped back into their familiar banter. "He never gave me his cell phone number, I don't know his middle name, and I'd never be able to pick his penis out of a lineup."

"Okay. I was wrong. So who *are* you seeing?"

"No one. I don't have time. I'm working, remember?" She headed toward the precinct. "Look, Linz. I've never been more frustrated in my life. We need a break. Something solid. I don't have to tell you with each passing day the trail gets colder and someone gets closer to getting away with this crime."

"I know, but you have to take time for yourself, or you'll get lost. Know what I mean? I can vouch, from experience, that life is too short. Don't get too caught up in this. Take a break. Why don't you go skydiving? That's always been your stress buster."

Kate checked her watch. "My shift is about over and I need to see Alvarez before he leaves."

"You're ignoring me." Lindsay frowned.

"I'm prioritizing."

"Isn't that a synonym for obsessing?"

"Don't start digging into your repertoire of shrink terms," Kate warned.

"Why not? I've paid a lot for them over the years."

"That reminds me. I need to call your therapist and cancel your sessions."

"Make sure you mention I didn't off myself. I'd hate for Dr. Spinozzo to take it personally."

"I never quite understood why you needed therapy anyway."

"Nightmares that started after Joe was killed. It got so I tried to avoid sleep because I dreaded the night terrors. I decided to get help when I began sleepwalking with my gun in hand."

"A nightie and a Glock. Quite a fashion statement."

"George didn't appreciate it. I almost nailed him one night coming out of the bathroom."

Kate laughed as she pulled the squad into the department lot. "Wish I could have seen that."

"He swore he'd never leave the toilet seat up again," Lindsay said, and grinned.

Kate cut the engine. "I'll have to remember that trick for my next relationship. But right now I have to find a better way to gain cooperation from a stubborn male."

"That's the most accurate synonym for Alvarez I've ever heard."

CHAPTER ELEVEN

When Kate decided to ignore my sage advice and visit Alvarez instead of going skydiving, I felt the familiar pangs of our edgy relationship resurface. Kate didn't like being told what to do—especially by me. So, I figured I'd join her in my ex-partner's office, to glean info *and* annoy the shit out of her.

Kate paced before Alvarez's rickety desk, ticking off reasons on her fingers. "For one thing, Lindsay was nude. Most suicides don't strip. My sister could be tough as nails, but she was definitely on the modest side. She'd never off herself in the buff."

Me? Modest?

She continued, "Her body was positioned, there were no prints, and no note. Not to mention the fact that the goddamned creep wiped up the mess and no one found any wet towels, which leads me to believe the killer is female. The whole thing reeks of a setup."

Alvarez glared. "I don't dispute anything you've just said, Kate. But the fact remains that there are a few details that point to the suicide theory."

"Such as?" Kate's eyes pinned him.

"No evidence of forced entry—for that matter, no evidence of anyone else being in the home at all."

"What about the spilled food in the living room? If she'd been in such emotional distress, I'm sure a ham sandwich and a beer would've been the last things on her mind."

Alvarez went on, "And then there's the hesitation marks on the wrist wounds."

"What the hell does that mean?"

"When someone slits their wrists, often there are hesitation marks near the wounds, as if they're trying it out first to see if they can follow through. It's rare to see clean marks.

"But according to the coroner's preliminary report, she'd been tasered. They found several marks indicating the guy zapped her more than once to keep her out."

"Any drag marks on the carpet?" Kate paced.

"None. She must have been carried." He rested a hand on her arm. "I know what you believe—that the person is a woman. But Lindsay was five-nine and . . . built."

I believe the term is toned.

He touched Kate's cheek. "Whoever did this had to have been incredibly strong to carry her limp body all the way to the bathroom."

Kate turned away. "You are such a chauvinist. Are you really naïve enough to believe a woman couldn't have done this? It makes perfect sense. Think about it. You're a single male, raising two teenage boys. How often do any of you clean up after yourselves?"

"All the time. There's no woman to do it for us," he said with a grin.

Kate realized her mistake too late. I saw her relax a bit and take a seat. She leaned over, burying her face in her palms. Then I watched in disbelief as my stone-cold ex-partner tenderly stroked Kate's head like a big brother comforting his sister. It touched me deeply. God how I missed my body, the Frost freckle included. I wanted it back so I could be there for Kate and the rest of my family. The best I could do for them now was solve the case.

Why couldn't I remember what happened? I searched for the

tiniest memory, but came up with nothing. Replaying what I remembered made for a very short flick. I recalled sitting down, feeling a sting in my neck, and the next thing I saw was my body in the tub. I made a lousy witness. How many times as a detective had I wished the victims could speak? The coroner, Thomas Stern, had told me repeatedly that that's what autopsies are for. It's the person's last chance to have his or her say. But I couldn't tell anyone anything, not because I couldn't speak, but because I really didn't know anything.

Kate sat up, asking the one question I knew she'd been gearing up to ask. "What about rape?"

Alvarez let out a long breath, and shook his head. "Negative."

Her facial tension eased a bit. "What's next?"

"We've put the word out to all our tipsters to keep themselves open for info. Her neighbors made poor witnesses; no one saw or heard anything unusual. We've questioned past arrestees of possible interest, but every lead has turned cold."

"What about women she's arrested?"

"No one stands out. You knew her best. Who'd do something like this?"

That was a loaded question. As a female dick, I'd made my share of women enemies both on the force and on the street. Some gals frowned upon other women in departmental positions, and sometimes it came down to the ugly green monster of jealousy.

Kate shook her head. "No one specific. The only person of interest that I can see is that damn George Anderson, but his alibi checks out."

"You sound disappointed," Alvarez said, grinning.

Before he could continue, one of the other detectives came in with a folded newspaper. "I think you should look at this." He handed it to Alvarez.

"*Mierda!*" Gerard cursed, scanning the paper twice. I watched his dark eyes turn black with anger. By the twitch in his jaw, I knew he was furious enough to level a city block.

Kate rushed behind him to read over his shoulder, the color draining from her face.

"Who the hell did this?" she yelled to the other detective.

He hung his head and shrugged. "Dunno. It's not lookin' too good for Frost."

Both Kate and Alvarez withered the man with a look and he turned tail to head out of the office.

"Not a word. Got it?" Alvarez called after him.

The man nodded and left.

I raced to see the paper before Alvarez folded it over.

My ghostly eyes widened in their ethereal sockets as I read the pack of lies for myself.

LOCAL HOMICIDE DETECTIVE COMMITS SUICIDE.

So much for damage control. Whoever wanted to dirty my name had succeeded, but it wasn't until I read further that I realized just how badly they wanted to tarnish the Frost name forever.

My eyes scanned blips of print, fueling my anger and spurring my determination to get this asshole: *no signs of forced entry . . . suicide . . . autopsy results pending . . .*

Then I spotted the words that confirmed my suspicions of motive.

Detective Frost's long list of accomplishments has been tarnished with speculation over hindered evidence collections and tainted suspect statements. Bribery questions in a recent murder-for-hire case have surfaced, leaving more questions than answers.

Kate thundered, "How could they print this bullshit?"

Alvarez reread the entire article with hooded black eyes and I knew there would be hell to pay when he got within a foot of the columnist who wrote it. He knew what I knew—that someone close to the guy, perhaps the killer himself, had planted this story. But why? Who hated me so much that my demise wasn't good enough for them?

While most detectives would think this a real blow, I saw it as another clue. Granted my name would suffer for it, but I knew now that this had been a vendetta. Someone really wanted to make me look bad, first by staging my demise, and now by publishing this load of crap for the whole world to see, or at least Taylor County. But that was my whole world, and it was slowly being taken away from me.

The look on Kate's face spoke of devastation and exhaustion, and I knew she was thinking about Mom and Dad, and the effect this would have on them.

Who wanted to destroy not only my life, but my memory as well?

I thought about Abner's warning at my wake and decided I'd done the right thing in not telling Kate about it. She had enough stress to deal with right now. Besides, I couldn't be sure of the information's worth. While Abner had given up his share of solid leads in the past, he held the notorious title of the Solemnly Swear Snitch because he couldn't always be trusted to get the whole truth, nothing but the truth, unless it helped Abner.

On the other hand, the snitch hadn't wanted anything that day—he'd said it was a freebie. So what was his angle? Unfortunately, he'd disappeared before I'd had a chance to press him further. Guess his navigational skills need work.

I followed Kate out of the precinct toward her car. Since I'd figured out that moving from one spot to another was a matter of willing myself in a certain direction rather than trying to make my legs take actual steps, I hit my target more often. As Kate took off in a hurry, I realized I still needed to figure out how to move faster.

"Hold up," I called as she slid into the driver's seat.

"I've got to get out of here, Linz. I'm going to the airfield."

Now, she takes my advice to go skydiving—just when I need to vent and use her as a sounding board after seeing my name fouled in print. Feeling abandoned, I realized emotions don't die with a person; if anything they become stronger. Left standing there, I decided to give her some space and go back to Alvarez.

CHAPTER TWELVE

The sun's reflection off the front bumper briefly blinded Kate as she stormed from the parking lot. No amount of talking, stomping, or shouting would soothe her raw temper right now. She had to get away.

It hurt to leave Lindsay behind, but she couldn't think with her sister's big blue eyes haunting her. Literally. The past week had been a roller coaster of events that spurred emotions she had no idea how to deal with. Lindsay is gone. Lindsay is not gone. Cold case. Slander. It was all becoming too much.

As she drove, her mind entertained thoughts of strangling the so-called journalist who wrote the piece of garbage for the local news rag, then she realized that would only fuel their fire.

LOCAL POLICE OFFICER MURDERS INNOCENT RE-PORTER.

Now there's a real oxymoron.

She knew there was more to the newspaper story than the obvious. It proved another way to hurt Lindsay and those she cared about, but most of all, it showed that the person responsible had no soul. In her time on the force, she'd met some rough characters and had seen people do things to other human beings she thought only Stephen King's monsters might conjure. But she'd never been involved with someone without a soul, and that frightened her more than any other criminal type, because this was a person who had nothing to lose.

She had no doubt that Alvarez would dig until he found the

worm responsible and put them in their place. He would have the newspaper recant its statements, and he'd probably scare the living shit out of the poor reporter, but would it be enough? The damage had been done.

Kate pounded the dash at a stoplight, frustration taking its toll. No new leads, no solid suspects, and now this. The only thing she knew, in her heart, was that the assassin had to be female. It wasn't much to go on and no one else agreed.

Her temper ebbed and flowed as she drove toward the airstrip. She didn't recall much of the drive when her car took the turnoff. Gravel and dust plumed behind her as she neared the Lansing Airport. It had serviced the northwest Indiana area for over a hundred years, and had been the site of her first sky-dive. She saw several familiar planes that she'd jumped from in the past, all polished and glimmering in the sun as if waiting for her.

As she pulled up to the south side of the building housing the small office, she saw her old instructor, Pat Turner. They'd become good friends over the years and she knew she'd never forget his patience and encouraging demeanor on her first jump. He waved her in, his contagious smile all but reaching both ears.

"Hey, look what the wind blew in!" Pat's forty-something paunch shook with a chuckle. "You here to jump?"

"Yeah. It's been too long, Pat."

The man pulled out a dog-eared logbook and scanned for her name. "Hmm. Looks like your last jump was in April." His faded blue eyes looked over his bifocals perched like a shelf across his large nose. "You checked your pack yet?"

"I always do. I learned from the best, remember?"

"Yes, I do. You were one of my favorite students." He reached for the phone. "I'll give Bowser a call. Looks like he's not doing much this afternoon flight-wise. He'll be glad to see you."

The name brought an onslaught of memories about a time, several years before, when she'd received a coupon for a free birthday skydive. A group of fellow officers had pitched in as a joke, but she turned the tables when she scheduled the jump and suggested they all go together. There were no takers in the bunch, forcing her to go alone, with the exception of a couple of guys who wanted to see her do it for themselves. Although she had serious second thoughts when it came time to get into the plane, she wasn't about to let them see her chicken out. Wind in her face and hands shaking, she jumped tandem with the instructor. After the initial panic passed, she opened her eyes and her love of skydiving was born.

Chuck Bowser had been the pilot that day, making her feel at ease as they'd slowly climbed to the right altitude, easing her mind when she considered calling the whole thing off.

The Lansing Airport staff had always made her feel like family, and today, especially, she felt the need for the added support of someone she trusted. Who better to fill that role than the pilot who carries your life in his hands?

Since that first day, parachuting had captured her heart, allowing her a quick way to get away from it all. She'd earned an advanced skydiving license, which meant she could solo and enjoy the greatest freedom of all. She loved the wind in her face and the free-falling feeling as she plummeted toward earth with nothing to restrain her, nothing to break into her thoughts. It was a way to leave her problems grounded and escape the earthly realm.

As she double-checked her chute, Kate thought about her two greatest passions, skiing and skydiving. They'd both given her hours of stress reduction, especially the yearly ski trip she took with her college cronies to White Crest Mountain in Wisconsin. The huge A-frame cottage set deep in a wooded area of pines overlooked a deep valley, offering a perpetual Christmas-like atmosphere even though the trip always took place in January. She'd tried for years to get Lindsay to go, without success. Her sister preferred mai tais served by a tall sun-bronzed pool waiter instead of thawing her fingers before the fireplace after a day of shooshing.

Snug inside her jumpsuit at the open door of the plane, Kate nodded to Chuck and he gave her the thumbs-up to jump. Crouched, hands holding the wing support bar, her heart pounded an adrenaline rush to her brain as she breathed in the fresh cool air. She mentally counted to three, then jumped.

Closing her eyes briefly, she began her free fall, allowing her frustration, anger, and fear to plummet to the ground. Back arched, arms and legs spread, she felt the familiar pressure against her body envelop her in a hug. She watched a car driving along the stretch of road away from the airstrip and thought of a shiny black bug.

For a few seconds, all her difficulties felt that small and she relished the feeling of strength and control. Caught up in the beauty of the fall, she didn't want to lose track of time and checked the altimeter. After a few more seconds, she'd be at fifty thousand feet. She enjoyed the last of her freefall, her last moments of high exhilaration.

When she pulled the ripcord it came off in her hand.

The altimeter reading dropped fast. Forcing down panic, she mentally reviewed emergency procedures. Pat's calm advice came to mind.

By now, she should be enjoying total calm and peace, drifting lazily toward land. She saw the ground coming up fast, and pulled the cut-away handle to release the main chute. Kate yanked the reserve chute's cord. Thankfully, it opened.

She maneuvered her way to the ground, cursing at her harsh landing.

Several airstrip employees rushed across the field to her aid.

"Kate. Are you all right?" Pat Turner asked.

"I'm fine." She shook off her backpack. "The main chute didn't open. The damn ripcord came off in my hand."

Pat examined the remains. "You might want to have a look. The ripcord was cut."

CHAPTER THIRTEEN

I saw Alvarez heading down the precinct steps toward his car. He wasn't alone, as Detective Elizabeth Copley followed close behind, getting into the passenger seat. The department had wasted no time pairing him up with a new partner, thankfully one with several years of detective work under her belt. Still, the idea rankled. I'd always thought of Alvarez and I as irreplaceable, like Sherlock and Watson, Starsky and Hutch, or, considering recent paranormal events, Scully and Mulder.

Setting my delusions aside, I settled for the back seat as Copley shut her door and buckled up.

They had no idea I sat in the rear of the Crown Vic wrestling my feelings of guilt into a tight corner of validation. I didn't like being the third wheel, and I liked the feeling that my actions were immoral a lot less. After all, my current condition prohibited me from fully performing like a detective, and there seemed to be no real point to my tagging along; other than the fact that I felt left out and jealous. Then I reminded myself that this was my murder and I had every right to be here.

Like it or not I was with them and anyone else whom I deemed necessary to "ride along" with in order to solve the case. If Alvarez had any idea I could help him from the great beyond, he'd appreciate the assistance. With my guilt neatly rationalized away, I tried to determine our destination.

As Alvarez drove, discussing the facts with Copley, I learned he'd been in contact with the journalist, and I use the term loosely, who'd written the article on me. Suddenly the car swerved to avoid a pedestrian who had the nerve to cross with the light.

"Jeez, Alvarez, can you slow it to the speed of sound?" Copley suggested.

"I want to catch Calvin Stokes before he gets too drunk. He has some explaining to do."

Calvin Stokes was a gun-shop owner, local drunk, and town asshole from our neighboring community of Dorian. He lived with his dowdy wife on the edge of town, where they mostly kept to themselves. I figured Alvarez's angle had something to do with the fact that Calvin Stokes and I had an unpleasant history.

We drove past the fairgrounds and into the historical section. The older Victorian-style homes rested proud along the rows of mature trees and the pristine sidewalks where people walk their dogs and wave to one another. I recalled this section of utopia from my patrol days, where nothing worse than the occasional parking violation occurred.

It took about twenty minutes to arrive at a drive leading to a white-pillared, smaller version of Tara from *Gone with the Wind*. Jade-colored grass carpeted its way across the wide hilly yard to meet a white Victorian mailbox facing the street. I wondered why we were here.

When the expensive white door opened, I recognized Calvin Stokes, with his bug eyes and bad comb-over, looking thinner and older than the last time I saw him on the courthouse steps. His son's killer had been set free for lack of evidence. I'll never forget his accusations and pointing finger as he followed me to my car that day.

Nineteen-year-old Jason Stokes had been gunned down during a drug deal in a nearby town a few years before. I'd lucked out, arresting the gunman for an unrelated charge that led to

Jason's passing. But somebody screwed up the evidence—a fact the accused's attorney, Marie Yates, had jumped on. With lack of sufficient evidence, we lost the conviction, and the bad guy walked.

Calvin didn't understand that I had nothing to do with the evidence after it was seized, and he remained convinced I was to blame. It hurt, because I'd known him for years.

Most of the cops bought their guns from Calvin, because he knew weapons and always gave an officer a deal. I'd bought an ankle pistol for extra protection several months before his son died.

Calvin had battled alcoholism for years, giving in shortly after losing Jason. I'd heard his wife, Janice, had come from old money, enough to support her husband's drinking and maintain the gun shop during dry spells. Janice was a strange woman, too quiet and mousy for my tastes, and she never seemed to cross her husband. Hey, whatever works. I'm no Dear Abby when it comes to romantic relationships, but I get the impression that Janice's devotion is out of fear, not adoration.

Months later, Calvin came around and got back on the wagon, but he never seemed to let go of the grief and anger, occasionally having one or two at the local bar.

Standing at his front door, I thought about how he certainly had motive to want me dead, and with his easy access to Tasers, he had means.

Alvarez introduced himself and Copley, and Calvin allowed them in.

"What's all this about?" Calvin frowned.

"Mr. Stokes, I'm investigating a story in the *Southfield Times*. The reporter who wrote the story said you were a source of information for him."

I saw Alvarez's jaw clench and knew he'd found the jerk who wrote the story about me.

Calvin's thin frame seemed to shrink as he slouched onto the couch.

Alvarez towered over him, waiting for a response. I swear he could teach a class on Intimidation. "Can you tell me anything about that, sir?" Alvarez pressed.

The man's sallow cheeks paled, but he raised a defiant chin. "What's it to you?"

"I'm trying to get the facts, Mr. Stokes. The story is pertinent to an ongoing investigation."

"What *kind* of investigation?"

"Detective Lindsay Frost—"

"That bitch! My son's killer went free because of her. She deserves what she got."

"What would that be?" Copley cut in.

"She's dead, isn't she?" Calvin wore a smug expression. "Just like my son. Now the score's even."

Alvarez's dark eyes pinned him. "Who's keeping score?"

"I am. I not only lost my son, but my wife has never been right since. I've lost everything because of that so-called *detective.*" He went over to the glass hutch and brought out a whiskey bottle.

"Can that wait, Mr. Stokes? We'd like to talk to you while you're lucid." Copley watched him pour four fingers full and down it.

"I haven't been straight since my son died. I sure don't intend to start now." He poured another round.

Alvarez ignored the man's behavior. "Where were you last Friday evening around eight o'clock?"

"I was sick."

"Where were you?"

"Here. Sick in bed. I just told you."

"Can anyone verify that?" Alvarez shifted his weight to lean closer.

"Yes. My wife."

"May I speak with her?"

"She's not here."

"When will she be back?" Copley asked.

"She's out of town for a few days. Am I under arrest?"

"Not yet," Alvarez answered.

"Then get out." Whiskey sloshed over the top of the glass as he motioned toward the door. "You people have done enough . . . no, come to think of it, you haven't done *anything*. So get out."

Alvarez nodded to Copley, and I watched him take his professional pride and leave, but I knew he would be back, because Calvin Stokes was lying.

Don't ask me how I knew. Maybe crossing over gives you some sort of second sight, but I could tell Alvarez felt it, too. Although Stokes didn't appear to be blessed with enough intelligence to plan a murder staged as suicide, I knew people were capable of all kinds of extraordinary feats with the right motive. But why now? His son died almost two years ago, giving Calvin's anger time to cool. On the other hand, it might have given it time to simmer to a boil.

In the car, Copley shook her head. "Too bad we don't have enough evidence for a warrant. Now that he knows we like him, he'll be watching for us. He'll get rid of any evidence if he hasn't already."

Alvarez nodded. "I want to talk to his wife. We need to know his whereabouts that night."

Alvarez answered his cell phone and suddenly turned on his car flashers. If I'd had a pulse, it would have sped up when I heard him say, "What do you mean, the chute didn't *open?*"

Chapter Fourteen

I know, I know. Kate is twenty-eight years old, self-sufficient, doesn't need anyone hovering over her—no pun intended. I realize it's time to let go of my big-sister act, especially since I'm only a spirit. But I can't. I'll be her guardian, her protector, her invisible shield if need be. It's a sister thing.

When we got back to Alvarez's office, Kate met us there. She'd survived, madder than a pit bull and just as likely not to let the incident go. I shuddered at the details of her near-fatal fall, and realized most people fear the jump when it's the landing that usually kills them. If not for her nerves of steel, quick thinking, and a back-up chute, I'd be instructing *her* on navigational skills.

"My equipment was sabotaged," she told Alvarez. "I packed my gear, like I always do."

"But you were upset. Maybe your head was elsewhere," he suggested.

"I know how important that final check is. I don't skimp on parachuting technique. Someone tampered with my stuff. The mechanic in the hangar said he saw a black, expensive-looking car leaving shortly after I went up for my dive. I say it was Marie Yates."

Alvarez stopped shuffling paperwork. "Number one, it's extremely difficult to tamper with someone's equipment with so many people around. Number two, Marie Yates wouldn't chance breaking a fingernail fooling around with parachute equipment that she knows nothing about in the first place. Three, why would Marie want to harm you?"

"I don't know. It doesn't make sense, but a description like that doesn't match many folks at the airfield. That's what caught the mechanic's attention—he'd never seen that car before and he knows everyone.

"And you're wrong about airport security. The smaller airfields can't afford all the high-tech equipment and guards. If the person knew where to look, it would only take a couple of minutes to sabotage a chute. And I know exactly when it happened. My pilot, Chuck, received a last-minute phone call when I hit the john before takeoff. There had to be at least a five-minute window, long enough for the person to get in and out relatively unnoticed."

"Did you talk to the pilot afterward? Was the call legit?"

"He wasn't sure. The connection was so bad he hung up."

"So what's Marie's angle? Why you?" Alvarez asked.

"Not just me. You're forgetting Lindsay."

"What? You think Marie killed Lindsay? I know there was no love between them, but murder? You're reaching."

"Never know. I might just grab something. It's more than we have so far."

Alvarez sighed. "I'll make some calls and find out what counselor Yates did today. But even if she was at the airstrip, it doesn't prove she tampered with your equipment. I'm afraid it's still a dead end."

Kate recovered nicely from her parachuting experience, enough to pay Marie Yates a visit the next day. What a way to spend your day off. I tried to convince her she should take it easy, but Kate remained adamant that she had nothing better to do than investigate my demise, and her *accident*.

Out of uniform today, Kate dressed in a red-silk sleeveless

shirt, black jeans, and dress boots—no one would have guessed her to be a cop. I wondered if this would be the style of dress she'd incorporate into her work as a detective. Personally, I always preferred something a bit more casual, because you never know when you'll have to hit the pavement.

Her goal to make detective hovered like a storm cloud, always threatening; the unmet goal was a constant reminder that she hadn't quite come up to her own success standards. I knew her desire to make detective was part of our ongoing competition, yet I also realize she just plain loves police work and wants to climb the ranks, with becoming detective being the next logical step. Still, not everyone can handle it, and we need good street cops badly.

As she drove, Kate and I tried to picture the self-assured criminal lawyer's expression when she learned she'd been seen at the airport.

"She might be out of the office," I suggested.

"She's probably at her weekly evil lesson with Satan." Kate cut the corner sharp.

"Yeah. I wonder what she charges him?" I pictured her browbeating the poor demon.

Kate tapped the steering wheel, waiting for a red light. "We've got her."

"She'll deny it," I said.

"Probably. But I want to see her face." Kate frowned.

"Are you forgetting what she does for a living? It's her job to hide emotions. She's had lots of practice over the years."

"A lie is still a lie. We'll catch her."

Kate pulled into a parking space close to Marie's office. The building faced what was known as "the square," which surrounds an old courthouse in the center of town. The Victorian-style courthouse, built in the 1800s, no longer served in a legal capacity—now it housed quaint shops specializing in everything from grandfather clocks to an old-fashioned candy store. Nestled among the shops, along the long red-bricked corridor, stood an old-fashioned ice cream parlor made to look like an outdoor café.

The building's upper level held chamber of commerce offices, a ballroom, and unused courtrooms where the public was invited take advantage of a free guided tour on select days of the week. I knew Kate had visited the place, always claiming an eerie feeling that it was haunted. My scoffing days had ended, now that I realized that that was entirely possible.

Facing the courthouse across the street, Marie's office sat on top of a shoe repair shop with a green-and-white-striped awning out front, which gave the place a carnival look—I wondered if Marie had tried to get the owner to remove it. Her tastes ran in the designer-Mercedes-hoity-toity circles. Still, with the modern main courthouse complex only five minutes down the street, it seemed the perfect location for her prestigious law office.

Passing a black Mercedes parked on the street, Kate stooped to check the tires.

"Shit." She glanced over the car. "It's been washed. No dust or gravel. I can't tell if she's been near the airfield recently."

"C'mon," I said. "Let's go talk to her."

Kate boldly headed inside and straight up the narrow flight of stairs to the office, where she entered without hesitation. Years of police work will do that to you—that and someone sabotaging your parachute equipment. The receptionist looked away from her computer screen through the glass partition, but Kate beat her to the punch.

"I'm here to see Marie Yates."

One of the receptionist's black eyebrows shot up. "Do you have an appointment?"

"No," Kate said on her way toward a closed door labeled M. Yates.

"Wait . . ." The forty-something woman jumped up.

Too late. Kate knocked briefly and proceeded inside, closing the door behind her. I followed.

Marie jumped up from behind her desk, toppling a cup of water into her lap.

"What the hell do you mean by coming in here without permission?" She reached deep into a side desk drawer and pulled out a tissue box. As she hastily blotted her clothing she watched in horror as the tissue disintegrated, forming tiny white wads on her designer skirt. Her brown eyes narrowed on Kate, summing her up.

"Kate Frost?" Marie seemed to relax a bit, still mopping the spill.

"Isn't that amazing, Marie? I'm still here."

"What are you talking about?" She straightened to her full height, which I'd guess to be about five-foot-eight.

Kate towered over her, edging up close with only the desk between them. "You visited the Lansing Airport yesterday."

Marie's frown deepened. "You're delusional."

I listened to their banter as I wandered about her spacious office. This proved the most fun I'd ever had in attorney Yates' presence. She could be a real buzz kill. I noticed her desk drawer hadn't closed all the way and realized she could easily do a half gainer over it as she decided to round the desk.

Marie tossed what was left of the soggy tissue into the waste can, and slammed the drawer. When it didn't catch, I saw that something inside prevented it from closing; my hopes for an acrobatic performance were still intact.

"Again, Officer Frost," Marie said, "I don't know what you're talking about. I spent the morning in court, then the remainder of the day tied up with clients here. You've wasted a trip."

"A witness says different." Kate moved closer.

"Your witness is mistaken." Marie reached for the phone.

Kate's hand slammed down, covering Marie's. "Don't."

The attorney never flinched, and I saw why she was considered the best criminal lawyer in the county. This had become a tea party for her; after all, she was used to dealing with razor-edged criminals and hard-nosed judges. It took more than a little intimidation to rattle Marie Yates. She thrived on it.

"Take your hand away or you will regret it," she cautioned.

When Kate didn't move, I came up beside her. "Just do it. You don't want her to call Alvarez, do you?"

Kate's hand slid back slowly and rested at her side. Good girl.

"I know you tampered with my chute. But I'm a better parachutist than you are a criminal."

"Someone tampered with your equipment and you think it was me?"

"Like I said, a witness places you and your car there."

"I wouldn't know the first thing about tampering with parachute equipment. Why don't you have it fingerprinted?" Marie toyed with her now.

"Already done. But of course, you've been around criminals long enough to know to wear gloves. I'm sure you've covered all your bases with this, *and* with Lindsay."

Marie's Lancôme-painted cheek offered a slight twitch. Perhaps Kate was breaking through.

"Are you accusing me of having something to do with your sister's demise?" Her tone seethed poison.

"Yes. I can't prove it right now, but you're definitely on my list, and I can't wait to take you down for it."

"I see." Marie shuffled a stack of papers and brushed at nonexistent dust. "Does Detective Alvarez concur with your findings?"

"He has nothing to do with my gut feeling."

"He might be interested to hear your take on things. I'll be sure to pass the information along, as well as your threat." She smiled and raised both hands in an all-finished-here gesture. "Well, then, since I'm not under arrest, I must ask you to leave."

With that, Marie turned her back on Kate and opened a file cabinet.

"This isn't over. I'll be watching."

"I said, you're dismissed, *Officer.*"

Kate stared at her a long moment. I could see the fury and hurt in her eyes.

"C'mon, Kate. Don't do anything stupid. You've made your point, now get out," I pleaded.

I saw my sister swallow her pride and leave without another word. The wheels of payback turned and I had no doubt that Kate would have her day against Marie Yates. Perhaps she was detective material after all. Part of the job is choosing your battles in order to win the war.

Across the street, a silhouette perched vulture-like, watching Kate get into her car and leave.

"The little bitch. We've failed," the commander observed.

"What do you mean? Your wish has been granted—Lindsay Frost is in a grave."

"That doesn't mean she's harmless."

"Of course she is. What more do you want?"

"Payment in full. A life for a life."

"I'd say the score is even. Why not quit while you're ahead?"

"Don't you mean, *we?* We're in this together, and I'm not going anywhere. As for Detective Frost, she's taken her share from you as well. You should be thanking me for including you in my plan. I want full justice and I would think you'd want the same."

"Can't we let the courts decide?"

"What good are they? The guilty walk free all the time. You

should know that from past experience. Can you really live with that?"

"You'll get caught, you know. I won't go with you."

"You're not that strong. Inside you fear me, as you should, *partner.* Our mission is far from complete. But this latest disappointment calls for further strategy and planning. I suggest you get ready for our next move."

CHAPTER FIFTEEN

"Daddy?" I moved behind my father in his garage.

Of course, he didn't respond. He couldn't hear me. His graying hair rubbed the back of his shirt collar in an unusual display of neglect. Perry Frost ran a tight ship of appearance, always telling Kate and I that if cleanliness was next to godliness, neatness lay hand and hand with happiness. A postman for thirty-five years, he still wore the uniform and prided himself in sticking to the old creed that mail gets delivered no matter what the weather.

"Dad?" I tried again as I moved around him to see what held his interest on the stained workbench.

As a kid I'd been fascinated by his woodworking miracles, everything from small cabinets to rocking horses. Today was no different. The ornate eight-by-ten frame rose from its base beside a carved replica of my badge. It was my father's tribute to me and I wished he could know how much I loved him for it.

It had taken me this long to go *see* my parents. Not that I'm very busy anymore; it just took a while for the reality of the situation to sink in. Finding Dad in his garage-turned-workshop made me feel that things might be getting back to normal; that perhaps both of my parents could eventually move on.

But now I felt guilty as a voyeur into his private grief, as tears rivuleted down his stubbled cheeks. He wiped his chin against his flannel plaid shirt and continued sanding the frame.

My anger roared like fire, at the pain the butcher had caused my family. I saw Dad's pale, bitten lips moving in a soft whisper.

"My Lindsay," he said to the empty frame.

Instinctively I stretched out my hand to touch and comfort him, then realized it was futile.

His cracked voice broke the silence. "Why?" He looked up past the rafters to an unseen God, unseen to both of us, so far.

"Why!" he shouted with a raised fist.

As a child, I'd been convinced there wasn't anything my father couldn't fix. I'd seen him perform miracles on broken dolls, bicycles, roller skates, and even one of my mother's chipped china plates, compliments of Kate.

Watching him so helpless to solve the problem sent me into a panic. If my dad couldn't fix it, it simply couldn't be done. I wanted to make him happy again, and in my confusion, I blurted out, "I'll fix it, Dad. I promise."

It didn't matter that he couldn't hear me; I had to hear it for myself.

"For every tear you wiped from my cheek, every softball game you attended cheering the loudest, and for all of your sage advice when I was too proud to ask, I promise I'll take care of this. It'll be all right," I said to his back.

I stopped when he suddenly said, "I love you, Lindsay." They were the magic words I needed to hear, the words I needed to gather my courage and collect my thoughts in order to get the job done.

One of my favorite childhood games had been hide-and-seek. My happiest memories are of Dad hiding his eyes, or at least pretending to, while Kate and I hid. Most of the time he'd let us win, but occasionally he'd find us, saying, "You're getting better, keep trying!"

I always worked harder after that, wanting to find a way to beat him. I'm still playing the game—only now it's hide-and-seek with brutal offenders. Once again, my dad's words inspired me to keep trying.

"I love you too, Dad."

I saw my mom come into the garage with a sweating glass of iced tea.

"Perry? You all right, Hon?"

" 'Course not." He wiped his cheek against a shirtsleeve and changed the subject. "I've just about finished with it." He nodded toward his masterpiece.

My mother's blue eyes brimmed as she grazed the carved badge with a finger. "Oh, Perry. It's beautiful. Wait till Kate sees it." She formed a tired smile and I saw the lines of her face had deepened under puffy eyelids. Although she was five-foot-eight, her petite bone structure sagged and she'd lost weight, making her look vulnerable and weak. I worried about her health.

How much more could my parents take?

"Here. Drink." Mom handed Dad his tea.

"I'm not thirsty," he said, then downed half the glass.

"I see that." She wore her I-told-you-so look.

"Carla?" my father asked. "You think Lindsay knew what happened?"

My mother paled. "What kind of a question is that?"

"An honest one. I want to know if she suffered, or if she simply got knocked out and never woke up."

"I don't suppose we'll ever know. The detective said they saw no signs of a struggle. That tells me it happened too fast for her to really know what was happening."

"I'd like to believe that."

"It's what I'm holding onto. I won't allow myself to think otherwise."

"Have you heard from Kate?" Dad asked.

"She's off today, so I don't expect a call anytime early. That girl is a late sleeper."

"She stays up too late. Remember when the girls were kids

and Lindsay would tell on Kate when she'd sneak out of bed to play?"

I remembered. It had been to my advantage back then to get my way with Kate. My parents never really knew how many times I'd let her slide in exchange for her doing one of my house chores, or giving up one of her toys.

"Yes, I'm afraid Kate is a night owl. But she's been putting in a lot of extra time trying to solve the case. I just hope she's getting proper rest so she's alert on the job. I couldn't bear to lose another daughter . . ." She stopped and my dad hugged her close.

His gaze seemed to find me standing nearby, and for a brief second I felt sure he'd seen me. Filled with hope, I started forward, but then his eyes closed as he held my mother and I knew I was forever lost to two of the people I loved most in my life.

After seeing my parents, I realized how unfairly I'd acted in recruiting Kate as my partner. They could easily lose both daughters if we weren't alert or quick enough to get this guy before he struck again.

If I'd stayed away from Kate, Alvarez would have done his best to keep her out of the loop—not that she would have listened, but perhaps she would be safer at this point. Then again, maybe not. It seemed my passing wasn't enough to satisfy the sick animal who'd taken my life. I just needed to figure out why.

I decided it was time to fess up about Abner's warning and hope that Kate would see the whole picture. We sat in her SUV in a fast-food parking lot, Kate biting into her double cheeseburger while I explained.

"You still don't trust me, do you?" she muffled around the mouthful.

"I made you my partner didn't I?"

"Wow. Thanks. You did me a real favor, huh? Well, I have news for you, big sister, I'd be working this with or without your permission. Truth be known, I don't think you have any business here. You're supposed to be at peace, eternal rest and all that. Why can't you ever do what's expected?" Tears brimmed her eyes as she shoved the burger to her mouth for another bite.

Shit. Now I'd done it. None of this would work if I alienated the one person I could communicate with, this person I loved so dearly.

"I didn't mean it. It came out all wrong," I apologized. "I don't want anything to happen to you. Do you realize what that would do to Mom and Dad? Think about it, Kate. If you die, I still get to keep you. They don't.

"Do I want to get this guy? You bet. But at any cost? No."

She'd pulled herself together, munching on a greasy French fry. "If this is going to work, you have to be up front with me Linz, about everything. You wouldn't have held back from Alvarez, right?"

I conceded with a nod.

"So, from now on I'm in on all info. Besides," she grinned, "since Alvarez isn't speaking to you, I'm all you've got."

I rolled my eyes, or at least, I think I did. "Deal."

"Good. Now about Abner. He's been known to lie. What's his angle in warning you?"

"Don't know. There's no angle that can make any difference now."

"I hate to mention it, Linz, but you're in the same boat. How can you be in danger? Could he be lying to somehow lead you astray?"

"I'm not sure, but your parachute attack seems to confirm that someone is still out to hurt me even if it's by killing someone I love. Maybe that's what he meant."

"Take a look at our possible suspects." Kate ticked off the names on greasy fingers. "We've got Buford Jones, part-time drug pusher with bad hygiene. But he's no killer.

"Next, there's Calvin Stokes, whose worst crime so far is being a belligerent drunk, but I don't think he's bright enough to pull off a murder. And then there's his strange wife, Janice."

"That gives us Stinkin', Drinkin', and Odd."

"So who would want us *both* out of the picture? We've never put away the same guy. Never actually worked an investigation together."

"Like I said, it all seems to come back to hurting me in as many ways as possible. First, I'm killed. Then my name is purposely dirtied in the press. Next, I'm warned about impending danger, and finally, you're attacked. Things seem to be escalating."

"I'm in no hurry to see what comes next." Kate popped the last of her burger into her mouth.

"Which brings me to the subject of Mom and Dad. They could be targets," I said.

"*Easy* targets," Kate agreed. "They've lived such uncomplicated lives until recently. Mom has bridge club and Dad tinkers in his woodshop. They've been through enough and I'd like to see them get back to normal. But they need to be alert for anything unusual."

"Talk to Dad," I suggested. "I think he has enough anger in him that he'll be able to handle it." His raised fist and bitter tears in the garage came to mind.

"I could talk to a few officers and ask them to drive by when they can. I'm sure they'll be happy to do it. There's an unspoken frustration from the lack of progress. No clues, no suspects. It's hard on everyone."

"Me included," I added.

She stuffed her empty food wrappers into the bag and started up the car.

"Where're we headed?" I asked.

"We have to work with what we have. And right now that isn't much. I say we head over to your neighbor, Mrs. Jenkins, and ask a few questions. She might just remember something that could give us a lead."

I followed Kate inside Mrs. Jenkins' Cape Cod, trying to recall the last time I'd actually visited the elderly widow. When I entered the small living room, I realized that in the five years I'd lived across the street from Gloria Jenkins, I'd only gotten as for as her front doorstep. It had been last winter, when I'd borrowed a can of chicken soup. She'd asked me in, but I declined since I was fighting a nasty flu. I waited on her porch with a 102-degree fever, bundled in long underwear, one of George's sweatshirts, and a hooded parka, worried that her memory had failed and she'd gone on to some other household task. When I became light-headed enough to see stars, I started to ring the bell again, but then saw her hauling a grocery bag full of flu combatants. She'd packed a portable pharmacy complete with fever reducer, mentholated rub, an ice pack complete with ice, and—God bless her—*several* cans of chicken soup. I would have kissed her but it might have meant the end for her at the age of eighty; her frail ninety-pound frame stood no more than four-foot-eleven in her orthopedic oxfords. I opted for several thank-yous with a promise to repay her soon. That had been six months ago.

Kate took the seat she'd been offered on the far end of the old, but comfy-looking, couch. Gloria leaned on a shiny wooden cane, offering to make tea.

"No, thank you, Mrs. Jenkins," Kate said. "I won't take up much of your time."

"I want to tell you how sorry I am about your sister." She took a seat on a wingback chair. "Lindsay was a good neighbor."

"Thank you, Mrs.—"

"Please call me Gloria. Life's too short for all that formal stuff. I'll be eighty-one in a few weeks."

"That's wonderful," Kate smiled.

"It sucks," Gloria stated, then chuckled. "I've always wanted to say that. My grandson Peter is staying with me while his parents are vacationing. He's thirteen and seems to be up on all the current teen lingo. I'm certainly getting an education. But I'm sorry, I know that's not what you came here to talk about."

"I don't know if you've heard the ugly rumors, but they're just that," Kate assured her. "Lindsay did not kill herself and the department is looking into it."

"That's terrible!"

"I'm here, unofficially, to ask you if you can recall anything, even a seemingly insignificant detail that might lead us to the killer."

"Well, I told that detective, the nicely dressed one, quite handsome, about what I saw. There was a black, expensive-looking car parked in front of my house that evening for a while, but then it left and later the police arrived. I didn't see anyone or any activity at Lindsay's house."

"You mentioned footprints in your backyard?"

"Yes, there were large prints near my gate where I keep the garbage cans. They certainly weren't mine. I wear a size five, and these had to be at least a nine or ten."

"Could they have been your grandson's?"

"He only wears what he calls high-tops. The footprints came from boots."

"I see. You didn't hear anything unusual?"

"I'm afraid my hearing is a little rusty, and with Peter's rock music blaring most of the time I probably wouldn't have noticed."

"Is Peter here?"

"He's at softball practice, and then he's staying overnight with a friend. At his age I would think he'd be too old for a sleepover, but frankly it will be nice to spend a quiet evening for a change. I can't take all that heavy iron music."

"You mean, heavy metal?" Kate hid a grin.

"Yes, that's it. Heavy metal. Whatever it is, it'll never replace the big bands of my youth."

Kate got up. "Thank you for your time, Gloria. I'm sorry to have bothered you."

"Not at all. Glad to be of help, although I really don't think I had much to offer."

She saw Kate out the door, saying, "Don't be a stranger. I could use some company."

"I'll do that," Kate said.

The ride back to the precinct held an ominous silence as both Kate and I courted our own thoughts. It appeared we'd run into another dead end.

"What are we missing?" Kate asked. "There's no such thing as the perfect crime. Somewhere along the way, this asshole has made a mistake and we just haven't found it. I'd give anything for a break, no matter how small."

I should have warned her to be careful what she wished for.

CHAPTER SIXTEEN

I planned to attend the Special Olympics softball game, hoping to coach my buddy, Richard Kelter, through Kate.

Richard captured my heart several years ago when I volunteered to coach softball through the organization. His smile never fails to light up my heart and make everyone feel at ease. I promised him he'd hit a run before the season ended, and I refuse to let a minor detail like dying interfere.

I could see the ballfield forming before me as I concentrated. I saw Kate and Richard talking before the game as the image grew clearer. Suddenly everything went dark. Pitch black.

I thought I was finished and on my way to the final judgment, alone with no backup. I've been before judges before, but not *the* judge. And I've always been on the right side of the law, but who knows how we'll be viewed when we actually get to the end?

I was shoved hard from behind into a gray fog. I figured it wasn't God I had to fear, as my hands hit what felt like asphalt and I actually felt pain. Up until this point, I'd been numb. No physical sensations, no sense of taste or smell. It made for a somewhat watered-down existence, but the sharp pain in my palms surprised me. I stood up and checked for blood, thinking this had all been a bad dream and I'd finally awakened. Hell, I was just glad to feel *something*.

Another jarring blow sent me sailing backwards into an invisible wall. My head bounced hard and I saw stars. The surrounding fog grew sparse, but was still too thick to see anyone coming. I lay defenseless against this unseen force, and chose to stay down and wait. It didn't take long.

A firm grip yanked me upward by my hair. Instinctively, my hands shot out in defense, cutting into the patchy abyss before me. There was nothing there. My eyes strained to see the overpowering shadow that held me, but it disappeared as quickly as it had come, causing me to stumble at its sudden release.

Before I could stand, I felt the effects of a sucker punch to my gut, then a brutal face kick.

I was down, and this time I wasn't getting up. I couldn't. Every part of my ghostly body cried out in spasm and I wondered what it all meant. How could I be a spirit and still feel physical pain? I might be a newbie to this world, but I knew this was wrong.

I groaned as a sudden weight straddled my chest, pinning me, my throat tightening until I thought I'd explode. The pressure increased as though something had a grip on my soul, squeezing it out of me.

Could this be my punishment? My final judgment? I couldn't fight, and panic took over as I struggled for freedom.

I managed to choke out, "Help . . . me . . ."

Rapid footsteps pounded the asphalt, and I waited to feel more pain. Then I heard a grunted punch and the pressure on my chest broke. I rolled out of my attacker's range.

By now the fog had started to clear and I saw a uniformed man raise his Glock, firing at the invisible attacker. The man, a little over six feet tall, had short brown hair worn fuller on top, a firm build, and—now I saw clearly—he wore a police uniform.

He started toward me. "You all right?"

"Yes," I stammered. "Thanks." I managed to get up, my ego bruised more than the rest of me.

"I'll stick around a while, if you don't mind. Never know

with these things."

"Right," I said, unsure of what he meant. I shook past the events and offered my hand.

"I'm Detective Lindsay Frost. And you are?"

"Oh, sorry. I'm Officer Michael Blake. Nice to meet you."

"Who the hell attacked me?" I asked.

"I couldn't see, but they sure have it in for you. You new here?"

I wasn't sure of anything at this point. "I guess. Where's *here?*"

His gentle chuckle filled me with comfort. In all this craziness, someone had the courage to laugh. I liked that.

"Not sure if this place has a name, but I know I died about a year ago. Robbery call. Zigged when I should have zagged." Again his laughter filled the clearing air.

I couldn't help but smile. "Well, Officer Blake, I owe you. I'd offer to buy you a drink but I haven't learned my way around yet and have yet to see a bar."

"You don't owe me; it's my job. Serve and protect, remember? And please call me Mike."

"Call me Lindsay."

"Detective, huh? What division?"

"Homicide."

"You're in the right place," he joked. "I'm sure there's a lot of that here."

"Homicides?"

"Well, victims anyway. Can I ask what happened to you?"

"I was murdered." It amazed me how matter-of-fact the words came out.

"How long ago?"

"I guess it's been about two weeks now. Seems a lot longer."

"Do you know who did it?"

"No. I guess I'm still on the clock, too. I intend to solve this thing. Still waiting for autopsy results, although I know it was staged. I would know if I killed myself."

"I might know someone who could help with that. He's a coroner."

"You mean . . ."

"Yup. He's here."

First Sally O'Shannon offers her services as the necro-tour guide; now I meet a cop with a coroner friend. My own task force.

"Hmm. I might need to see him."

"Could you use some help? I'm not doing anything for the rest of my life." He grinned. "That sounded more like a proposal, didn't it?"

I laughed, probably for the first time since I got here. It felt good. "And I accept—the assistance part, anyway."

As we stepped out of the fog, I wondered who would have attacked me here. It seemed I had two people after me. I had a feeling this was just the beginning, but how do you take down an attacker who's already dead?

I did a quick rundown of every horror flick I'd ever watched. Silver bullet? No gun.

Stake in the chest? No beating heart.

Exorcism? It wasn't Satan I feared. After all, he'd had his chance with me when I died.

It looked like I had a new partner on this side, too, and I realized I needed all the help I could get.

"So what's a girl do for fun around here?" I asked.

"The same thing a guy does. Wander around looking for a kindred spirit."

"If our professional backgrounds qualify, then I guess you've found one. How long were you on the force?"

"Nine years."

"Long time. I have four years as an investigator."

"I thought about making the move to detective, but I really

like the streets. I spent most of my time on motorcycle patrol, which appealed to my rebel side."

"Do you miss it?" I asked him.

"Not as much as I miss my family. I have an eight-year-old daughter, and a wife. It's been a year, but it doesn't feel like it. I'm still adjusting."

"I'm single," I confessed. "No kids. No pets. But I really haven't had time to miss anything. I'm still trying to figure out navigational skills."

He smiled. "That takes some work. You know what I miss most, with the exception of my family?"

"What's that?"

"Action movies and Chinese food. I know it sounds weird, but if I could have one thing here, I believe it would be a heaping plate of kung pau."

"Moo goo gai pan," I countered. "I'll tell you what, if I ever find a Chinese restaurant here, it'll be my treat. I owe you."

His expression turned serious. "You haven't been here long enough to make enemies. You'll need to watch yourself, because it looks like someone has been waiting for you."

CHAPTER SEVENTEEN

Kate adjusted her baseball cap against the blinding sun and rested her hands on her knees behind the chain-link barrier next to the dugout. The bases were loaded as Richard Kelter ambled up to the plate.

The Special Olympics softball league had started without Lindsay this year, but Kate had decided Richard wouldn't be alone. Lindsay had taken to the twelve-year-old a few years before, during her first time helping with the Olympics. Her athletic nature had taken over when she saw the boy repeatedly struggling to hit the ball, then ambling back to the bench looking sad and defeated. She'd taken him under her tutelage, working with him at the batting cages when she had the time. Finally came the day when the crack of the bat hitting the ball echoed throughout the indoor practice area. He'd done it. Kate recalled Lindsay's excitement when she described the look of sheer joy on Richard's freckled face. Her enthusiasm had been contagious, luring Kate to several games to watch the fun.

After Richard's first big hit, his goal had changed to making a run for his team, but sadly, Lindsay never saw that accomplishment while she was alive. Kate hoped he would do it this season, knowing her sister would be there in the stands.

She feared her sister's passing would devastate the boy and ruin his spirit for trying, so she'd made it a point to show her support for him to quell some of the feeling of loss. The kid didn't deserve pain like that. With butterflies in her stomach and carrying an extra bottle of Gatorade, she'd met him at the field to explain her sister's absence. To Kate's surprise, Richard had taken the news in stride, saying, "Yinsay's not gone. She's right here." His hand rested over his heart.

Today the anxious crowd looked on as Richard raised the bat into position.

"C'mon, Richard! You can do it!" Kate called over the noisy softball crowd.

The boy gave her a wave, and grinned wide as he stepped up to the shouts of his teammates.

Kate jumped when a familiar voice called from behind, and she turned to find Gerard Alvarez standing in the bleachers.

"Go get 'em Richard. Sammy Sosa better watch his back!" Alvarez caught Kate's glance and waved.

She returned the gesture, puzzled by his presence.

Richard swung hard at the first pitch and missed. The crowd applauded and shouted encouragements.

The boy's smile never faded as he raised the bat once more.

Kate's heart sunk when he missed again.

"Tighten up on the bat, buddy," Alvarez shouted from behind.

The next pitch flew too high and Richard held his swing.

"Good eye! Good eye!" Alvarez grinned.

Kate turned back to look at the detective. His firm jaw had relaxed, allowing a smile to soften his hard look. Strange to see him in jeans, and a short-sleeve shirt that exposed tanned muscular arms. She felt the heat rise in her cheeks when his dark eyes caught and held her in the burning sun. Kate quickly checked on Richard's progress.

"Concentrate, buddy. You can do it!" she shouted.

The pitch came fast and hard, hitting the boy in the leg. He yelped, dropping the bat to grab his shin.

Kate flew to the field in a flash. She bent and inspected the injury as Richard regained composure. "Are you all right?"

115

"No big deal, Kay," he said and frowned.

"What's wrong?" She examined his leg.

"I didn't hit it."

"You'll get it next time." Kate helped him up.

The umpire called a walk and the boy made his way to first base, bringing in a run from third.

As Kate applauded with the crowd from behind the fence, she felt a presence beside her and knew without looking that Alvarez had joined her.

"He's a terrific kid, isn't he?" he asked.

"Yeah. I can see why Lindsay was so taken with him."

"You're doing a great thing, Kate. Lindsay would really appreciate it."

"I know, but it's not just for her. I'm concerned for Richard, and what kind of negative effect Lindsay's passing might have on him. She wouldn't want that."

They watched the teams change for a new inning, and Kate searched the dugout and field for any signs of her sister. It surprised her that Lindsay would miss the game, even if she couldn't take part.

She saw Alvarez staring in her peripheral vision.

"Are you looking for someone?" he asked.

"Not really." She turned back to the field. He was staring again. Kate broke the awkward silence. "Where are your boys today?"

His smile came easily. "John is working. He's the top fry guy at Burgerama. And Paul's with his mom today. With no kids at home, I decided to show up for Richard. But I see he already has a cheerleader."

"I'm not as softball savvy as Lindsay, but I can offer moral support."

"Kids need to feel that. Raising two boys has taught me a lot about love and support."

"How old are they now? I haven't seen them since the police picnic a few years ago."

"John is seventeen, and Paul just turned fifteen."

Kate grinned. "I don't envy you. You've got a lot on your plate."

He nodded. "We've had a few rough times since the divorce, but we're working them out." He paused as if he'd said too much, then changed the subject. "How are you holding up?"

The question caught her off guard. There hadn't been a moment when her thoughts and nightmares hadn't centered on Lindsay.

She took a draw from her water bottle to ease the sudden tightening in her throat. "I'm getting there. This is actually therapeutic. You?"

"Handling it."

"We're all *handling* it. The question is, how well?" She stared at him.

"Right. I'll let you know when I find the animal who did it."

"That makes two of us."

"Kate, I know you want to get this guy . . ."

"But?" She turned toward him. "I hear a 'but' in there."

"Let us take care of it. I promise you'll be the first to know when we get a solid lead, or take someone into custody."

She smiled, knowing how hard this must be for him. He actually looked uncomfortable talking about it. Maybe Lindsay was right and Alvarez wasn't so bad after all.

Without thinking, she rested her hand on his bare forearm, feeling his sun-baked skin. "Thanks. I'm glad you're on our side." She pulled back, embarrassed.

"Our?" he questioned.

"Mine and Lindsay's."

"Always."

"*But,*" she emphasized with a grin, "I'm a police officer, and as a public servant, I not only owe it to my sister to try and find the guy, I have a promise to keep to the people of this town." She raised a palm to stop his rebuttal. "Wait, I'm not finished. It sounds corny and clichéd, but it's who I am. I'm not asking for a badge and a SWAT team, all I want is your blessing to work this on my off hours. There'll be no stepping on your toes, or anyone else's. I would think you'd appreciate all the help you can get."

He let the ballpark sounds fill the silence, eyeing her carefully.

Kate took another swig of water, trying to shake off his penetrating stare. If she drank any more, she'd have to brave the Port-a-potty.

"You're stubborn like Lindsay. I miss that."

"Stop stalling and give me an answer."

"Kate . . ."

She fought to keep the edge from her tone. "Police officers solve crimes too, Detective."

"*Mi Dios*," he said under his breath. "Don't forget I was a beat cop for many years, and have nothing but respect for the job. All I'm saying is I see your potential, Kate. You're Lindsay all over again. You have her passion, her drive, and most of all her determination to do the right thing.

"I know there's nothing I can do to stop you from working this. But dealing with a violent crime can uncover ugly details. You need to be ready and willing to handle whatever comes up. I'm not sure this should be your first taste of investigation. One day, when the time is right, you'll be a great detective and I look forward to working with you."

Dumbfounded, Kate gulped down the last of her water. "Thanks. I'll hold you to that." She pitched the bottle into the trash.

"That's a pleasant thought."

"What's that?"

"You holding me to something," he said with a grin.

Warmth flooded her cheeks when she realized he was flirting. A mix of emotions from confusion to butterflies swarmed her. She had to admit, he hadn't been the only one feeling the attraction. Touching his arm moments ago had stirred a desire she hadn't felt for months. She knew her response could set things in motion and create an awkward hurdle between them, hindering their work.

He moved close, heating the air between them. Her mind wandered through the forbidden valley of lusty intentions, until she realized Alvarez waited for her to say something.

Emotions versus common sense had been the last conflict she'd anticipated at today's game. Surprises remain the spice of life, but this had taken her completely off guard.

Levelheaded. Grounded. These were adjectives describing Lindsay's relationship decisions, while Kate had always enjoyed a more adventurous approach, never taking things too seriously. But this *was* serious. She couldn't risk unbalance between her and the lead detective of the investigation.

"Kate?" Electric warmth surged up her arm from his fingertips. She wanted to move but didn't.

Blessedly his cell phone rang.

When he stepped away to answer she noticed the breeze felt cooler, and she shivered under clouds of emotion warning her not to get involved.

Alvarez pocketed his phone, his flirtatious expression replaced by a tense frown. "I have to get going. Parental duty calls."

Kate watched him go with a mix of relief and disappointment, wondering what her answer might be next time.

The umpire made the call. "Play ball!"

CHAPTER EIGHTEEN

Dr. Warren Saint heartily shook my hand, or at least he tried. "Five-foot-two, eyes of blue" came to mind. He still wore the spotless white lab coat he'd had on at his passing in the morgue. According to Mike Blake, the good doctor had had a massive coronary at work and had never regained consciousness.

A sudden thought hit me at the sight of his white coroner's jacket. So far, the spirits I'd met had been in the clothes they'd died in. No wardrobes changes here. I had a feeling that the way you die is the way you spend eternity. The lack of wrist wounds on my spirit body and the fact that I still wore the clothes I'd come home in that night proved I hadn't killed myself. If I'd bled out in the tub, I'd be eternally naked. Thankfully, whoever did me in also did me the favor of seeing to it that I'd been deceased before I entered the tub. Too bad there was no way to share that enlightening info with Alvarez.

Mike introduced the coroner, watching me closely.

Dr. Saint's bushy mustache lay like snow on his upper lip, twitching when he spoke. "Detective Frost. What a pleasure," he grinned. "Where are you from?"

"Southfield Heights in Taylor County. I worked Homicide."

"Ah, yes. You and I are kindred spirits, no pun intended. What I mean is that we both serve the deceased." He chuckled softly.

"Yes, I suppose that's true. But for now I have to be selfish and serve myself. You see, I'm working my own investigation."

"Good for you, Detective. I'm at your disposal. Of course, I don't have a morgue or access to lab equipment, but I'll do whatever I can."

"Thank you," I said, wondering just how much help he could provide.

Mike Blake looked on as I filled the doctor in on the details. The officer's eyes roved like scanners over the surrounding area. He still didn't trust whoever had attacked me. I found comfort in having a bodyguard and relaxed a bit, enjoying the stout little man before me as he went on about some of his most disturbing cases.

My mind wandered to Mike, who was standing close by. I guessed him to be early thirties; too young to die. The hole in his police uniform told me he'd been shot in the chest, almost a direct hit to his heart. Strength and a muscular build are no match for a bullet.

As the good doctor reminisced about an old case involving Vaseline and a gerbil, I spotted the gold band on Mike's left ring finger. That might explain the deep look of sadness in his eyes that never quite faded with his smile or laugh. I knew he missed his family.

"Have you been autopsied yet?" Dr. Saint wanted to know.

"Yes. About two weeks ago, I think." I couldn't actually recall what day it was. No calendars here.

"Those results should be in by now. Have you seen the prelim?"

He meant the preliminary report of findings that gives law enforcement officials a quick idea about the cause of death.

I nodded. "Unfortunately, the guy thought of everything, right down to hesitation marks on my wrists."

"This wacko is good," Dr. Saint offered. "Who did you piss off, Jack the Ripper?"

Mike flinched, checking my expression. I wanted to tell him

I'm a lot stronger than that. Years on the job and then viewing your own corpse tends to build a tough hide.

"Wish I knew," I told Dr. Saint.

"We'll get him." He polished a gleaming scalpel with the sleeve of his lab coat, and returned it to his pocket. "He'll get what's coming to him, and the person who attacked you here as well."

Sally O'Shannon cut in from behind, "I wish I believed that bunk."

She moved into our circle and I made the introductions all around.

"Sally has opted to be my personal tour guide and teacher," I explained.

The doctor studied her a moment. "You don't believe there are penalties here?"

"Not really. Maybe a paranormal wrist slap. No different than the other side. There's no justice anywhere."

"That's not true, Sally," I cut in.

"Oh yeah? Those assholes who toasted me will be out one day on good behavior."

"They committed manslaughter. I'm sure their sentence reflects that," I countered.

"Yeah, but I'll always be dead. Where's the fairness in that?"

Mike, who'd kept quiet during the conversation, spoke up, "I gave my life for the justice you say doesn't exist. I only hope you're wrong, Sally, or my wife and daughter don't stand a chance. They're banking on the punishment of the men who did this to me." He pointed to his chest wound.

"Perhaps it will come on *this* side. We don't know what happens after our tags are given up," Dr. Saint offered.

Sally's dark eyes narrowed. "Maybe you're right. If I wait it out, I can track them down when they get here and serve the proper punishment. For once, I'll have the advantage. They'll be on my turf, at my mercy."

Her words struck a chord. If my spirit-world attacker was on a vendetta, it could be a clue to the identity of my real-world murderer. I doubted they were one and the same, but couldn't deny a possible connection.

Instead of hiding, I had to find and confront my phantom attacker, and that meant forming an offensive.

"Sorry about the negative talk," Mike said, following me from the group. "Keep in mind that Sally seems bitter."

"Actually, she's given me an idea," I said.

"Uh-oh."

"Probably. Want to hear it?"

"No. But go ahead."

"I think it's time to stir the pot and flush out a turd."

"That might work if you knew the turd's name."

"Let me worry about that. All I need is a foolproof trap."

"I'll do all I can, but you need to be cautious. I've done battle with your attacker and I can tell you he gave me pause. You should allow yourself more time to build strength."

"Time is a luxury I don't have."

"We have eternity, Lindsay."

"Do you really believe that, Mike? Can you afford to wait that long, for your family's sake?"

"It's not the same. No one is stalking me."

"The longer I wait, the less likely we are to find the guy and I'm convinced this attacker is connected to my demise. I just have to find the link."

"I'm listening," he said.

I knew I'd started this conversation but never intended it to get this far. I wasn't ready to share more than I already had. Still, Mike had risked his safety to save me. I probably owed him an explanation.

I filled him in on what I had so far, which didn't take long, with no leads or solid suspects, a spiritual warning and an attacker. When I'd finished, he agreed things looked grim.

"So you believe whoever took your life is somehow connected to your stalker?" he asked.

"It has to be. The whole thing is too coincidental. But that in itself might be a clue. That's why I need to find the stalker."

"What makes you think he'll tell you anything?"

"There's no guarantee but I need the chance."

"I get why it's personal to you, but sometimes crimes go unsolved; I'm sure you've seen it before. What will you do if that happens? What if the guy goes free?"

My hand gripped my badge on its cord. This went beyond personal. Sure I wanted to bring closure to my family and myself, but if it went unsolved, it would be another incident where I'd let people down. Like I had with Joe.

My shrink would love this. After the countless hours he'd spent trying to get me to open up and explore my feelings of guilt without much success, all it took was one session with a complete stranger to start the flow. Rage burned inside when I pictured Joe's mutilated body. Why hadn't I saved him? I saw his children's pained expressions at the funeral and felt my own helplessness in wanting to make things right for them. Although we'd found Tanner, she'd still escaped punishment. Taking her life had been too easy on her.

This time I had to make things right.

I answered Mike's question as honestly as I knew how. "That's not an option."

CHAPTER NINETEEN

My plans for an offensive against my attacker simmered while I joined Kate on a trip to Alvarez's office. True to his word, he'd called her when the autopsy report came in. I asked Dr. Warren Saint to take a look, and of course, the good doctor was eager to oblige.

Officer Blake, or Mike, had offered to come along to Alvarez's office, but I declined. I likened it to going to the doctor and felt odd sharing such personal information. He seemed to understand, although I thought I detected a momentary look of hurt.

Kate paled when she saw the good doctor beside me in the empty corridor down the hall. As I made quick introductions, she offered a subtle nod his way, still looking confused. Likewise, the doctor raised a caterpillar eyebrow in question at her ability to see him. A hurried explanation satisfied his curiosity and we set off to view my autopsy results.

Alvarez slid the report across his desk toward Kate, and Dr. Saint and I perused over her shoulder for the official ruling.

Homicide.

Toxicology showed no drugs, and there'd been no defensive wounds or skin under my fingernails, suggesting I hadn't fought. From what I recalled, there hadn't been time. The original theory had been put to rest by several facts. First, my right wrist had been crushed. The crime-scene photos showed a boot pattern on the top of my hand. Second, the burned areas on my neck and chest proved consistent with Taser marks. Reading further, I learned I'd died of a heart attack due to the Taser's, prolonged current.

Dr. Saint shook his head beside me. "That device had to have been pressed and held over your heart to cause arrhythmia."

That explained the lack of fighting and blood at the scene; I'd been deceased before I hit the water.

It cleared my name to those in the room. Still, the damage had been done. The visual would forever remain with the crime team and my fellow officers.

If I knew one thing, it was that my attacker was a coward. I figured he'd intentionally left the Beretta strapped to my ankle to prove that my gun expertise had been futile over his power. Another message.

Dr. Saint tried to soften the blow with his reassuring smile and professional tone. "Excellent job. This Dr. Thomas Stern certainly knows his stuff. He's spared your good name."

I didn't agree. "Nice try, Doc, but to some folks, there will always be a question as to whether or not I really offed myself and the department simply covered it up."

Kate picked up the cue, telling Alvarez, "This isn't good. What about the original findings?"

"It's been ruled otherwise." He rubbed his bloodshot eyes, then reached for an aspirin bottle in his desk drawer.

"You okay?" Kate asked.

"Yeah. Just stressed." He attempted a smile that didn't work.

"I appreciate what you're doing," she told him. "You've put in a lot of extra hours and have kept me up to speed on the investigation."

"Wish there was more to tell."

"Me too." Kate smiled. "Can I get a copy?"

"Sure."

I followed Kate toward the door with Dr. Saint close behind. "Kate?" Alvarez stopped her. "I'm sorry."

"Thanks, Gerard."

Watching Kate copy the report in the main office, I contemplated our next move. We had to find the key clue, the one that would turn everything around. In my four years in violent crimes, I'd never known an investigation without one. Sometimes the clue came easily, within a day or two; other times it came too late and you ended up a complete dead end. I hoped that wasn't happening now.

Earlier Mike Blake had suggested we re-visit the crime scene, but I didn't see the point. I'd spent far too much time there myself, going over every inch of the house as well as reviewing the parts I could recall. I can't explain why I'm drawn to the place, but I figure it's time to stop reliving the past. The crime lab has already covered it, as well as Kate and countless others. I trust my co-workers' expertise and figure a return visit is a waste of time we really don't have.

Kate nearly jumped over the copy machine when I blurted beside her, "I hope you don't mind Dr. Saint's presence; there wasn't much time to warn you."

She looked around, mumbling, "No problem. Is there anyone else I should know about, in case you have a demon chasing you or something?"

"How did you know?"

"Know what?"

"I was attacked earlier by some kind of ghostly stalker."

"Why didn't you tell me sooner?"

"No point. It's over and there's no APB system in the spirit world. Besides, I don't even know who I'm looking for. Any ideas who might want me deader than dead?"

"You mean someone who's died with a vendetta against you?

That could be a long list."

"Very funny. By the way, we need to re-interview Calvin Stokes."

"Any other *impossible* requests I can say no to?"

"Look, if anyone wanted to pin my hide to the wall, it was Calvin. He had the motive, the means, and he knows where I live—lived, whatever. We just have to poke a hole in his alibi."

"And you think he put an otherworldly hit on you?"

"No, but I think it's all connected."

Her look of confusion sparked my frustrations. This wasn't how I worked. I sounded like a novice detective grasping at straws. My independent nature had a real problem with relying on others to get the job done. I wondered if this was some sort of punishment invoked for my often-cocky attitude and bullheadedness. Perhaps fate had decided I needed a lesson in humility. My badge lay against my chest, reminding me I still had a job to do, whether on this side or the other. Either way I'd sworn to make it work.

I considered my options and they all led back to Stokes. If I wanted another interview with the snake, it would mean pitting Kate against Alvarez to give the go-ahead, and that meant that I had to come up with a good reason to re-interview him or he'd cry harassment.

I realized I needed more information, and just like old times I knew where to go.

CHAPTER TWENTY

It amazed me how Abner Taute's longish hair still looked greasy and unwashed in the afterlife. You'd think the process of dying might clean up the body a bit, but that sure wasn't the situation with ol' Abner. I tried not to stare at his pistachio-colored teeth, grateful I no longer had a sense of smell.

This time I took Officer Blake up on his offer to tag along, in part because I needed someone who could navigate well enough to locate Abner, but also because I figured Mike's presence might be persuasive.

Mike explained that part of the trick to getting where you want to go is concentrating on past experiences enough to re-create them. That's why our memories are so important to hold on to. It wasn't long before we reached an abandoned storefront that looked similar to the part of town where I usually met with Abner.

The more I imagined, the clearer the details became.

I saw the graffiti-sprayed, boarded-up storefronts lining Western Avenue, where ghostly gang members patrolled their turf wearing their colors. They saw me but paid no attention. I no longer held any threat.

An abandoned car complete with smashed windows and an orange tow sticker rested in an alleyway between the barbershop and the liquor store.

"Home sweet home?" Mike asked, skirting a rat.

"I've had better first dates," I said, trying to lighten the mood.

"I'll keep that in mind."

It wasn't long before Abner Taute appeared, trudging along the littered curb looking for change. I felt like I'd returned to my element, back on familiar turf, and I approached for information.

The ghostly snitch shook his head, still clutching his whiskey bottle. "I told you I don't know who's out to git ya. All grapevine stuff. Nothin' definite."

"You're lying," I pressed. Normally, I would have had him begging to spill information by now, with various threats and bribes, but on this side, I had nothing to bargain with. When it came to manipulating my new environment, I was as green as his teeth.

"C'mon, Abner. What are you afraid of? They can't kill you." Mike crossed his muscular arms over his chest.

The stubborn old man raised his chin. "Don't matter. Bein' here doesn't end your worries ya know. Have you considered we might be in hell?"

"Maybe we are," I cut in. "I feel like I'm riding the same ride over and over again and getting nowhere. What's it going to take? Tell me and I'll find a way."

His faded gray eyes took on a glazed look and I knew he wanted a drink—bad. "You can't help me," was all he said.

"What if I can? What if there's a way to get you a swig of your favorite whiskey?"

"You're good, Detective Frost, but not *that* good."

He was right. I barely managed navigation. How could I get him a shot?

"There is one thing I've always wanted and never had a chance at," he continued.

"Name it." I tried to sound sure.

"Always wanted to be a hero like John Wayne. Now *that* was a real man. Nothin' fake about him. But, as you know, things didn't quite work out that way for me. I'd give up the whiskey for a taste of being the Duke."

Good Lord. He wanted to be John Wayne. I had a better chance of getting him drunk. Then I realized what he really wanted was a chance to be *like* John Wayne.

"Now *that* I can do," I said.

"How's that?" Abner narrowed his eyebrows.

Mike gave me a wary look, but I went ahead.

"What do you think John Wayne would do if he knew someone, especially a woman, was in danger?" I hated to play the gender card, but I knew it would work.

Abner's eyes widened. "He'd kick their asses, by God."

"That's right. Now there's someone after me and I need your help to find out who, so I can stop him. Will you do that for me? For John Wayne?"

He shifted his stance a bit while he thought it over, and I wondered if the element of time worked the same on this side. Eternity seems awfully long.

Mike shortened the distance, towering like a skyscraper. Finally, Abner nodded.

"All right. I'll help ya. But I'm being honest when I say I really don't know who it is for sure. All I got is a reason. I hear it's about a killin' some years back. Somethin' about your old partner, Joe. Don't know if that helps, but it's all I got. Really."

His eyes looked from me to Mike and back again. I knew he was telling the truth. If his information was right, my stalker was Tanner Jean Hoyt, the woman who'd slaughtered Joe.

After Abner left, Mike navigated us back to our starting point, which seemed to have become my home base. The small clearing resembled an area where my parents took Kate and I to picnic as children. What Mike had said earlier about memories made sense now. I wanted to spend eternity in a place of peace and happiness.

"I like this scenario better. No rats." He leaned against a tall oak. "So, what are you thinking?"

"That Abner is telling the truth and if he is, I'm up against a real sick pup."

I'd filled Mike in earlier on Tanner and how she probably had a vendetta against me, since I'd been the one to kill her. She'd always thought herself invincible, and in a way, I guess she'd been right. Even in the afterlife, she proved a formidable foe. But was it really Tanner, I wondered?

"If it is?" he asked.

"Well, that means I have to stop her all over again."

"Just like that?" He grinned.

"What do you mean?"

"You're too new at this. You'll need help."

"Ah, and you're the man for the job."

"I think so."

"Look, I'm not used to being pampered; I've always taken care of my own problems."

"Too good for help?" he teased.

"I didn't say I don't appreciate backup from my fellow officers when needed, but as a woman detective, I've learned you have to be able to hold your own or you can lose credibility and possibly your life."

I'd already done the latter and didn't plan to give up anything else.

"Thanks Mike," I said, "but this is something I have to do alone. I have to set her up in order to take her down. Go on the offensive."

"And what are you going to do?"

"I'm not sure yet, but you'll be the last to know." Now it was my turn to grin.

"Why is that?"

"Because you'll try and stop me, or you'll want to help. I can't allow either."

He moved closer, and I found myself taking a step back. His eyes held mine and although neither of us had any real physical presence, I swear I felt heat emanating between us.

"A good cop always knows when to call for backup." He leaned in. "I promise not to overstep my bounds."

And a smart cop knows when to make a hasty exit. Distance, shielding, and movement came to mind from my police training. I forced a picture in my mind. Before Mike could move any closer, I felt myself fade from the scene, leaving my would-be backup behind. I had some serious planning to do.

CHAPTER TWENTY-ONE

I ended up inside my house, feeling guilty for leaving poor Mike back at the picnic area, but relieved I'd actually ended up where I'd planned. It looked like my navigational skills were improving. Too bad my relationship finesse seemed lacking. The buzz between Mike and I made me nervous, first because I seemed to be a poor judge of character in men, and second, I was too new at this whole thing to even consider a relationship. Besides, he was married.

Okay. Weak argument. Marriage vows are "till death do us part," so technically he's single again. As a detective, I've been trained to spot the little things and add them up to bring an arrest. It's all in the details. I can spot a drug dealer by the way he wears his pants, but I couldn't see that the man I lived with had lost all feelings for me and had planned to end it. I'm unqualified in the relationship arena. Best stick with what I know.

Although I'd vowed to stay away from my own crime scene, I wandered about in my bathroom, looking for a missed clue and contemplating how to handle my paranormal stalker. I recalled what I knew about Tanner Jean Hoyt.

Self-trained in military-style fighting, including significant weapons and tactical knowledge, she was considered dangerous. According to her psychological history, she had problems stemming from her father's desire to make her the son he'd never had. His influence as a hard-nosed Vietnam vet shaped Tanner into more than a tomboy. I'd learned from her profile that she'd shown up in her high school counselor's office complaining she'd been placed in the wrong gym class because they were all girls.

Any hopes of salvaging Tanner slipped over the edge when she was seventeen; her father abandoned his family and was never heard from again. Her remaining high school career brought more isolation; she had several run-ins with the law that earned her the label of rebel. Eventually, she'd taken advantage of her muscular build and tomboy image, protecting some of the weaker kids from bullies. It had earned her the title "Guardian Demon."

When a Marine recruiter visited the school in her senior year, she'd made the decision to turn her life around and join the military. Unfortunately, her plans shattered when she learned that women Marines don't see combat. From there, she'd headed for college and the police academy, where she failed the psych evaluation. Something snapped and she formed a personal mission to serve her own brand of justice. Her third-degree black belt, knowledge of weapons, and bad attitude made her extremely dangerous. If she had been psychotic in life, God knew what she'd become now that the threat of dying had been removed.

My plan to lure her was simple; return to the scene of the crime. If she were truly stalking me, she'd be watching and would know when I was alone. Leaving Mike behind was the surest way I knew to accomplish my goal. All I had to do now was wait.

Roaming through my house, I reviewed the facts.

We had no solid suspects, except Calvin Stokes, who had motive and means, but the evidence was too weak. The only crime-scene evidence had been the razor blade belonging to neither George nor myself, and it proved nothing. Besides, Calvin Stokes preferred the stubbled look.

The fact that I'd been Tasered didn't necessarily point to Calvin, but since he owned a gun shop he shot to the top of my list. In my mind, Calvin Stokes had everything to do with everything. I just couldn't prove it.

I moved on to the second puzzle piece, Tanner. Could the two of them be connected? If so, my guess was that it had something to do with weapons. I had to get her to talk, and I figured the best way to rattle her cage was to get her mad enough to make a slip.

I took in what used to be my refuge, now an empty battleground. From the looks of things, nothing had been moved or changed and I made a mental note to ask Kate what she planned to do with the house. It broke my heart to think about selling, but I really had no use for it now. Maybe I'd haunt it for fun.

A violent shove from behind sent me sailing over the bathtub—literally. I shot up and turned to defend myself but found the room empty. Before I turned, an arm tightened around my neck, yanking me backwards and down to the floor. When I looked up I saw Tanner Jean Hoyt's camouflaged face inches from my own.

"Better change your title from detective to prisoner of war," she spat, tightening her grip.

"The VA rejection committee called. They mentioned you by name," I managed to get out.

"You're mine," she said, and grabbed me by the throat.

"You're not my type. I prefer someone with less chest hair."

She held me secure as she searched my body.

"Give me a break. I'm unarmed." I squirmed, trying to figure out what she could possibly be looking for.

"Where is it?" She jerked me up onto my feet. "Give me your badge!"

I remembered Sally saying something about giving up our tag and moving on to the next level. I wasn't ready to do that. Tanner wanted my badge to send me off to oblivion and perhaps to my final judgment. With me out of her way, she would be free to wreak whatever havoc she pleased.

"Silly reject, shields are for cops." I formed a mental image of her going down as I forced a thrust kick to her face. To my complete surprise, she hit the tiles.

Her cheeks flushed red between lines of green and black camouflage. I wished I'd brought a camera.

She jumped to her feet in a karate stance, ready to pounce.

I bent and rushed her. This time she hesitated before getting up. I knew I was onto something. "Tell me who did it, Tanner. Who killed me? Was it Calvin Stokes?"

"Is the great Detective Frost stumped?" She landed a punch and I went down hard.

I tried to stall before she reached me. "What difference does it make if you tell me? There's nothing I can do about it, right?"

I rolled right, avoiding another hit.

"I see you've been working out, Frost. Too bad we can't work as allies."

The bathtub lay between us. Not much of a defense, considering she could dive right through it.

"C'mon Tanner. Be a hero for once. Didn't your father ever teach you honesty is the best policy?"

She lunged, taking me down. Her black eyes emanated pure hate as she overwhelmed me with her strength. Shoving a hand under my shirt, she yanked the cord that held my badge.

I saw the victory in her expression as she held it up like a trophy. Suddenly helpless to retaliate or to retrieve it, I wondered what had happened to my sudden rush of power.

My grand plan to piss her off had only fueled her fire, making her stronger. The bathroom dimmed around me and I fought a consuming weightlessness. Panic set in as my body began fading before my eyes.

Tanner hissed close to my ear, "You were present at my execution. Now I'm returning the favor."

A loud whir filled my ears and I tried to recall the Lord's Prayer.

Chapter Twenty-Two

Kate maintained her distance along Main Street as she followed Marie Yates. She frowned at the vanity plate: CRIM LAW. Marie was as arrogant as they came, but that might be a good thing if it caused carelessness. The sleek Mercedes cut like a black knife through the midday traffic of downtown Southfield Heights. So far, the lawyer didn't seem aware of Kate's presence only a few car lengths behind.

Kate braked suddenly as the Mercedes' taillights flashed; a minivan shot out unexpectedly from the dry cleaners.

No matter how many times Alvarez put down her idea that Marie Yates was responsible for Lindsay's death, Kate couldn't let it go. Something was going on with the defense attorney. Marie had changed. Of course, a few bad hair days and weight gain weren't probable cause, but it had her attention.

Alvarez had called it *wishful thinking* and *grasping at straws*, but she preferred to think of it as instinct and intuition. The feeling that the too-rich, too-cocky, and too-smart criminal lawyer had gotten away with her sister's death gnawed at her.

She'd gone over motive, means, and opportunity a dozen times, finding means and opportunity easy for a woman in Marie's position. If she didn't have the actual "means," she had access to enough criminal types who would. The same held true for opportunity. She knew where Lindsay lived and could easily find out her schedule. Who would question Attorney Yates? Her record gleamed spotless, her trial success unmatched in Taylor

County, and she'd made herself available to prominent politicians and local organizations. What a woman. She probably had a cape tucked into her designer suit.

While Marie had made no bones about the fact she didn't feel any remorse over Lindsay's death, it didn't prove she'd killed her. Kate knew that if she could find a solid motive, it might make Alvarez and Lindsay consider her theory. Eventually, Marie would give herself away, either in words or actions. Kate was banking on the latter.

She slowed when the Mercedes turned into the alleyway behind Stokes' gun store. Her pulse accelerated when Marie parked close to the back door and got out.

There was no way to follow her into the alley without being seen. Kate cursed as she drove to the next traffic light and made a right in order to circle back. A garbage truck blocked the street to make its pickup, costing Kate valuable time. She waited for an oncoming car to pass, then swerved around the truck into the alley. The Mercedes was gone.

Stunned by the disappearing act, she failed to see a car behind her, and jumped when the driver tapped his horn. She swallowed hard when she recognized the driver as Gerard Alvarez. She watched his approach in the side-view mirror, trying to gauge his demeanor. He didn't look happy.

His knuckle tapped her window hard enough to made her jump once again.

She rolled down her window and tried for nonchalant. "What's going on?"

"Why don't you tell me?" He glared.

"Just hoping for a lead."

"Find anything?" Alvarez scanned the inside of her SUV.

For the first time, Kate understood why the man seemed so successful at interrogations. Every muscle, every movement, every nuance seemed intimidating, and *she* was one of the good guys. Kate nervously checked her passenger seat. What was he looking at?

"I'm waiting." He moved closer.

"Well, no. I haven't really found anything, but I haven't been looking that long." She felt like a schoolgirl in the principal's office.

"That's funny. I received a call a short time ago from Marie Yates. Says she was being followed by someone who looked an awful lot like you. What about it?"

"Oh, that. Small town. I was out for a drive and our paths crossed."

"In an alley?"

"Right." She knew she'd been busted and shrugged. "I wanted to say hi?"

"Don't ever play poker."

"What?"

"You're a lousy bluff." His gaze traveled over her bare legs.

"I'm off duty," she said, explaining her shorts and halter. "Just out for a drive."

"Kate, you can't keep doing this."

She was out of the car in a flash, her frustrations at a peak. "Doing what? Trying to find leads? Looking for the one break we need? I'm on my own time, driving around town, not hurting anyone. For all you know, Marie saw me and decided it was an opportunity to get me in trouble." She backed up against the car as he closed in.

"She claims you tailed her for at least twenty minutes. That's not just a drive around town."

"That manipulative bi—"

Before she could finish, Alvarez kissed her. Her eyes widened as his cheek brushed hers and she saw the length of his silken ebony lashes. She tasted a hint of cinnamon and breathed in his spice cologne as heat ignited and spread throughout her body.

To her amazement, she kissed him back, wanting to enjoy his flavor and feel.

When it ended, she felt the sting of remorse replacing the fire within. What had they done?

When he pulled away, she could barely look him in the eye. Should she apologize? Should she just get in her car and leave?

He saved her the trouble.

"I shouldn't have done that. I'm sorry." He stepped back.

Kate stared, not knowing what to say. She wasn't sorry, not really. It felt good to release the pent-up tension she'd felt around him for so long. Major attraction.

For as much as she'd like to explore their couple potential, an uneasy feeling in her stomach signaled a warning. That or she'd skipped lunch again. Either way, she knew she had to get out of the alleyway because now wasn't the time to get involved.

She decided to let him off the hook. "I'm going to visit Lindsay's grave. Care to come with me?"

"I really should get back." His expression pleaded forgiveness.

"See you at the station then." Kate got in her car, hiding her disappointment.

She watched him leave, his taste lingering as she closed her eyes, reliving the memory. Damn him, and her choice of off-duty clothes this morning. Grinning, she started the car, realizing it had been neither. As much as she hated to admit it, she'd wanted him to kiss her, had even seen it coming when he'd moved close. She'd had her chance to stop it, but chose to play it out.

His reaction afterward had surprised her. Hadn't he been the one to start the flirtatious behavior that day at the ballpark? She'd simply called his bluff. Apparently Detective Alvarez wasn't accustomed to that. If anyone should steer clear of poker it was him.

She didn't fear challenges and didn't back down easily. Any inhibitions over a relationship with Alvarez stemmed only from possible job conflicts.

A groan escaped her when she anticipated their next meeting. There was no way to assess the damage until then and something told her that *awkward* wouldn't begin to cover it.

"You've really done it this time, Frost." She pulled out of the alley, knowing things would never be the same between them.

CHAPTER TWENTY-THREE

Kate placed flowers on Lindsay's grave, offering a silent prayer. She knew her sister wasn't here, and in fact was probably out scouting for leads, but somehow she couldn't help visiting the place where Linz *should* be resting.

She forced thoughts of Alvarez and their kiss out of her mind and thought about the beautiful surroundings. The Shepard's Garden Cemetery offered rolling hills carpeted with lush green grass, where statues and mausoleums surrounded the majestic white marble fountain in its center. Even the more traditional plots looked well kept, with bronze nameplates gleaming under the bright sun. It reminded Kate more of God's backyard than a cemetery and she knew that had been the reason her parents had chosen this place to inter their daughter.

A woman startled her from behind. "*Narcissus jonquilla.* What a lovely choice."

Kate turned to find Janice Stokes squinting in the sun, as she made her way closer.

Her low-heeled Hush Puppies seemed too big for her feet and clumsy with her modest skirt and blouse. She clutched her oversized handbag with both hands, as if it might get away, and let the silence fall between them.

"I'm sorry, I didn't get what you meant by *jonquilla* . . ." Kate stalled, trying to keep a lid on her anger. The woman's husband had been responsible for the newspaper's vicious lie about Lindsay, and Kate fought the urge to start questioning her about it.

Instead, she chose to see where the conversation led.

Janice blushed. "I'm a part-time horticulture buff, part-time gardener. You brought jonquils and I was just spouting off their formal name. *Narcissus jonquilla*."

Kate stared, wondering what to say to the woman whose husband stood out as the number-one suspect. "Jonquils are . . . were . . . Lindsay's favorite." She forced an awkward smile.

"Yes. Their scent is one of the most beautiful in any garden, that's what they're known for. It's too late to plant them now. You'll have to wait until autumn for a spring garden. If you're thinking of selling your sister's place in the future, you might want to consider them in the front. They do so much to dress up a barren yard."

"Right." Kate wondered why Janice thought Lindsay's front yard needed dressing up. Suddenly, this mousy woman seemed incredibly interesting. "So I take it you're visiting your son's grave, Mrs. Stokes?"

"Yes. Jason is right over that small hill." She pointed a bony finger to the south. "I try to come weekly, but it's hard. Although he's been gone a while, the pain is still fresh. But I guess I don't have to tell you. How are your parents holding up?"

As far as Kate knew, her parents had never met Janice, yet the woman talked as if they were well acquainted. What was she up to?

"They're dealing with it," Kate answered. "It's the not knowing that's hard. We're all looking for closure and we'll never have it until it's solved."

Janice stared a moment, her gray eyes faded against the bright sun. "I thought . . ." she trailed off.

"That my sister took her own life?" Kate finished.

"Yes." Janice's cheeks colored.

"You can't believe everything you read in the local news rag.

Autopsies don't lie and we're waiting for the paper to retract their statement. Of course it's too late to undo the damage your husband's comments made."

Janice straightened. "I'm sorry, but you know they're more or less true."

"An investigation cleared my sister of any wrongdoing, including the loss of evidence."

"I'm sure Calvin didn't know the facts were false at the time. He was merely stating what he'd heard."

"Heard from who?" Kate pinned her.

"I couldn't tell you. He has many more acquaintances than I do. Besides, what does it matter? The paper will amend its mistake and you and your family can move on."

"That hardly seems fair."

"Life is sometimes unfair, Officer Frost. As with Jason, it was bad enough he was so brutally taken, but then to watch that animal go free . . . it's just too much."

Kate knew she'd have bite marks on her tongue before this conversation ended. "I'm sorry for your loss, Mrs. Stokes," she forced out evenly, "but we need to find the person or persons who attacked Lindsay. She was ambushed in her own home."

"That's horrible." Janice looked truly astonished at the news. "And they have no idea who might have done it?"

"There are several strong leads," Kate lied.

Janice thought a moment and said, "They say a few extra lights left on in a home can help deter potential attackers. I use a light timer when we're away. But you probably know all that, being a police officer."

"No one mentioned her house being dark, Mrs. Stokes. Why do you think that?"

"I just assumed if someone broke into her home, they must have thought it empty. Don't mind me, I'm only a civilian."

Kate knew the woman was lying. Maybe Alvarez and Lindsay

were right in believing Calvin Stokes had something to do with it. "One thing I can assure you, Mrs. Stokes. We will catch whoever did this."

Janice's timid demeanor suddenly fled, replaced by an acidic tone. "And then what? A botched trial complete with missing evidence? I pray you and your family don't have to endure the pain and humiliation of injustice as we did."

Kate felt stunned at the woman's sudden anger. The conversation had taken more ups and downs than a roller coaster. The woman gave the impression of being quite unstable.

Janice stalked off down the small hill toward the paved road, and Kate watched as she sped off in her black Beemer, spattering gravel and dust.

Kate jogged to her car, in a hurry to let Alvarez know Calvin's wife was back in town, supplying them with the strongest lead so far.

CHAPTER TWENTY-FOUR

Just as my memory came up with, "Our Father, who art," I saw Tanner go down as if plowed over by a bulldozer. Mike Blake jerked my badge away from her and tossed it to me as he dodged her combat maneuvers. By the time she scrambled away from him, fading into the void, my form had taken clear shape again and I realized the officer had once again saved my ass.

He bypassed the I-told-you-so formalities, saying, "If you won't let me help you, at least let me show you how to defend yourself. It's no longer a physical world. You need to know the rules."

I felt like a rookie.

"Agreed. I'm all yours," I said, quickly adding, "as a trainee."

"Good. We'll start with the basics." He moved closer.

My ethereal hackles rose, hoping he'd stop before he got too close.

"Relax," he coaxed. "I'm not going to do anything improper."

I must be more transparent than I thought. I forced myself to stand still.

"I'm going to show you how our spirit bodies work when we will them into action. That's the key, Lindsay, you have to use your will. Ready?"

I wasn't sure, but I nodded.

He placed his hands on my shoulders and closed his eyes. Suddenly I moved forward, against his chest. He tilted his head to catch my look.

"You didn't even see it coming. I pulled you close with my arms, even though neither one of us has any physical properties. All it takes is picturing your intentions. Now you try."

"So why is it we can't shake hands?" I figured I had him.

"Because it's more of an implied gesture. No one puts a lot of thought into a handshake." He moved closer.

"Oh." I tried to recall my promise to stick with what I knew, but it seemed long gone. His body, physical or not, had me intrigued. Definite attraction.

I felt comfortable with the idea of moving closer under the pretense of a return demonstration; it gave me the excuse to get close. Couldn't find a thing in my Emily Post data bank about breaching student-teacher relations so I went ahead.

I closed my eyes and found the will part easy, with the right motivation. What I didn't expect was the sudden rush of warmth his closeness brought, nor the feelings of arousal. I realized God has a sense of humor and this must be my punishment—horny in hell. What a great reality show that would make.

"Wow," he observed. "You're a quick study."

I didn't move back, which meant I had to look up to answer him. Although I stood five-nine, he easily stood six-two.

"I've had to be. It's a job prerequisite for a female detective."

Mike lowered his arms and stepped back. "Okay. Try this."

I pictured what I wanted to *see* happen when he lunged for me, and countered with a move that landed him on the floor.

He lay prone a moment, grunting, "I think you're getting the hang of it."

"Next time I'll be ready for that commando wannabe."

"Next time?" he questioned, getting up.

"What? You think I'm going to avoid her, or run away when she comes after me again? You don't know me very well, Officer Blake. If I've come away with anything from police work, it's a determination to get the bad guy, and sometimes that means smoking them out of their holes."

"Lindsay."

"You don't understand—"

"No, *you* don't get it. You're not immune to destruction. Losing your life isn't the end."

I stopped. "How do you figure? No body, no blood. Can't do much damage to a spirit."

"Wrong. Remember what I told you? You no longer exist in a physical world. There are other ways to destroy a being, whether they're flesh and blood, or otherwise."

"Explain." I started to pace the shiny tiles of my john.

He tapped his forehead. "It's all in the mind."

"Great. I thought I was through with mind games. You're telling me that's all that's left for me?"

"No. There's much more, but for now you need to remember Tanner's been here longer than you, she has more experience, and she won't hesitate to take you down. She came close today."

"So what would've happened to me if she'd taken my badge for good?"

"We wouldn't be having this conversation. I can't really tell you what happens because I've never lost my tag, but I know of those who've resolved their issues and given up their tags."

"And?"

"I've never seen or heard from them again."

"They just fade into a poof of nothingness?"

"Something like that. Tell me what it felt like today when you were without your tag."

I didn't want to remember. It frightened me to the core. "I became weightless, and I know that doesn't make much sense given the fact that I'm only a spirit, but this was completely different. Like being washed over the edge of a high precipice with no net. I saw my form begin to fade. I guess it was the not knowing what to expect that scared me the most.

"When I was alive I kind of had expectations about what I might see when I passed. God, my grandmother, a white light. The usual stuff. But now that I'm here, I can't even fathom what might be beyond this world. It's overwhelming."

Mike reached for me, and although I had plenty of time to counter his move, I didn't want to. I let him hold me for what seemed like a long time, but who knows what that might have been. I have yet to see a clock here.

The sensation of warmth spread through me, even though I can't say my form has any sense of temperature. When I held him back, I didn't feel his body, but I knew my arms were encircling something with energy.

Call me a hopeless romantic, but the moment should have ended in a kiss. Nothing like that happened. I'm not even sure it could. After we parted, I considered that although my relationship track record is nothing to boast about, I've always maintained the hope that one day I'd get it right. George had been the last in a series of bad choices, but he'd been the only man I'd allowed myself to get serious with—serious enough to consider a name change, anyway.

Of course, now the rules have changed and I really don't know what to expect with regard to getting romantically involved with another spirit. Typical dating problems such as bad breath and feeling bloated have been eliminated, along with the morning-after breakfast and phone call. But it raises new ones such as, marriage, children, and of course, "till death do us part."

I came away from my first paranormal self-defense lesson darn sure that there might be a lot more to learn about the physics of the spirit world and that Mike Blake might just be the one to teach me.

CHAPTER TWENTY-FIVE

The uncomfortable thought of seeing Alvarez face to face after their alley encounter didn't deter Kate from bursting into his office unannounced.

"I've got something." She felt her cheeks warm when he looked at her.

"Ever hear of knocking?" He shoved some paperwork aside, avoiding her eyes. "Let's hear it."

She adjusted her shirt, tugged at her shorts, and mentally chastised herself for feeling self-conscious about her looks in front of him. *It was just a kiss,* she reminded herself.

"Well?" He stared.

She paced. "Okay, here it is. You're not going to like this, or probably even believe it, but I happened to run into Janice Stokes at the cemetery."

"You're right times two."

"Just listen. I swear I didn't follow her. I brought flowers to Lindsay's grave, remember I invited you to come when we . . . well, anyway, I went. She approached me and struck up a conversation."

"What about?" He gave her his attention.

At least he hadn't thrown her out.

"She mentioned she was there to visit her son's grave, and asked how my parents are holding up. From there I steered the conversation where it needed to go."

"You interrogated a grieving mother in the graveyard?" His

eyes widened.

"No. I questioned a potential suspect's wife. I simply went along with her conversation, leading here and there."

"Leading where?" He pinched the bridge of his nose against closed eyes.

"If you're getting a headache, I have some aspirin in my purse. Believe me I've already taken some."

As she repeated part of her conversation with Janice Stokes, she watched Alvarez's expression turn from *what have you done now* to *I think you're onto something.*

"We should talk to her," Kate told him.

"We?" He leaned back in his chair. "I'd planned to question her when she returned from out of town, but it looks like you've beaten me to it. What happened to your promise not to overstep your boundaries?"

"I know you're annoyed, but you won't be when you hear the rest of the story. It will give you a reason to haul her in for questioning."

"Thank you. I'll let Detective Copley know we have a suspect."

"Aw, come on, Alvarez! Give me a break."

"I'll see what I can do. Now tell me what you have."

"She talked about Lindsay's house, right down to her empty flowerbed, and she went on to suggest there'd been no lights on that night. And if that's not enough for you, Janice drives a black Beemer."

"That matches the description the neighbor gave of a dark sedan." Alvarez grabbed his jacket. "We'll see where this goes."

A short time later, Kate watched the interview from behind the interrogation room's one-way glass. She fidgeted with her hair, tugged at her shorts, and paced, itching to be on the other side. Alvarez had argued she'd done her part, and done it well. *She'd* argued that since she'd established a rapport with Janice, it might be smart to let her talk to the woman first. When the fireworks ended, she'd found herself on the wrong side of the one-way glass, biding her time until she made detective.

Lindsay showed up in time to see the show, and they watched as Elizabeth Copley entered the room behind Alvarez.

Kate felt a tug of jealousy and wondered if it stemmed from her desire to be in on the questioning or to be with Alvarez.

"We just have a few questions for you today, Janice." Elizabeth smiled. "Are you comfortable? Do you need water?"

"No. What's all this about?" Janice picked at a fingernail.

"Gerard?" Elizabeth turned the interrogation over to her partner.

"Gerard?" Kate shot a questioning look toward her sister.

Lindsay shrugged, motioning back to the interrogation room.

Mousy Janice looked like she might puke any minute. Her pallor had lightened several shades, to the point where no amount of makeup could have helped her. Kate took note of her feelings of pity for Janice and considered how this was lesson one in the detective codebook. Never let your emotions get the better of you. Not an official rule as far as she knew, but it was fast becoming her personal motto.

She watched Alvarez saunter back and forth behind the woman who was sitting in a dilapidated wooden, uncomfortable-looking chair. Janice jumped at the sound of the detective's voice behind her.

"Tell me once more why you were at Detective Frost's home that night."

"I've already told you. I wanted to talk to her but chickened out."

"Talk to her about what? Did you have a relationship with Lindsay Frost?"

"Well, no, but she'd been the detective on my son's investigation, so I knew who she was."

"So you sat across the street watching her house?"

"Yes," she stammered.

"And how did you know where she lived?"

"My husband keeps excellent records and I was able to get her address from the form she filled out when she purchased a gun from him. I didn't break any law, did I?"

"That's what I'm trying to find out. So, you were watching the house?"

"Well, not exactly. I was only trying to get up enough nerve to go up to the door, but when I saw that there were no lights on and that her garbage hadn't been taken out for the night, I figured she wasn't home."

"And what else did you notice, Mrs. Stokes? Any movement, any other cars parked nearby?"

Her gray eyes wandered over the tabletop as if she'd find the answer there.

Alvarez rounded the table and leaned across, closing the distance between them. "Are you with me, Janice?"

"Yes. I'm not deaf, Mr. Alvarez."

Kate lowered her gaze with a smirk. The dowdy woman had a temper when pushed.

Janice straightened and looked him in the eye. "I didn't see anything else. Nothing unusual."

"Can you tell me what you might have said to Detective Frost had you been given the chance?"

Her eyes filled as she thought a moment. "I think . . . I think I would have told her that I didn't really blame her for the way things turned out at the trial."

"Go on," Alvarez encouraged.

"You see, it's mostly my husband who has a grudge against her. Oh, I did up until recently. I even talked with that reporter who wrote the story about Detective Frost's unfortunate end."

"I thought your husband was responsible for that," Alvarez pressed.

"Not exactly. The criminal attorney for the man who killed my son phoned me and suggested I speak to the press to get the true story out, that it might be a good way to vent and heal. The attorney told me, 'At this point, it's the only justice your son will ever see.' So I told the newspaper reporter everything. But I'm sorry about it now, because I don't really feel that way.

"See, Calvin blames Detective Frost for the missing evidence that set our son's killer free, but I don't."

"And why is that, Janice?" Alvarez asked.

"Because I know what it's like to lose a child, and when I heard about Detective Frost, I couldn't help feeling sorry for her parents. Then I thought about the trial and the devastated look on Lindsay's face when the guy went free. She couldn't have been more horrified."

Kate swiped hard at the tears that streamed down her cheeks. *Don't get emotional.*

Alvarez reined her in. "What about your husband? Where was he the night Detective Frost died?"

"I, uh, well, he was out."

Bingo. Kate found herself moving closer to the glass. Calvin Stokes had lied.

"Where?" Alvarez never flinched.

"He was at his shop. Why?" She helplessly looked around the room.

"No reason. Except there is no one to vouch for your whereabouts on the night in question and he lied to us. All we know is what you've told us—that you were in front of the victim's house."

"You think *I* killed her? With what, my ninety-pound frame and a SWAT team? Look at me, Detective. I'm forty-five years old, five-three, and I don't work out. What makes you think I

156

could kill anyone, let alone a six-foot detective?

"Let me tell you something, Detective Alvarez. I have remorse over Lindsay's passing, but not because I killed her. I feel for her family because I know what it's like to lose someone you love. Nothing more. And I resent that my attempt to show compassion today has been twisted into an attempt to frame me." The woman's cold stare penetrated the dark glass and Kate knew the last comment had been directed at her.

At that moment, Kate knew the entire interview had been a waste. The only thing they'd accomplished was the revelation that Calvin Stokes had lied to them about his whereabouts that night. She shook her head at Lindsay's insight. Here was the *hole in his alibi* she'd wanted.

Elizabeth answered a knock at the door and read a slip of paper from an officer. She whispered something to Alvarez.

"Saves me the trouble of going to get him," he replied.

A moment later, Calvin Stokes entered.

"Just what the hell's going on here? Why is my wife being questioned?"

"We're almost finished, Stokes." Alvarez pulled out a wooden chair for him. "Have a seat. We're just getting started with you."

"Oh? Why's that?"

"You're suspect numero uno."

CHAPTER TWENTY-SIX

My new body had proven its disadvantages, but standing behind the interrogation room's one-way glass, I found a benefit. Kate grinned when I slid through the glass unharmed and unnoticed by a frightened but cocky Calvin Stokes. When I looked back, I saw the one-way glass worked both ways for me, and I could see Kate through it as if it were an open room. Just a death perk, I guess.

Taking in the familiar territory, I smiled. Home sweet home. I'd spent countless hours with and without my partner, questioning, cajoling, and bullying suspects in this room. For the first time since my passing, I felt back in my element, in on the action, and most of all, alive—if that makes any sense.

Elizabeth had taken Janice Stokes out of the room, leaving the unshaven gun shop owner to stare daggers at Alvarez.

Calvin's expression didn't intimidate Alvarez; in fact, I knew Gerard thrived on challenge. He paced behind the man's chair like a hungry tiger, toying with its prey.

"Your wife has made some startling revelations about your whereabouts on the night in question. It seems you lied. What's up with that?" He leaned across the scarred wooden table. "What size prison jumpsuit should I request for you?"

Up close, I saw a thin veil of sweat clinging to Calvin's upper lip as he twisted it into a sneer. "You got shit."

"We've got *you*," Alvarez countered, rereading the slip of paper Elizabeth had handed him. "It seems one of our detectives had a nice chat with your hunting buddy, Jerry Hanson. He said you and several others returned from your annual hunting trip the night before the murder."

"So?" The man looked skeptical. "What about it?"

"He also told him that you'd had a few beers too many and had carried on about how you blamed Detective Frost for losing the evidence in your son's investigation. I quote, 'He kept saying how that Frost bitch would get what's coming to her.' End quote. Is that true?

"Tell me Calvin, where were you while my partner became a sacrifice in her bathroom? Where!" He slammed his palms on the table in front of the man, causing him to jump.

Calvin tried to appear unshaken, saying, "Easy there, Detective. You don't want to harm your only suspect, do you? So far I've been patient, putting up with your harassing, ridiculous questions, not even asking for a lawyer. But I'm real close, *amigo.*"

To my surprise and disappointment, Alvarez backed off. I caught Kate's expression through the glass and knew she wanted to bust through it.

"Okay, Mr. Stokes. Message received. You want a lawyer."

"I didn't say that." The man fidgeted with his shirt cuff.

"Oh, but you did. You said the word *lawyer* in a police interrogation room, so that ends our conversation until you can secure counsel. Shall I call one for you?"

"No!" His eyes showed a momentary flicker. Was it panic?

"Why not?"

"I'll decide when or *if* I want a lawyer. Am I being charged with anything?"

"I don't know yet. You haven't answered my question. Where were you that night?"

"I've already told you—"

"A lie. I know. Try again."

The man sat back, steepling his fingers over his chest. I saw Alvarez circle around behind him, then shoot up close to Calvin's left ear. "Where!" he shouted.

"All right! Jeez, give a guy a heart attack. I went to my shop that night."

"What time?"

"About eight, I guess."

"Don't guess."

"Eight."

"What did you do there?" Alvarez briefly glanced at the one-way glass.

I caught Kate's unreadable expression as she stared at him and wondered what she was thinking.

Calvin sighed. "Is this really necessary? I didn't kill that woman, so why don't you just check for prints or DNA or something?"

When Alvarez stared him down, he caved. "All right, all right. I had to set a couple of mousetraps. It was a good excuse to get out of the house for a while. I was bored."

"Did you know your wife had gone out too?"

"No. She tell you that?"

"She went to Detective Frost's home with the intention of talking to her. Surely she mentioned it after seeing the news in the paper the next day."

"I don't read the paper." Calvin's upper lip brimmed with sweat again.

"Why did you lie, Calvin? What's the big deal about mouse-traps?"

The man wouldn't look at Alvarez. "I can't believe she went out."

"Why not? You did. I think you're lying. Again."

"But she never goes out after dark," he said, more to himself than Alvarez.

"Right now you have bigger problems unless you have someone who can verify your whereabouts that night."

"Why does everyone think I did it?"

"The motive became clear the minute you opened your big mouth to your hunting buddies. In police circles, that's known as intent. You certainly had access to Tasers, and now you can't prove your whereabouts. It's not lookin' too good for you right now, Calvin. So I'm going to ask you one more time before I arrest you, where were you that night?"

Calvin's ruddy color had turned gray. He shook his head and mumbled, "Sheila Blackman. You can call her. She'll verify my whereabouts."

"I'll do that. Who is she?"

"Please don't tell my wife. I'm beggin' ya. Sheila will tell you everything and then you'll have your proof that I didn't do it. There's no reason to let on to Janice."

At that point, I left the room and headed back beside Kate.

Kate thought a moment, then asked, "What do you think?"

"He got more than a mouse caught in his trap, but he's not our man. I still haven't given up on his wife. There's just something about her goodie-goodie presentation. No one could be that naïve."

Alvarez came into the viewing room, stripping off his tie. "Damn! I thought we had him," he told Kate. "But I'm getting a search warrant for the wife's car and their home. I can place her at the house and she had plenty of motive."

Kate caught him before he left the room. "Do you know who the defense attorney was for the guy that killed Calvin's son?"

Alvarez shook his head. "No, but I can find out. Why?"

"Just a hunch."

"I'll be right back." He brushed a lock of hair from her face. "We're getting close, I can feel it."

I waited until I heard his footsteps echo down the hall. "Okay.

What gives between you and Alvarez?"

"What?" Kate blushed and avoided my eyes.

"Oh no. You didn't."

She looked down at her shoes and pretended to swipe a smudge. "It all happened so fast."

"*What* happened?" I could hardly contain my excitement. "Hurry up and tell me before he gets back."

"Just a kiss, all right?" Her smile said the rest.

"I knew it! You never could hide that stuff from me."

"Look, don't turn it into something it's not. It was a mistake. A one-time thing. I'll never wear those shorts again."

Alvarez stuck his head in the room, saying, "The criminal attorney against Calvin's son was Marie Yates."

"Yates, huh? So she's ultimately responsible for the newspaper story urging Janice to tell all." Kate flashed him an I-told-you-so look.

He shook his head. "In a roundabout way, but unfortunately we can't pin it on her."

"Isn't that a breach of ethics?"

"It won't work. Janice would never turn against her."

Kate glanced my way and I nodded. Janice slipped when she'd mentioned the idea source for the story, but it wasn't a crime. The fact that Janice had run with it made her naïve, not a criminal.

Alvarez started to leave. "I'm going to check out the Sheila story before we turn him loose. The warrant will probably be served this afternoon."

"What are you looking for?" Kate asked.

"Towels and the Taser."

Kate's mouth opened to say something, but he'd already gone.

"So," I asked with a grin, "what about Boden?"

"Boden who?" Kate said softly.

Chapter Twenty-Seven

"Fool! You were almost caught. I can't let you out of my sight without problems. You cannot talk to the enemy, especially Kate Frost! Now our plans will have to wait until everything settles down," the commander decided.

"*Our* plans? I told you I don't want any part of this," said the woman.

"You're already a part of it. But from now on I'll be watching you carefully. You, and them." The commander pointed toward an older couple sitting on a bench in Southfield Park. "Pay attention, because they're the key to our plan now."

"You can't do that. They're innocent. Whatever Lindsay Frost did, her parents had nothing to do with it."

"Every war has its casualties, innocent or not. Surely, you know that from personal experience. Life and *death* are not fair."

"Let it go. It's time to move on. Don't you want peace in your life?"

"I've never known peace, and you will never see it again unless our goals are accomplished. I'll see to it."

"What if I go to the authorities?" Her tone turned defiant. "They'll lock me up and then you'll be alone. You need me. There's no way to accomplish your goals without me."

A firm hand knocked her to her knees. Held by the hair, her head repeatedly pounded the hardwood floor. The commander screeched in her ear with each strike. "You will not disobey me!

Not ever! Did you think there were no consequences for misbehavior? You are no match for me. Humble yourself now!"

She knew from experience what came next. Her head throbbed in pain and warm blood oozed down her forehead. On shaky knees, now sore and bruised, she lowered herself with arms spread out before her. She said the words that had been ingrained in her head and had become the only source of relief from the beatings.

"I apologize for my haughty nature and ask for your mercy as my superior. Thank you for leading the way in order to serve the law of the land and right all injustices."

With that, she vomited and passed out.

CHAPTER TWENTY-EIGHT

The bad news was that ol' Sheila came through for Calvin and the search of Janice's car and home turned up no evidence. Calvin had been released and we had nothing. Personally, I still liked Janice, but Kate didn't agree, of course, setting her sights on Marie Yates.

"Will you let it go? Marie has better things to do than commit manslaughter," I reminded Kate as we drove to my house.

"You always told me about the importance of a hunch. Why can't you follow my lead for a change?" Kate sped up along the main street of town.

"Okay, let's say Marie did it. What's her motive?"

"She hated you."

"Well, I have to admit, I've seen people kill for less. I'll give you that one, but what about means? She wouldn't know a Taser from an Uzi."

"C'mon, Linz. She's a criminal attorney. She spends most of her time with criminals who would know exactly what to use and where to get it."

"Okay," I said, pulling out my last trick. "What about opportunity? Yes, she knows where I live, but there were no signs of B and E, not even that anyone had been in my house. She's not that good."

"Two out of three?" Kate grinned. "I don't know, maybe I'm looking for something that's not there because I don't like or trust her. But you've taught me too well, big sister, and I'm not letting go of this feeling until it lets go of me."

Kate's theory was more than anyone else had at this point. I watched my driveway come into view. "So tell me why we're here again?"

"It all goes back to the damn lack of water around the tub. Someone cleaned up afterward. Unless they brought towels or sheets with them, some of yours should be missing."

"All that proves is that they preferred not to get their shoes wet on the way out."

"Maybe. But we never found any wet towels. Something Janice said about your garbage not being on the curb for pickup the next morning gave me an idea. Since your trash wasn't out, the guy probably took the soggy towels with him. That's why we have to make sure you have some linens missing."

She cut the engine in my drive and we headed inside.

It didn't take long to find that the embossed *Lindsay* and *George* towels were absent from my linen closet. Kate had given them to me as a gift when we'd announced our engagement.

She checked the hamper and the laundry basket to be sure, but I knew she'd come up empty. I had placed them on the top shelf so I wouldn't use them until after we were married. I realize we lived together, but I wanted to save them for our first day as a married couple. That bit of foolish sentimentality had been a stroke of genius but I kept that insight to myself.

Kate shoved the closet door closed with her hip. "Find the towels, find the killer. Come on," she said on her way to the car.

I wasn't pleased with her next idea, although I have to admit I couldn't see any other way.

"I have a real problem going in without a warrant," I objected.

"*I* would need one but you don't. That's why you're going in and I'm not." Kate turned the corner and headed for Marie Yates' house.

"If Alvarez gets wind of this, you'll be suspended," I warned, knowing it was futile.

"If those towels are there, the warrant will write itself."

Right. It sounded so simple.

"You'll have trouble convincing him. There's no reason," I said.

"I'll think of something," she said, and grinned.

"How's it going between you two?"

"I told you it was a one-time thing. It's over."

"Why is it I don't believe you?"

"Because you don't *want* to. Quit playing matchmaker. You're a ghost, not Cupid."

"I wish I knew Cupid," I mumbled.

"Why would you . . . wait. You have something you'd like to share?"

"Not really. I'm trying to find a way to talk you out of this crazy idea."

"Have you met someone?"

"Forget it, Kate. He's a ghost."

"So are you. Gives new meaning to *soul mates.*"

"You know I'm no judge of men. Look at George."

"He is *no* man. Don't get me started. He's been dead for years but no one has told him."

"He wasn't *that* bad."

"Oh yeah? Remember the department softball game?" Kate chuckled.

I'd never forget it. George had agreed to fill in on our team during the annual police and fire department softball challenge. It became clear why the man preferred golf, but I'd loved him for his efforts.

"Running isn't his thing. Golf is his game. All things considered, I don't think he did too bad around the bases."

"Right. Ever see a Jesus Lizard run across a swamp?" She stopped at a red light. "C'mon, details about the new guy."

I quickly told her what little I knew about Mike Blake and our close encounter.

"I can't let this go any further," I said. "Like you and Alvarez, it's a one-time thing and won't happen again."

"If you say so. Now stop stalling." She pulled the car over several houses down from Marie's. "The good counselor might be back anytime."

I sat a moment, trying to come up with an argument for why I shouldn't go in the house. Why was I so skittish? It bothered me that I couldn't place my fear. "Kate, you have to understand, my skills aren't quite polished yet. I won't be able to move stuff to look."

"Good. Then she won't suspect anyone was inside."

I can do this, I told myself. But did I want to? Inconvenient morality issues popped into my head and I realized my fear stemmed from the upcoming final judgment. It would come sooner or later, and since I'd made it this far, it was the sooner part that bothered me.

"Go," Kate urged.

"Just like that? Give me a minute. I'm still considering how this might turn back and bite us."

"Time's up."

A few seconds later, I found myself inside the elegant two-story Georgian that Attorney Yates called home. Wow. She left no detail unattended to, from the oriental rugs to the antiques, including a grandfather clock that had stood the test of time better than I had. Every piece said mint condition, every picture frame dusted and perfectly aligned. By the time I made it to the upstairs bedrooms, I figured Martha Stewart probably called her for decorating ideas.

Peering out the French doors into a spacious backyard, I saw that the landscaping looked as meticulous as the inside of the home.

The bathroom fixtures sparkled and shone like polished gems; even the half-empty shampoo and conditioner bottles showed no gooey signs of use. The words *clean freak* came to mind, when I realized she probably cleaned and dried them. I would imagine there are less antiseptic surgical suites.

The rest of the home proved to be the same, without dust, dirt, or germ. I stuck my head inside her refrigerator, partly to see what a criminal attorney kept inside, but also to perform the final test. The absence of putrefied red gunk on the ketchup lid and a spotless butter tray convinced me the woman had definite issues. Unfortunately, that's all I found.

With no sign of the missing towels, I decided to try the garage, hoping Marie had slipped them into a garbage can. The spotless cans turned up empty. I knew Kate would be disappointed. She seemed so sure.

Then it hit me. If Marie were germ phobic, she'd never touch bloody wet towels or have taken them anywhere. She probably wouldn't have slit anyone's wrists either.

I wished my feelings could have died along with my body, so I wouldn't have to deal with the disappointment of false leads and suspects, and the idea that no one would ever pay for the evil they'd done. Add, to all that, the look on my sister's face when this promising lead fell through, and the week couldn't get much worse. That is, until I saw Marie Yates' car beside Kate's along the curb.

CHAPTER TWENTY-NINE

An hour later, Kate helplessly watched in horror as her job slid down the proverbial toilet. Police chief Grady O'Connor's office reeked of strong aftershave and stale coffee, neither of which helped his argument with Marie Yates. His tough Irish nature did little to sway the high-strung, pissed-off attorney.

Kate realized she probably deserved what she was getting and what she might eventually get, but she hadn't done anything illegal. It served as O'Connor's only argument against the ranting attorney. Thankfully, without a legitimate argument, the most she could do was threaten to press stalking charges. After some fast-talking, he managed to calm the woman down with the promise that Officer Frost would be chained to his hip from now on.

When at last the attorney received a call and had to leave, Kate knew better than to breathe a sigh of relief. The wrath of O'Connor would be next on the playbill.

No amount of talking would convince the chief that Kate hadn't been watching Marie's home. He was too smart and too devoted for that. The tough part for him, she imagined, was the fact that he probably would have done the same thing under the circumstances. But he had to act appropriately in front of his superiors, and that left no place for favoritism. She'd forced his actions with her latest attempt at overstepping her bounds.

Chief O'Connor's expression looked tired around the deep blue of his eyes. Today they didn't sparkle; instead, they seemed filled with disappointment. "Frost, you leave me no choice. I'm putting you on suspension until further notice. Personally, I think you came off bereavement leave far too soon. If I were you I'd take this opportunity to get my head on straight and set my priorities in order. I'm sorry."

"Not your fault, Chief. I brought this on myself." Kate suddenly realized an opportunity. Time off meant more time devoted to the investigation.

He ran a pudgy hand through his thick white hair, looking like Santa with a migraine. "I hope you learned something in this. Tough lessons often end up teaching us something."

"You're right." She grinned. "Next time I won't park so close to the house."

Twenty minutes later, Kate took a sip of her large mocha coffee at the Main Street Café. The quaint coffee bar housed about fifteen petite round tables, serving up strong java and some serious band entertainment on the weekends. The raucous music wasn't Kate's preference, but she'd patrolled the teen hot spot often. Today the crowds seemed absent, and she smiled to see she had the place mostly to herself—until Alvarez walked through the door. She choked on the hot liquid as he removed his sunglasses and zeroed in on his intended target—her.

He took a seat at her table, saying nothing. His dark expression spoke volumes.

Kate fanned herself with a napkin. "Is it hot in here? I feel intense heat, searing me to the bone. Oh, it's you, staring."

"Why, Kate?" He wasn't smiling.

"You know damn well, why. It was a chance to get something on Marie. I never went near her house. Frankly, I don't know how she saw me. It's as though she has a sixth sense, like . . . Satan."

"I know you don't like her. Believe me, the feeling is mutual on her part. But you cannot tail her. Without me."

Kate's mouth opened, snapped closed, then opened again. "What? I thought I heard you agree with me for the first time. Shall I call the media?"

"If you'd like, but I think you've received enough attention for one day, don't you?"

"I don't care if I have to swing butt naked from the clock tower. I can't let Lindsay's butcher go free."

"Naked, huh?"

"Stop it." Her cheeks warmed with the memory of their kiss, still fresh in her mind. "Why can't you take me seriously? Is it a gender thing? A personal thing? The fact that you know I'm right and you can't admit it?" she teased.

"I wish you *were* right, Kate. I'd like nothing better than to get this guy, or gal, if your theory is correct. But detective work doesn't play out like that. It's a giant puzzle and it has to be put together one tedious piece at a time."

"Okay. So tell me about the not-tailing-without-you part."

"I know what you'll be doing on your suspension time. I'd hate to see you get into more trouble, *Lucy,* so I've got a proposition for you."

Kate raised an eyebrow. "Really?"

He ignored her insinuation and continued. "I'll help you if you promise not to go off on your own, unsupervised."

Kate bristled. "You mean like a two-year-old? What are you, my nanny?"

"No. I can see you're no child." He let his gaze linger on her lips.

"We'd work together, as equal partners? My ideas legitimately considered? What's in it for you?"

"Kate, you have some great instincts. You need to learn the procedure and protocol in dealing with touchy investigations like this one. There are too many frayed nerves to go poking at them. But there *are* ways to get the information without ruffling feathers."

"In other words, I need to learn how to be sneaky."

"In a manner of speaking, yes," he said, and smiled. "Other than that, I get to spend time with you."

Kate's cell phone rang, and she frowned at the precinct's number on the caller I.D.

"This is Kate Frost," she answered, and her whole world fell apart.

Kate left her SUV at the café and rode with Alvarez. He turned on his car flashers and sped down Main Street. She shared what scant information she'd received from her frantic mother at the jail.

"My dad has been brought in for questioning about a stolen gun. Can you believe that? The man hesitates to use a flyswatter, says he feels sorry for the little fellas. Why would he steal a gun?"

Alvarez frowned. "Did he have it on him?"

"Mom didn't say. The poor woman is near hysterics. God, how could this happen? It has to be a mistake."

"Try and keep calm—we'll straighten it all out when we get there."

Less than five minutes later, Kate pushed through the precinct doors with Alvarez close behind. She keyed in the code to open the inside door and saw Chief O'Connor waiting. His expression looked grim.

"What happened? Where is he?" Kate followed the man to his office.

"Close the door, will you Alvarez?" O'Connor asked.

"Where is my father? I need to see my parents."

"Sit, Kate. They're both fine. Let me fill you in. First of all, your father hasn't been arrested; he's just being questioned. An anonymous tip came in about a gun spotted in his mail truck."

"Did they find a gun?" Alvarez asked.

"No gun. But a short time ago, Calvin Stokes reported that his security system had been disabled and a gun had been stolen from his store."

"So why is my father the suspect? Anyone could have stolen the gun from his shop."

"The gun in the truck was described as a .45 millimeter, same as the stolen gun. The two incidents coincide; I have to check it out."

"It's a setup," Kate said.

"There's a team processing Calvin's store right now. I'm sure your dad's prints won't be found; meantime, I'm trying to *protect* your father because I don't believe he had anything to do with it. Like I said, it's too coincidental. I want to nip this in the bud before it gets out of hand."

"What does Mr. Frost have to say about it?" Alvarez asked.

"He won't say anything." O'Connor shook his head.

Kate frowned. "Why?"

"He's waiting for his lawyer."

"Lawyer? He hasn't been charged."

"Looks like he's been watching too much television."

"Let me talk to him, Chief," Kate pleaded.

A knock at the door revealed a young female officer. "Sorry to interrupt, but Mr. Frost's lawyer is here."

"That's fine, Teresa. Send him in," O'Connor said.

Kate froze at a familiar voice just outside the door.

"Thank you," said Marie Yates, entering the office.

CHAPTER THIRTY

After Marie busted Kate, I decided Sis could probably handle the fallout with Chief O'Connor. If she wanted to be a detective, she needed to learn how to take the heat for her mistakes. I should have listened to my instincts and not gone into the house. Now Kate would replace my butt in the chief's office, receiving a lecture meant to ensure the offending officer would think twice the next time. It usually worked, too. I always thought twice before going ahead with an unsanctioned plan.

I decided to work on my navigational skills in preparation for Tanner Jean Hoyt. I hadn't abandoned my plans to lure her out. A brainstorm had taken shape enough for me to realize it might actually work, but I would need help from my supernatural crime team, including Sally. If everything went as planned, Tanner would soon become a distant bad memory.

As far as I know, there is no great-beyond handbook, and therefore some of the rules fall into gray areas. For instance, when I hear my name called, I tend to head in that direction. When Kate sounded off loud and clear, I thought I might be hearing things, until I heard it again.

"Lindsay. Come!"

Suddenly, Sally turned up to stop me.

"Hey, you might want to watch out. Unless you can see who it is, don't go," Sally warned.

"I know my sister's voice."

"Yeah? Close your eyes."

I have real trust issues after an elementary school *friend* told me to close my eyes on the school playground for a surprise. She quickly yanked my pants down and ran. I swore I'd never get caught with my drawers down again, literally.

Sally tapped her ever-impatient foot. I reluctantly obliged her, shutting my eyes.

"You steppin' out tonight, Sis?"

My eyes bolted open. Sally wore a smug expression.

"See? It's a gift."

"How'd you do that?"

"Another skill you'll eventually develop. I just wanted to warn you. You never know who's out there on this side."

I heard Kate call again and looked helplessly at Sally. "I have to go to her."

She shrugged. "Hey, it's your funeral."

"Funny," I said, and went in search of Kate.

No one was more surprised than I to find Kate, my mother, and Alvarez sitting in an interrogation room waiting to see my father. Kate excused herself to the ladies' room and I followed. She checked the stalls to be sure we were alone, then filled me in on what she knew.

"A short time ago, Calvin Stokes reported one of his guns stolen. O'Connor has a team there now, but then Dad went and lawyered up. God, this looks bad.

"And to add insult to injury, Marie Yates is his attorney! I almost swallowed my tongue when she walked in." Kate paced before the sinks.

"How did that happen? I know Mom wouldn't call her." I refrained from joining her. Pacing is a family trait.

Kate snapped her fingers. "Earlier today, when I was in the chief's office, getting reamed . . . by the way what happened to you?"

"Paranormal nature call," I lied.

"Really?" She frowned. "Anyway, Marie received a phone call and rushed out. It saved my ass, because she had to cease her tirade and settle for a simple promise to keep an eye on me from O'Connor. Whatever that call was, it had to be important for her to give up seeing me squirm. I bet someone tipped her off that Dad had been taken in, and she rushed over to offer her services. She's good, I'll give her that."

"It's just her way of showing you she has more power than you do. We need to slow down and analyze this. Number one, Dad is innocent."

"Right," Kate agreed.

"Two, I think we can safely assume it's a setup."

"That's what I say," said Kate.

"I still like Calvin and Janice for everything, and I wouldn't put it past Calvin to try and set up Dad. It's just one more way to enact revenge."

"Maybe." Kate looked doubtful. "But I can't give him that much credit. He's too dumb and drunk most of the time to think like that."

"Did they find out who called in the tip?" I asked, watching her wear down the dull floor tiles.

" 'Fraid not. What'll we do now?"

"I'll stay and watch Dad until they figure out his prints are nowhere inside that grimy gun shop. If something happens, I can find you. Meantime, you need to find out what you can about that false tip. And light a fire under Marie's ass to get him out of here, will you?"

"It'll be my pleasure. Got a blowtorch?"

After Kate left, I sat beside my dad in the interrogation room. He sat hunched, with face in his hands, looking pale and beaten. My father had always been the castle defender, at the ready to slay dragons or crawl under the bed in the middle of the night to kick the boogeyman's slimy green ass. It hurt to know I seemed helpless to do anything for my hero, my forever friend.

Marie had left him alone to speak with the chief in the hall. I watched her prissy demeanor, the plastic-looking no-muss hair, the designer suit, and the lipstick that never smudged or faded. I much preferred the more natural, bitten look.

Again, I tried to figure out who would be so cruel as to set up my poor father for a crime he didn't commit. Again, my mind came around to Calvin Stokes, but I quickly realized Kate was probably right about him. Calvin couldn't have acted alone in this, or my death, and I couldn't see Janice being much help.

Then an idea hit that would have sent chills down my spine if that were possible. I got up to pace, considering the idea that Tanner and Calvin Stokes might be connected. They both wanted their revenge on me for different reasons, but that might be part of the connection. The old adage "misery loves company" came to mind. They made the perfect couple, one evil enough to plot, the other supplying the physical presence needed to get the job done. But how did they know one another?

Guns. In life, Tanner had been into guns and other weapons, and it was a sure bet her father had known Calvin from his interest in military-style weapons. There was a solid chance that she'd bought a gun or two from him over the years. But even if we proved that, it wouldn't prove they'd planned my murder. There was a piece missing and I needed to find it fast.

The interrogation room door opened, and Marie Yates took a seat beside my father, resting a hand on his arm.

"It won't be much longer, Mr. Frost. There's no weapon; therefore, no reason for you to be here."

"They're checking Calvin's for my prints, but they won't find any," my father said.

Marie's expression burned with annoyance. "What they *will* find are hundreds of prints from countless patrons, including mine." She smiled.

I couldn't tell if she was serious or simply trying to make him feel better. Since Marie lacked an empathy gene, I assumed she was telling the truth in a roundabout way. As much as I appreciated her attempt to reassure my father, I tucked that bit of info in my mental Rolodex of reasons to suspect her. So far, it was the only one and was weak at best.

It did, however, give me a connection between her and Calvin, and that's who my money was on. In order to find out for sure, I knew I had to find a way to get to Tanner. Sally's mimic demonstration came to mind and I wondered if it would work on my stalker.

First, I had to determine who she'd be drawn to, and I immediately thought of her mother. Although I didn't have much background to go on, I knew she'd cared for her at home during her cancer battle. Still, I wasn't sure what their relationship had been. What if she'd simply taken care of her mother out of a sense of duty? If that were the case, she'd probably ignore her mother. I'd only get one chance to draw her out. I needed a sure thing.

I recalled the story floating around town at the time of Tanner's father's disappearance in 1996. Although I'd graduated high school three years before, I still kept in touch with my younger friends. Tanner, only seventeen at the time, had told everyone her father had been called into military action on a secret mission, a story that earned her a lot of teasing by her schoolmates and several detentions for defending his honor. John Hoyt had lost a leg in the war, ending his tour early and forcing him home, where he eventually ended up running an auto repair shop in town. But in Tanner's mind he'd gained hero status. If anyone could get her attention, it would be John J. Hoyt.

But in order to mimic him, I'd have to know what he sounded

like, and I'd never met the man. I needed sound archives to go back and study his manner of speaking, inflection, and accent, if any. If anyone knew where to find that kind of info, it had to be Sally.

I decided to leave my father in Marie's cold but capable hands. It looked like he would be released before long, and I needed to find Tanner before she caused any more trouble.

Navigation had become easier each time and I managed to find Sally quickly. I watched her pace the perimeter of the parking lot of her last job at Tri-City Labs, finally catching her attention with a wave.

She headed my way, taking her time, with teddy bear in arm. I noticed her usual lack of enthusiasm at my appearance.

"Hey, Sally. I thought I'd find you here."

"Yeah. Where else, *paradise?*" Her scarred lips twisted into a tight frown.

"What's wrong?"

"I'm here. Isn't that enough?"

Her emotional claws shredded my enthusiasm. I tried a different approach. "I need your help, Sally. Do you have time?"

"All the time in the world. You might just say eternity. What's up?" She sighed as if she might die all over again, this time from boredom.

"Remember when we talked about mimicking?"

"Yeah. Have you been hearing voices again?"

"Not exactly. This time I *want* to hear them."

"You don't have enough trouble?"

"I can see you're in a rotten mood; maybe I'll try you later." I started to leave.

"Wait," she called. "I'm sorry. I've got some personal problems I'm trying to deal with, but I said I'd help you. So, shoot. Who is it you need to hear from?"

"Tanner's father, John J. Hoyt. I need to learn to mimic him, but I've never heard him speak. I noticed you mimicked Kate's voice without ever hearing her. What's the trick?"

"No trick. I eavesdropped on your conversation with her at your wake."

I should have been annoyed, but didn't have the time. "Is there a way to learn John Hoyt's voice?"

"Hmm, the only way I can think of is to visit his residual haunt, if he has one. Many ghosts do, especially if they have unfinished business."

From what I'd learned of John Hoyt, he had plenty. His Vietnam service had ended after only a few months due to his injury. I can only begin to imagine what kind of hell that plays with a person's mind.

I had no idea what Sally was talking about though, when it came to a residual haunt. "I missed the newbie class on that kind of haunting. Care to explain?"

"A residual haunt is a past act or scene from the ghost's life, where they revisit and play out their previous actions. It usually involves talking to whoever played a part in their past. It's kind of like rehearsing for a play, but the scene never ends."

"Thanks. Clear as mud." Death only complicates life.

"Okay. Give me a minute." She paced, with the bear hanging at her side. "It's likened to when a person says they wish they could go back and redo, or undo, a past mistake. For a ghost, it's a good place to work out their past. But it can get monotonous and some spirits get caught up in the residual, never finding their way out."

"So it's not the same as revisiting the place you die?" I asked.

"No. We all do that, but not every spirit has a residual haunt, and it isn't always where you crossed over."

"How do I know if John has a residual?"

"First we have to find him."

I motioned with my hands for more info.

"What do you think his residual might be?" she asked. "For example, if he was a surgeon he might revisit a surgical suit, or a lawyer might seek out a courtroom. Got it?"

"I think so. John was a Vietnam vet injured in the line of duty. How about a Vietnamese jungle?"

"If he has a residual haunt, I'd say that's a good bet. Now picture it."

"Should I tap my ruby slippers three times?"

Sally tried to raise an eyebrow in annoyance, but only succeeded in raising her entire forehead. "Do you want my help or not?"

"Sorry. I picture the jungle and then what?"

"You hope he shows up. He won't be able to see you, so don't worry about interrupting him."

"You coming?" I asked, feeling skeptical. I was used to carrying a gun and taking backup if needed. This time I'd be solo, with no weapon.

"Not this trip. I've got some thinking to do. You can handle it."

"Thanks for the vote of confidence. I'll remember that when winged monkeys are ripping my guts out."

"You don't have any guts."

"Something tells me I better get some fast."

CHAPTER THIRTY-ONE

At first glance, I thought I'd found Tanner among the jungle vines and heavy brush, and I crouched low, watching someone in mud-covered fatigues move north toward a small clearing.

M16 cradled and ready, the figure motioned to another soldier behind. He was sweating profusely over facial camouflage under a blanket of humidity. The two men followed a dirt path through deciduous trees as they talked. The taller of the two men removed his helmet and swiped rivulets of perspiration from his face with a shirtsleeve.

The black buzz cut, dark brown eyes, long angular jaw, and cocky saunter convinced me I'd found John J. Hoyt.

I pressed ahead, hoping Sally was right about a ghost's inability to see others outside of their residual haunt. As we neared a small village ahead, the men continued to talk and joke without any reaction to my close proximity.

I'd only seen Vietnam in photos and on television. Images of soldiers bleeding among the tall elephant grass and napalm explosions jumped out as my most vivid memories, but this scene seemed removed from the horrors.

Farmers worked in their rice paddies, where water buffalo were trudging slowly through the mud. I hurried to catch up with the two men, as John Hoyt spoke to his comrade.

"Linh told me she's pregnant." His eyes scanned the brush to his left, stopping briefly to listen.

The private readied his M16 and waited.

John nodded the okay and they moved on.

"No shit. Pregnant? You gonna marry her?" the other man grinned.

Hoyt glared at him. "Right. I'm going to carry her off on my steed and bring her home to Mom."

"You love her?"

"Christ. I'm barely nineteen." He gazed upward, checking the trees. "But Linh said she knows in her heart it's a son. A son. Jesus, I can't imagine what that's like."

"What do you mean?"

"*My* son. A boy to teach all the things I've learned and watch him turn into a man."

"Can you handle it?"

"Screw you."

"So? What're you going to do?"

"I'm sure as hell not leaving her in this godforsaken jungle. I'll find a way to get us both out of here in one piece."

"Congrats, man. Can I be the best man?"

"You gotta *become* a man first, Taylor." Hoyt tugged a Polaroid photo from the shirt pocket of his fatigues. "Take a look."

"Damn, she's beautiful. Her eyes could melt glaciers."

I peeked over their shoulders to see a young girl, no more than eighteen, smiling beside Hoyt near a low-standing hut. Her hair flowed like ebony silk over creamy shoulders; a haunting pair of almond-shaped black eyes stared back at me. Cover Girl had no idea what they'd missed.

Before the two men took another step, I heard a squeal of laughter and recognized the girl from the photo running toward them through the brush along the narrow path. Her petite frame flew faster as the white folds of her dress fanned in the tropical breeze. Bare feet pounded the dirt before her.

"John!" she called, arms outstretched.

"Stop!" he called, his words trying to send her back. His eyes widened in horror. I followed his gaze and saw the trip wire.

The air exploded, sending dirt and weeds flying in a flash of light.

Taylor shoved Hoyt into a thicket of brush, diving after him. I watched helplessly as John struggled against his comrade for freedom, as steel fragments rained down in a wide arc, cutting down everything in its path. Including Linh.

The booby trap had most likely contained metal, creating shrapnel once exploded. C-4 was my guess, although I'm no explosives expert. I watched it spray about one hundred meters. Hoyt and Taylor had been lucky.

When the dust settled, John set out down the path, toward the blood-drenched pile of clothing.

"Linh!"

Taylor ran after him. "Hold up. Let me go ahead, there might be another trap."

Hoyt stopped to collect a severed hand, crying out as he stumbled on.

He began tearing aside the large palm leaves thick with mud that littered the narrow path. A pair of battered legs stuck out from underneath.

Panic etched the camouflaged lines of his face and he dove inside, fumbling for her body.

"Linh!" He tore the debris from the pile, then suddenly stopped.

Taylor caught up with him, viewing the carnage. "John, wait. Let me."

Hoyt dropped to his knees beside Linh's legs, his eyes staring blankly.

Linh's upper body lay across the path a few feet from her legs.

Hoyt crawled to her shredded torso and cradled what was left, his blood-slicked hands smearing her cheek bright red.

"Damn you!" he cried to the sky above.

"We'll get 'em." Taylor squinted into the nearby brush. "We'll take them all down."

"No, we won't. There isn't enough justice in this world for that." Hoyt's voice broke. He bent and kissed Linh. "Can't you see? There's no justice anymore."

Suddenly, I found myself standing where the scene had begun. Like a replayed movie, the entire spectacle started again from its beginning. The jungle had repaired itself; Hoyt and Taylor started down the path. I saw Hoyt remove his helmet and heard him tell Taylor about Linh's pregnancy. The residual haunt had restarted.

I guess we all have our private wars to battle. This was John Hoyt's. It explained a lot about Tanner. Why she'd turned out the way she had. Why she'd gone on her own avenging rampage. But most of all, why she sought me out now. Her father had ingrained the idea of serving punishment, and although they were both ghosts, they were still reliving their missions.

In a way, I had my own war to fight. The one that fate had waged against me when it allowed my life to end prematurely. Holding my badge, I decided I wouldn't let my past difficulties drag me into a residual haunt, turning my time in limbo into a visit to a doomed vision of the past. I was in for the duration, whatever that might be, but I'd make damn sure it would eventually be resolved.

After I made my way out of the jungle, I realized Sally had probably been right. It seemed that John Hoyt had become stuck in his residual haunt. It wasn't something I wanted to happen to me and I knew how important moving forward had become. Dwelling on the past seemed just as unproductive here as it had been in life. Time to move on.

Now that I knew what Hoyt sounded like, I had to perfect my mimic in order to lure Tanner. When I gave it the ol' college try, however, I heard my own voice instead, and I realized I had no clue what to do next. I needed to find Sally.

I knew she'd been in some sort of emotional funk before I visited Hoyt's residual, and wondered what had triggered it. She'd suffered from loneliness since before her passing and I wondered why she hadn't been able to beat it. And why did it bother her so now?

My own loose ends seemed cut and dried; find the bad guy, find peace. But I knew it wouldn't end there for me. I'd never be able to give up my tag and move on as long as criminals haunted both sides of eternity.

I found Sally at the Tri-City Lab parking lot, bear in hand. She called to me from the handicapped space in front.

"Hey. How'd it go?"

She seemed to be in better spirits. No pun intended.

"Interesting," I said honestly. "I need to work on the mimic."

"And then what?"

"Then I'll try to call Tanner out by sounding like her father."

"What if it doesn't work?" Her eyes wouldn't meet mine.

"What do you mean?"

"She might already know he's unable to get out of his residual. If so, she'll probably be waiting for you."

"You didn't tell me that."

"Sorry. I was preoccupied. But I feel better now."

If she was right, my excursion to Vietnam had been a wasted trip. I would have strangled her if possible.

Instead, I pushed aside my disappointment, asking, "What happened to you? You had me worried."

"Yeah?" Her smile was genuine.

"Of course. We're friends, right?"

If I didn't know better, I'd have sworn I saw tears in her eyes.

"Right. I knew that," she nodded. "Listen, here's the truth if you're interested. I don't want to bore you or anything, but you asked."

I nodded for her to go on.

She clutched her bear as she paced. "I keep reviewing my life but can't see that I've ever done anything worthwhile. I never saved a life, never even had a boyfriend, or kids. It's like I never contributed.

"And I'm finding this side isn't any easier. A person has to have a purpose in order to feel worthy. It's no different here. I just haven't made a difference."

"That isn't true, Sally. You've helped me a great deal. Without you who knows where I would be right now. You've been my guide throughout this whole mess. I need you."

"Really?"

"Yes. Try not to be so hard on yourself, okay?"

"I guess. Thanks, Lindsay."

"So tell me honestly, Sally. What are the chances that the mimic will work on Tanner?"

"Guess I should have told you up front. It's a long shot. She's been here long enough that I'm sure she's already sought her father out. If so, she knows that isn't possible. I'm not saying *don't* try it, but you might end up in trouble."

So much for my ventriloquism gig. That meant I had to come up with another plan. Until I could find a creative, foolproof way to get to Tanner, I had to keep vigilant and that meant watching over those I loved. I thanked Sally for her insights and headed back to check on Dad.

CHAPTER THIRTY-TWO

Kate cursed, because locating the gun tipster was proving futile. When she interviewed the officer who'd taken the call, she'd learned only that the caller had been female, with a bad lisp. Since the call had come in on the non-emergency line, the address hadn't come up on the screen and callers aren't required to leave a name or number. Her father had become a victim of the system intended to help stop crime by encouraging citizens to call and maintain anonymity.

Perry Frost had been released after a couple of hours. There'd been no prints, or evidence at Calvin's, and no gun found in the mail truck. The surveillance tape from Calvin's security camera glimpsed a dark shadow that'd known enough to stay out of the eye's view. Whoever had stolen the gun knew the shop well enough to stay out of sight and still get the job done. The whole episode had been another slap in the Frost family's face.

Kate circled the block once more, biting her lip. The setting evening sun threw Alvarez's neighborhood into near darkness, save for a few houses with porch lamps. She pulled next to the curb in front of his house. The living room window glowed yellow and inviting behind closed drapes. What if he was in bed? Hmm, boxers, briefs, or au natural?

Before she could talk herself out of it, she paced at his front door and rang the bell. One of her favorite childhood pranks, called "Ding-dong Ditch," came to mind, and she held tight to the screen door handle so she wouldn't run.

Everything in her world had spun out of control. She needed grounding, a solid boulder to hold onto as things fell apart. She needed reassurance, even false hope at this point, that everything would turn out all right. She needed—

"Alvarez. Hope you don't mind, but I was in the neighborhood . . ."

He wore a faded AC/DC T-shirt, stone washed jeans, and a skeptical expression. "Of course. You only *live* a couple of blocks over."

"Three." Kate shrugged.

"Hey, have you eaten dinner yet? We were just sitting down to my mother's homemade tamales and I cooked up a little Spanish rice. There's plenty."

"Really? I'm sorry, I didn't even look at the clock. I didn't realize it was dinner time."

Alvarez held open the door for her, calling over his shoulder, "Hey, Paul, set another place. We have a guest!"

"Mmm. Home cooking. It's been a while." Kate removed her shoes and followed her nose to the kitchen.

"What? You don't cook?" Alvarez feigned shock.

"It's hard to cook for one person. One meal can last a week."

"I'll have to send over my crew. They devour like locusts." He nodded at his two sons in the kitchen.

Kate greeted the youngest boy, Paul, and then John, who scooped rice into a large bowl at the stove.

The boys looked more like young men than children. Paul glanced her way, a slight blush creeping up his neck.

"How've you two been? How's school?" Kate asked them.

Both boys talked at once, but quickly stopped after a sharp glance from their father. John let his younger brother answer.

"We'll be out next week for summer break. But I liked my first year of high school; it's more mature than middle school.

And next year I can get my license." Paul noted his father's frown. "Well, not too much longer."

Kate couldn't help notice how much both boys resembled Gerard, with thick black hair, flawless bronzed skin, and dark eyes that danced in excitement when they spoke. Alvarez watched them with a father's pride; a relaxed grin hugged his lips. Quite a beautiful family.

"In your dreams, little brother," John said, setting a bowl on the table. "I'm seventeen and I *still* can't get the car."

"At least you have your license," Paul countered.

"Hey, guys. I'm sure Kate doesn't want to hear your woes. Let's talk about something that isn't an appetite killer."

They all took their seats and after Paul's quick prayer, they dug in.

Kate let the food and small talk soothe her nerves. Before long she joined in with the playful family banter, and then washing the dishes.

"I thought you said your mother made dinner?" she asked Alvarez as she scraped a plate.

"She did. My mother prefers quiet at her meals, so she occasionally drops off our dinner and leaves."

"Wow. Homemade carryout. Can't beat that."

"She's a good woman, devoted to her family. But the boys can test her nerves sometimes."

"I think they're wonderful. You've done well, and should be proud."

"Sometimes I wonder. It can't be easy on them, growing up without much input from their mother."

Kate rinsed another plate. "I hope I'm not intruding when I ask why."

"She has her problems, which have everything to do with our divorce last year. I'm hoping she'll come around and be a parent to them, but for now I'm doing my best."

191

A loud thud sounded from an upstairs bedroom, sending Alvarez to the foot of the steps. "Hey you two! Get started on your homework."

When the last dish had been dried, Kate and Alvarez retired to the family room and left the television sound on low as they talked.

Kate felt comfortable sitting beside him on the couch, enjoying the quiet and the company.

"You want to tell me what's bothering you?" Alvarez said, looking her way.

"How did you know?"

"You look a lot more relaxed than when you first got here, but I know something's on your mind."

When she looked at him, she suspected he might be thinking she'd come to discuss the alley incident. His questioning expression held her.

"You're right. When I arrived, I wanted to vent and pace, about my dad and how helpless I feel and how unfair this whole thing is."

"But?"

"But you eased the demons by simply being you. I realized how selfish I'm being."

"Selfish?"

"When Lindsay died, you lost a partner and I can only imagine your frustration level when each lead turns sour. And then today we were dealt another low blow, but you kept your wits. I'm impressed but envious at your levelheaded attitude. Care to share your secret?"

He shook his head. "No secret. Just years of practice. You'll get there. Police work is a patience game sometimes. It's part of the job."

"I don't know if I'm cut out for this."

He touched her cheek with his fingertips. "You're a good

cop, Kate. Don't underestimate your talents or instincts. I wouldn't have offered to work with you if I didn't think so. But like I said, sometimes we have to wait for the right time, the right signals, even though we want answers right now."

She held his gaze. "And that's when it's time to make your move."

"Yes," he said, leaning in.

"Where did you learn all that?" she asked softly, his lips inches from hers.

"Boy Scouts," he mumbled against her cheek, grazing her mouth.

Her promise not to let it happen again evaporated at his touch. She took in the scent of his cologne and the warmth of his arms around her. A long-forgotten heat rekindled deep within, as he trailed his tongue along her neck. She allowed the pleasurable sensation to fill her, drawing into his embrace.

Then a round of raucous clamor above sent them apart. Paul trampled down the stairs.

"Dad! Tell that jerk to stop borrowing my CDs."

Kate adjusted her hair and looked over at Alvarez. He, too, had some rearranging to do and waited a minute before heading up to take care of business.

When he returned, she giggled.

"What's so funny?" He checked his look.

"Us. Like two teenagers."

"A real riot." He sat back down beside her.

"Oh, back for more?"

He checked his watch. "It's getting kind of late. I don't want to keep you up."

She leaned back against the couch. "I can sleep in if I want. I'm being punished, remember?"

Alvarez grinned. "Not anymore."

"What do you mean?"

"I guess Marie Yates got what she wanted out of you. She doesn't have to rake you over the coals anymore, because she has all the revenge she could want by becoming your dad's lawyer. I heard she's dropping her complaint against you."

He handed her the portable phone. "You'd better call in for your schedule."

CHAPTER THIRTY-THREE

My dad's release from questioning did nothing to sooth my ruffled feathers. The damage had been done and I watched him leave the precinct with my mother, a sad, defeated-looking man who seemed to have aged ten years during the two or three hours he'd been held. I vowed to get the bastard responsible. I needed to make a move before anything else happened. Screwing with me is one thing, but my family is off limits.

I couldn't get the Tanner-Stokes connection out of my mind, and since Calvin wasn't talking, it left one name on my list. Short on time and ideas, I located my spiritual allies to help form a plan.

Sally joined Mike Blake and Dr. Saint, looking pleased she'd been asked to participate. Her lopsided grin took the pained look out of her facial scars as she surveyed the picnic spot I'd chosen to meet at.

"Nice place you've created. Mind if I visit once in a while?" She leaned against a tree.

I wasn't exactly sure what she meant. "I didn't create it; it's more of a pleasant memory for me."

"Right, and because it doesn't really exist here, you've re-created it. Got it?"

Mike Blake and Dr. Saint nodded in agreement.

"You mean like the virtual reality Holo-deck on that space show?" I asked.

"Something like that." She frowned as if she wasn't quite

sure what I meant.

"We can re-create scenes from our pasts?" Another amazing fact I'd picked up before Ripley's.

Sally shrugged. "It's just one of the perks."

"And it will be real to those who are here, right?"

"You got it," she said, picking a jonquil. "Remember when we first met?"

"Yes. Why?"

"That Tri-City Lab parking lot was where my life ended. I revisit it all the time. Know why?"

"I couldn't say."

"A spirit is drawn to their place of death until their past life problems are resolved, especially if your passing isn't from natural causes."

It made sense except for one thing. "So why did I end up at your scene when we first met?"

"Because you were searching for help. Fortunately, your navigational skills sucked and you ended up with me. It could have been a lot worse."

"That's why I want to revisit my scene? I thought I was being a good detective."

"I'm sure that's part of it," Mike said. "But Sally is right. I'm drawn to mine as well."

"What do you think about luring Tanner to her own death scene?" I was pumped, pacing. This had to be it. I finally had a way to lure Tanner right where I wanted her.

"It might work, but you still need to be careful," he warned.

Dr. Saint smiled. "I think I know where you're going with this, Detective. You're setting a trap for her. Brilliant!"

"Mike," I said, "I'll need some pointers."

"Be glad to help."

Sally stepped up. "I'm in."

"Of course you can count on me," Dr. Saint said.

For the first time in my career, I pushed pride aside and accepted the offered assistance. There were too many variables and unknowns in *this* world for me to try and take on Tanner by myself. She'd already proven I was no match for her. Twice. I looked at it as having my own supernatural SWAT team.

Suddenly Sally looked doubtful. "I've never done anything like this before, and I'm not even sure it will work. I'd hate to let you down."

"Sally, I trust you. You've been my guiding light since I've been here."

"But I don't know what will happen if we create someone else's scene. Maybe that's going too far. If something goes wrong . . ." She frowned.

"Look, we'll do this together. Don't forget, I was there when Tanner died. I'll get all the details right. Especially the part about Joe's demise."

"That's what I mean. This isn't just about Tanner. Your partner died in that house, too. What if he's at peace? Would you want to relive it all over again and risk bringing him back?"

"Is that what will happen?" I felt guilt pangs at the thought.

"Like I said, I'm not sure."

I stared at her a minute, trying to justify what I wanted to do, trying to convince myself this wasn't as selfish as it seemed. What if it affected Joe's rest in some way? What difference did it make if I solved it? I'd still be here.

"Damn! A handbook would be so helpful right now. Any ideas?" I asked the other two.

"If Joe is at rest, I would assume he's there to stay. The problem is between you and Tanner," the good doctor reasoned.

"Yeah, but if Joe was at the original scene, wouldn't he be re-created too?" Mike asked.

"You're right," I said, feeling defeated. "We can't do it until we know for sure. And there's only one way to do that. Find Joe."

We agreed to meet at my picnic spot on a daily basis to compare notes and form future plans, and I put Sally in charge of summoning everyone in the event of an emergency meeting. I expected one day soon, she'd be asking for a badge.

As the meeting broke up, Sally cornered me saying, "It seems I've let you down again. Don't worry about anything. I'll figure out something."

She disappeared before I could tell her how wrong she was.

I leaned against a tall oak with Mike nearby, feeling like I'd hit the final roadblock. None of the pieces fit, we had no leads, and each plan had fallen through. The others left us to do whatever spirits do on their downtime.

My own schedule hadn't changed much since I'd crossed over. I was still chasing bad guys, talking with snitches, and not getting any rest. The whole "rest in peace" thing is overrated.

Mike's hand touched my shoulder. "Are you going to search for Joe?"

"No." The answer came out before I realized I'd decided against it. "It's not right. I've done enough to him."

"How's that?"

I wanted to take back my words, knowing they would require an explanation that I probably didn't have. "I guess I'll always blame myself for letting him get killed."

"How could you have altered fate? I don't think that's what's expected of us as officers or human beings."

"You're right but that doesn't change things. There's no way I can go forward with a plan that might disturb him."

"We can still keep an eye out for him without actively disturbing him. I'm not the only cop around here. I'll ask around. But that still leaves you with no way to draw Tanner out." He moved closer.

"I'll just have to deal with it. Sooner or later, she'll come after me." I hesitated, not sure if I should bring up the subject on my mind.

"What is it?" He looked alarmed.

"Would it be too personal to ask about your situation? What happened to the guys who took your life?"

"They're serving time."

"Is that enough for you?"

"I guess it'll have to be. At least it brings some closure to my family."

"Tell me about them." I sat on the ground.

He hunched down beside me, plucking grass. "Kathy and I were high-school sweethearts, and got married after college. My daughter Michelle was born a few years later. She's eight now." His smile lingered.

"Have you seen them since . . ."

"Yes. I watch Michelle at the bus stop every day."

"What about Kathy?"

"We had our problems. Toward the end, there wasn't much left between us except our beautiful daughter. Police work can kill a relationship. I've seen it a lot."

"I know. The job hasn't been easy on my love life, either."

I told him about George, noting his look of indignation at my fiancé's attempt to come on to my sister. "So, I'm hanging up the relationship gloves. I don't even know how it works on this side. Do you?"

He grinned. "No. But it could be a lot of fun learning."

"Look, Mike . . ."

His smile faded. "I know. I've been thinking about things. It's too soon for both of us. There are still some things I have to work out over my life. And I'm sure you have your own concerns to deal with.

"Still, I miss the closeness of a relationship, the bonding. It can be lonely here sometimes. Am I making sense?"

"More than you know. Look, we can have the bonding and friendship; I need it, too." I managed to take his hand. "I hope you'll keep working with me."

"Of course. You know, we have eternity to work things out."

"I'll be here." I fanned the grass with my hand, noting the absence of weeds in my created scenario. "This might sound odd, but George was the first guy I'd ever gotten serious with. I dated in college, but I was having too much fun to get tied up with a relationship.

"During academy, I didn't have much time or energy for a social life and lost touch with most of my dating contacts. It seems I've spent the past decade climbing the police ranks and chasing the bad guys instead of seeking out one good one."

Mike stared at a bee hovering over a nearby flower. "Have you ever considered that *you* might be the good one being sought?"

I grinned, wondering where he'd been all my life. "Schmoozer."

"What are friends for?"

CHAPTER THIRTY-FOUR

Kate stared across the desk at Alvarez. Up until this point, her morning had been filled with pleasant thoughts of the previous evening with Gerard and his boys. Their goodnight kiss at the door had stayed with her afterward, enough to cause her trouble falling asleep. She'd struggled to put her racing thoughts to bed long after she'd climbed in for the night. Luckily, she'd drawn the afternoon shift for her first day back, which meant she had the luxury of sleeping in. For the first time in weeks, she'd slept peacefully, without nightmares, and had awakened this morning refreshed and ready to take on the day.

Dressed in full uniform, with the start of her afternoon shift still another forty minutes away, she wished she could start early. Her smile faded when Alvarez broke the news.

"You're kidding, right?" She tried unsuccessfully to get comfortable in the wooden office chair.

He shook his head. "Sorry. It was O'Connor's idea. What could I say?"

"He's really called in a psychic?" Kate said, needing to hear it confirmed.

"It's not uncommon for a police department to utilize psychics when we're stumped. We've used this woman before and she has a high success rate. We've reached the end, Kate. At this point I'm not opposed to trying everything we can, no matter how crazy."

"I'm not saying it's crazy." She considered her recent paranormal experiences. Her belief in otherworldly entities had been proven correct by Lindsay's circumstances. But it went deeper than that, and included her reliance on her own personal psychic, Mona Fitzpatrick Divine.

She'd met her two years before, at the Taylor County Fair, where Mona read palms and tarot cards. They'd kept in touch after her reading, and it had proven a lifesaver for Kate on the job. Since then they'd become close friends.

"It says we've given up. It's admitting defeat before we've had the chance."

Alvarez shook his head. "Look, I don't believe in hocus-pocus. To me, if I can't see it, it's not there."

He moved to her chair, saying, "I'm a realist. Proof is in touch, scent . . ." He leaned close to her face. "And most of all, taste . . ." He touched his lips to hers. "That's how I know something is real."

Kate jumped when his desk phone buzzed, her lips still tingling when he reached to answer it.

"We'll be right there," he said.

Ten minutes later, she and Alvarez sat in front of Chief O'Connor's desk. A tall, reed-thin woman of about fifty entered behind the chief, wearing a black blazer and skirt with a red silk blouse. Kate's gaze caught on the gold chain that held a large crystal, which was dancing in and out of the woman's skimpy cleavage. Kate glanced at Alvarez, whose only response was a questioning eyebrow.

After brief introductions, the psychic, Julia Parsons, made herself comfortable in the chief's leather chair. She brushed a fiery auburn lock of hair from her cheek.

"Thank you for having me, Chief O'Connor."

He motioned for her to continue, taking a seat behind Kate and Alvarez.

"In case you're not all familiar with the way this works, let me brief you," the woman said. "I can usually get a reading about an unsolved crime if I have access to a personal item of the victim. Most of the time the reading takes the form of a scene or object in my mind that often leads to pertinent and otherwise unknown information. That's what we're hoping for today.

"I'd like all of you to remain as quiet as possible. I've already discussed the details with Chief O'Connor and have seen the crime scene photos to try and get a preliminary reading. So far, nothing has come through."

"You've seen the photos?" Kate looked at the chief, feeling violated.

"It's procedure," he offered.

"I understand you're the victim's sister?" the woman asked Kate.

"Yes. Why the need to see the photographs?"

"I promise you it won't influence my readings." She changed the subject. "You're a police officer."

"You're good." Kate felt her temper flare. This had turned into a carnival sideshow. Kate had met legitimate psychics, extremely gifted people, Mona among them, and could spot a charlatan. Julia reeked of fake.

"Kate." Alvarez stopped her.

She felt the heat of his hand on her arm, and saw his eyes silently pleading cooperation.

Taking a deep breath, Kate said, "I'm sorry, Ms. Parsons. I know you're trying to help, but this is all so personal. Please go on."

The woman nodded and removed a small object from a manila envelope.

"What I meant," Julia said to Kate, "was that since you're a police officer you probably understand the need for me to see the crime scene, as well as the victim's personal effects."

Kate recognized Lindsay's wristwatch. Her hand tensed on the chair's arm.

Julia closed her eyes holding the watch.

Kate wished Lindsay would show up to give this fraud the ride of her life, but then she realized that a fake like Julia Parsons probably wouldn't be able to see Lindsay anyway.

Finally, the psychic looked at Chief O'Connor. "I'm sorry. I'm not getting the usual readings."

"What do you mean?" he asked.

"The vibration I'm receiving is from the living. For example, it feels more like a sensation I get from a missing person or kidnap victim, who is eventually found alive. I don't know what to make of it."

Kate straightened in her chair at the unexpected twist. Maybe Julia was more tuned in than she'd thought.

"This may take some time," she reassured Kate.

"Go ahead," Kate said, interested in the findings. So far, the woman was right, Lindsay's spirit hadn't gone, not completely anyway.

Julia concentrated for several more minutes, until she slowly opened her eyes. "I believe I have something. It's quite unclear, but it's definitively a signal of some sort."

"Can you tell us what you see?" the chief wanted to know.

"It's dark, but I think I see a gun."

"Lindsay wasn't shot," Kate blurted.

"I know. I'm only stating what I see." Julia's penciled eyebrows crooked. "Yes, there's a gun, but I can't tell what kind."

"Anything else?" O'Connor asked.

"I'm getting an overwhelming sense of fear and uncertainty. Panic."

Alvarez turned to Kate and whispered, "Are you sure you

want to hear this?"

She nodded, touched by his concern. "I'm fine," she said softly.

Julia continued, "There's something else. I almost hate to ask."

"Please don't feel intimidated by my presence, Ms. Parsons," Kate cut in.

The woman shrugged and looked at O'Connor. "Can you verify cheese at the crime scene?"

"Cheese?" O'Connor asked. "Alvarez?"

"*Jesu Cristo*," the detective cursed under his breath. "No cheese, sir."

CHAPTER THIRTY-FIVE

The good news that Kate was back on the job meant Marie had come to her senses. I hoped Kate had learned her lesson about overstepping her bounds. We are too much alike when it comes to getting the bad guy, and look where that had gotten me.

I'd kept the morning meeting with Sally, Mike, and Dr. Saint short. There'd been no signs of Joe or Tanner, and frankly we'd all run dry on ideas. Finding my old partner had proven futile, even with the help of my experienced ghostly crew. We came to the bittersweet conclusion he'd probably gone on to the next level, but we couldn't be sure. I wanted to find him, not only because it would give me the go-ahead to kick Tanner's ass, but I could have used his cool attitude and street smarts right about now.

Mike had kept his distance, only staying around long enough to make contact with everyone and see that nothing pertinent had changed. I got the impression he'd decided to make good on our decision to remain friends. Deciding that might be best, I forced myself to move on and formulate a plan. After all, like Mike suggested, we had eternity to work out our relationship.

I decided to visit Calvin Stokes' gun store, looking for a lead. The chances I'd hear a confession from him while he sold guns and filled out forms was as likely as Bin Laden winning the Nobel peace prize, but with my plans to lure Tanner out of hiding on hold, I had nothing better to do than pester the living. Who better than my old buddy, Calvin?

Stokes' gun shop looked the same as I remembered, with rows of guns pinned to a Peg-Board wall behind the glass counter housing the more expensive firearms. He'd run the shop for years, and I'd purchased several weapons from him, the most recent a 9mm Beretta that I kept strapped to my ankle for emergencies. Turned out to be a waste of money.

Calvin worked at the counter going over paperwork while Janice swept the floor with a frayed straw broom.

"Calvin, we have to do something about the mice. Your customers won't want to come here if they see mouse turds." Janice twisted her thin lips into a frown.

"This ain't Victoria's Secret. I'm sure most of my customers have seen mice before," Calvin waved her on.

Mice? Ghost or not, I checked around my feet, catching sight of a corner mouse trap loaded with cheese, cheddar to be exact, according to the open package on the counter.

"Cal, I'm serious," Janice insisted. "If you don't call an exterminator, I will."

"Go for it if it makes you feel better. They'll just be back. Right now I have other problems, like who stole that gun? How in the hell could they have broken in without doing any damage?"

"Maybe the mice took it," she teased. But Calvin wasn't laughing; in fact, he looked to me like he might belt her. I never would have guessed he had much speed in him, but he rounded the corner in a flash, grabbing the broom.

"Stop worrying about the stupid mice! Don't you get it, Janice? The police are already watching me because of Frost, and now one of my guns is missing. Doesn't that seem too coincidental to you?"

"I guess, but how could that be trouble for us? We were robbed." She backed up a step.

"They might think I tried to plant it. Did you ever think of that?"

Suddenly, Janice's face twisted into a pasty wash of runny watercolor and the store blended into blackness. A deafening whir filled my ears and I fought to stay in place as my legs melted from under me, with my body following. The total dark silence had me convinced I'd graduated to the next level, and I clutched my badge tight. I wasn't ready to go.

CHAPTER THIRTY-SIX

Kate felt her hope dissolve into anger as Julia struggled to explain her cheese vision. She checked her watch for a good excuse to leave. "I'm late for my shift."

"Johnson won't mind covering you. I'll take care of it." O'Connor left the room.

Julia took a long drink of water and a moment to relax. "I'm sorry," she said. "This is highly unusual."

Kate barely heard his reply, distracted when she saw Lindsay's form take shape in the far corner. She noted her sister's painful expression as she slowly materialized. When Lindsay became clear, she looked around the room in confusion. Finally, her gaze landed on Kate and she motioned for her to get out of the office.

"Excuse me," Kate said. "I'll go see what's keeping the chief."

Inside the ladies' room, Kate learned Lindsay wasn't in pain, only annoyed.

"What happened?" Lindsay demanded.

"I don't know what you're talking about. You popped in like Jeannie. What are you so pissed about?"

"I was at Calvin's shop trying to get information, and I was onto something when suddenly I'm here."

"Uh-oh."

"Uh-oh, what?" Lindsay asked.

"The chief called in a psychic. She's in there now, but so far all she's come up with is cheese."

"Julia Parsons?"

Kate nodded.

"Actually, she's quite good," Lindsay said. "Wait, did you say 'cheese'?"

" 'Fraid so. Sorry."

"No. That's not bad. I think I know what happened. She summoned me."

"As in a séance medium?" Kate scoffed.

"Exactly. Since I haven't stepped off to the next level, she ended up summoning instead of reading me. Makes sense and confirms her abilities."

"I certainly had my doubts, especially when she said she saw cheese."

"Calvin and Janice were talking about their rodent problem right before I left. Julia picked up on my whereabouts and what I saw. Try and cut the session short, though, I want to get back."

"She did say she saw a gun. Guess I owe her an apology."

"Do it quickly, and get rid of her."

"What did you find out so far?" Kate asked.

"They don't have a clue who broke in and stole the gun. The robbery is legit."

"It had to be someone with a key. Do they have any employees?" Kate asked.

"I don't think so. I've been there several times and the only one that ever waits on me is Calvin. Janice's main job seems to be clean up."

"Then she has a key."

"That's what I need to find out. Get rid of Julia."

In O'Connor's office, Kate took her seat, apologizing for making them wait.

"That's quite all right," Julia said, "I was just about to get restarted . . ."

"I really appreciate all you've done, but perhaps this isn't the right time. It seems you're struggling to get the proper readings, and I'm concerned this could somehow disturb my sister's rest," Kate tried.

"That's not how it works. I can assure you this won't take long and if it becomes too uncomfortable for you I'll stop. Please allow me more time."

Lindsay held up five fingers from the corner.

"Let's give it five more minutes, okay?" Kate forced a smile.

"Thank you," Julia said and closed her eyes, once again clutching Lindsay's watch.

Kate saw her sister impatiently pacing behind the woman's chair.

Minutes ticked by and Kate checked her watch for the last time. Enough was enough. Suddenly Julia startled her.

"My God. It can't be."

O'Connor jumped to his feet. "What is it, Julia?"

The psychic paled and slumped back in the chair. "I can't . . . I can't . . ."

"What? What can't you do?" He clasped her shoulders.

"Give me a minute."

Kate caught Lindsay's confused expression, then looked at Alvarez, who returned her glance with a shrug.

"Do we need medics?" he asked O'Connor.

"No. I'm fine," Julia said. "I'm afraid I've never experienced anything like this before, and I'm not sure you should hear this, Officer Frost."

"Tell me." Kate gave Lindsay a nervous glance.

"I received what I believe to be a warning, a serious warning. It involves your sister, and as strange as it sounds, I feel compelled to tell you your sister is in danger."

"Wait a minute, Ms. Parsons. How could she be in danger?" Alvarez looked ready to pounce from his chair. "Chief, I think this has gone too far."

"I realize that, Detective Alvarez," Julia said. "I'm only the messenger. This warning is so strong I can't ignore it. Lindsay Frost's spirit is in imminent danger."

Kate ignored Lindsay's wrist-tapping motion across the room. She wanted to know more. Before Julia could say another word, the chief sprang into action.

"I think we've heard enough, Ms. Parsons. We all have our off days, and this appears to be yours. Kate doesn't need to hear things like that. Perhaps you could come back another time."

He quickly showed the psychic out the door, leaving Kate alone with Alvarez.

"I'm sorry you had to hear that, Kate. She's never gone off like that before."

She tried to hide her disappointment with a shrug. "I can handle it. I told you it was a waste of time."

Lindsay gave her a thumbs-up and disappeared from the corner.

"Want to grab something to eat before your shift?" Alvarez asked.

"Thanks, but I really hate to stick Johnson with my time. I better get going."

On her way out, she replayed Julia's warning about Lindsay's safety. As crazy as it sounded, she found herself trying to come up with a way to protect her sister.

CHAPTER THIRTY-SEVEN

I watched the paranormal party break up soon after Julia's revelation, but I never made it back to Calvin's. As a detective, I'm used to receiving messages via Post-it note, phone, or Chief O'Connor's bellow, but this one had me stumped. The words *Seventy-fifth and Main. Back alley* repeatedly filled my head. I recalled Sally's warning about answering unknown sources, but the address was one I'd visited often when I needed information. I pictured the street, hoping I'd actually end up there, and that it wasn't a trap.

Graffiti adorned the faded brick of the abandoned buildings on Seventy-fifth and Main. Debris littered the alleyways from overflowing Dumpsters, providing housing for rodent and cockroach families, and sometimes, sadly, also providing temporary storage of unwanted humans. I recalled an incident a couple of years ago when a Dumpster turned into a crime scene after some kid found a body inside. I'd taken the call on my way out for the day, anticipating some much-needed time off. It had been the first and last day of my vacation, and I'd never had one since, unless you consider my current situation. What a way to get time off.

About half a block down, I saw the familiar dingy overcoat hanging on hunched shoulders. The figure moved in a staggering gait, driven by frayed tennis shoes. I waited to be sure it wasn't Tanner playing some sort of shape-shifting game; after all, I still didn't know all the rules. When Abner Taute stood a few feet away, I noted that his hooked nose dribbled, and I wondered how that was possible, given the fact he had no bodily fluids. I figured I still had a lot to learn.

He saluted with his whiskey bottle. "Hey there, Detective. I see you're finally getting your sea legs."

"Sea legs?" I asked.

"Gettin' used to your new body. You made it."

"What do you have for me, Abner?" I got down to business. I usually made my visits with Abner short and sweet, partly because he didn't like being seen talking to cops, but mostly because the stench of rancid sweat and stale whiskey turned my stomach faster than a sun-baked corpse. That was no longer a problem for either of us.

"Just wanted to give you a heads up. Somethin' big is about to happen."

"Where do you get your information? Who's your source?" I regretted the question before I finished it.

His expression turned wary and I knew I'd overstepped my bounds. Rule one when dealing with an informant, dead or alive—never pry into their business. That's like asking a hit man for a list of job references. It can easily put them out of business. Permanently.

I never would have asked him in life; why did I think I could get away with it here? I expected him to fade on me, but he stuck around.

"You losin' your touch, Detective? You know I can't tell ya."

"Sorry, that was rude." I couldn't believe I was apologizing to a man who openly panhandled and pissed on street corners.

"Forget it. You've got bigger problems."

"So I've heard."

"All I can tell ya is to watch yourself. I don't know the particulars, but there's a dark cloud hangin' over your head."

"Would this have anything to do with Tanner Jean Hoyt?"

I didn't know a spirit could turn pale, but he did.

"Who?" He tried to play coy.

"You heard me. I know she's stalking me. I've had the pleasure of her company recently, and let me tell you, I've met nicer serial killers."

"She's no one to mess with."

"Did she send you?"

"Not exactly." He clutched his whiskey bottle tighter.

"She threatened you."

"I'm just here with a message."

"So give it to me."

"Let me get it straight. Oh, yeah. 'Your favorite poet has less than a mile before he sleeps.' " Abner shrugged. "Couldn't tell ya what it means. I guess that's your job, you're the detective."

At first it didn't register. "That doesn't mean anything to me. Are you sure that's it?"

"Yup. That's it. But I'll tell ya something else." He looked around before continuing. "She's got help from the outside. You better be ready for that."

I didn't know what he meant, but he'd not only come through for me, he'd risked skin he didn't have. "Thanks, Abner. You're a real hero, just like John Wayne."

His face grew suddenly serene and his green-tinged teeth smiled at me as he began to fade. It wasn't until I saw his empty hands rise upward that I realized his whiskey bottle had disappeared. He'd given up his tag.

I watched him go until there was nothing but the graffiti-filled wall before me.

That was the last time I saw Abner Taute. In silence I considered the day when I'd give up my own tag and move on. The thought terrified me and I decided to hold out long enough for science to find a cure for death and eliminate the problem.

My happiness for Abner was cut short as I considered his

message. The original poem had been Robert Frost's, but Tanner had twisted the quote to accommodate her message. And suddenly I knew what it meant.

Growing up, my father had been a closet poet, occasionally sharing some of his work with family members only. He'd boasted that we were related to the famous poet, Robert Frost. One day, having nothing better to offer in my sophomore English class, I bragged about my literary lineage, and of course no one in class believed it. There hadn't been enough floor tiles to crawl under that day at Southfield Heights High. At home, my parents almost wet themselves laughing when I asked for proof to show my friends. My sister, Kate, actually did pee her pants, but it stemmed from her excitement over having something on her big sister. I vowed I'd never read another poem by the man.

It was a painful lesson, but not nearly as devastating as this one. I realized Tanner's words, "Your favorite poet has less than a mile before he sleeps," were in reference to my father.

I wasted no time in finding Kate patrolling the residential district on the south side of town, where she'd be guaranteed a quiet day, unless someone decided to snuff out a mailbox or steal a pool floatie. Patrolling the area proved blessedly boring if you had a lot on your mind, and I had a feeling that was the case with Kate. Thankfully, it would give us time to come up with a plan to ensure our dad's safety.

In order to give her fair warning of my presence, I zeroed in on the squad's radio hard enough to cause static. She immediately adjusted the frequency, cursing.

I formed in the passenger side.

My plan didn't work and she jumped, nearly rear-ending the minivan in front of her.

"Jesus, Linz. You've got to do better than that." She turned the corner and pulled over.

"Sorry. I thought the static might be a good signal between us." I saw the tension in her expression and figured it had nothing to do with my sudden appearance. "You still upset about Julia?" I guessed.

"Aren't you? We know she's psychic, and I tend to believe her. You've already been attacked. What if she's right?"

"I'm watching. And this time I'll be ready."

I told her about Abner's visit and the poet message. "Kate, you've got to convince O'Connor to put a watch on Mom and Dad. They're in danger."

"He'll never go for it. There's been no threat," Kate frowned.

"You have to try. If that doesn't work, go to Alvarez. He has a way with the chief."

"I'll catch him this afternoon after my court date."

"Anything big?"

"Just a traffic ticket dispute. The guy doesn't stand a chance, but I still have to waste my time at the courthouse."

"Great. Meantime, I'll keep an eye on Mom and Dad. Good luck."

I left Kate, heading for my childhood home in hopes that I'd misread Tanner's poetry.

CHAPTER THIRTY-EIGHT

The gavel banged, ending Kate's court session. Her case had been called last, costing precious time. She checked her watch and noted that she needed to hurry in order to catch O'Connor before he took off for the day.

The violator who'd disputed her ticket flipped her the bird as he left, clutching a fistful of paperwork that had proven futile in winning Judge Bricket's sympathy. The ticket stuck like she knew it would.

"Back at ya," she called as the courtroom emptied.

Hurrying to the ladies' room, she vowed to drink less coffee. This was another stop she didn't have time for, not to mention public johns made her want to wear a Hazmat suit.

Inside, restroom tiles the color of blue fungus complimented the overpowering smell of disinfectant, bringing to mind a brothel on Bastille Day. The stalls themselves supplied bladder-extended patrons with excellent reading. Kate hurried to finish and get out.

She heard the door open and the sound of heels clicking sharply into the stall beside her. Her eyes widened when she noticed the shoes were turned backwards as the woman in question straddled the facility.

Kate attempted a hasty exit to avoid an awkward confrontation. She suppressed a fit of giggles hurrying to wash her hands. Before she could reach for a paper towel, the stall door banged open and Marie Yates came up behind her.

"Officer Frost," she frowned. "That explains the foul odor in here. I was going to complain, but I see it's not the janitor's fault." She hoisted the top of her skirt and gave it a hearty yank to straighten it.

The attorney's insults didn't even register as Kate tried to comprehend what she saw. Marie's palm hit the faucet handle, causing water to splash on the floor and all over her designer suit. Without a second thought, she wiped her hands on her backside and stepped closer to the mirror to pick something out of her teeth.

"Do you have any floss? I see I have some opposing counsel leftover."

"I *thought* you looked like you'd put on some weight." Kate eyed her up and down.

"You have all the answers. Just like Lindsay." The Katie Couric look-alike closed the distance between them, standing inches from Kate's face.

Kate held her ground, hoping the attorney would make the wrong move. She'd like nothing better than to haul the little bitch in for assault.

"At least my sister had the *right* ones. I heard you fouled up a big trial last week, Marie. You losin' your touch?" She flashed an acidic smile.

Too smart to take the bait, the attorney stepped back.

"I'd love to stay and shoot the bull, but I have other commitments. You know how it is; the war on injustice never ends for a gal like me. Oh, by the way, my condolences."

"For what?" Kate forced herself to remain calm.

"The recent death in your family."

With that, Marie swung open the door and left.

Twenty minutes later, Kate finished venting before Alvarez's desk.

"I'm telling you that bitch threatened me."

"Why didn't you arrest her?"

"Ughh! Because she stopped before she got that far. She knew there wasn't anything I could do. But there's something going on with her. She's different."

"Maybe pissing backwards is her only pleasure in life."

"You don't get it. I think she could be dangerous. And what about her parting comment?"

"Sounds like she was rattling your cage. Any excuse to get you going and she knew bringing up Lindsay would do it."

"I didn't get the impression she was referring to Lindsay."

"Right now the only thing she's guilty of is penis envy."

"No. It's something else, and I think my parents should have some protection." Kate hoped this would be enough to secure his help.

"O'Connor will never go for it; she didn't threaten anyone. We're using extra manpower as it is."

"Will you at least talk to Marie? You'll see for yourself that she isn't right." Kate made her way around his desk and rested a hand on his shoulder. "Won't you at least talk to her?"

Alvarez shook his head. "No way. You've done too much to her and she'll cry harassment for sure. Until she actually does something that I can pin on her, she's off limits, especially to *you.*" His stern look startled her and she realized her mistake.

Kate closed her eyes in humiliation. The intimacy they'd shared had gone to her head and now she'd made a fool of herself by expecting special treatment. Their relationship had turned into a conflict of interest like she feared it might, and she wondered if her reasons for wanting to be with him held true. Until she figured it out, she decided to stay clear of Detective Alvarez. There was too much to lose both professionally and emotionally if things backfired.

His phone rang, giving her the chance to make a quick exit.

In the courthouse cafeteria, Kate watched as lawyers, officers, and civilians gathered to talk about the day's business over wilted salad and rancid coffee. While this place didn't offer the best food in town, Kate knew that at least she'd be left to sit and think without interruption. Here, police uniforms blended with the scenery—and she was just another cop. She opted for the hygienic safety of a vending machine candy bar, and then sat at a corner table.

She cringed when Officer Jake Tucker appeared, carrying a bright orange food tray and searching for an empty table. While he'd been kind enough not to mention her bar episode and the ride home, she still felt awkward about it and had avoided him until now. His eyes zeroed in on her and she knew she had no choice but to call him over.

Grinning, he set down his tray, which was filled with enough food for two. His six-foot muscular stature probably called for mega calories, but even Superman fears Kryptonite. Someone should tell this guy about salmonella.

"Hey, Kate." He popped open a carton of milk. "Care to join me? There's plenty."

"Thanks, but I just ate." She slid the candy wrapper into her pocket.

"So how's it going?" He shoveled in a mouthful of gravel-colored mashed potatoes. "Need any rides lately?"

"No. And thanks again." She hoped this would be the last she'd hear of it.

"Not a problem. I know you were hurting." He finished his milk. "I heard about your dad. Is he okay?"

"Better. Now that he's home."

"I guess that Marie Yates is some attorney. It's good she was available for him."

"What do you mean?" Kate wasn't sure if her nausea was

due to the topic or the gristle of cube steak he popped into his mouth.

"She's considered the best defense attorney in the area," he said.

"I don't know much about her."

"I hear she's tough to work for. My sister used to be her secretary. Said Marie was a clean freak."

"What else do you know?"

"Well, you know she lost her daughter a few years ago. Suicide. She divorced her husband after he abandoned her when their daughter was five. Oh, and get this, my sister said she goes to the gun range for target practice. Can you believe Miss Priss can actually fire a gun?"

"I suppose she feels it necessary in her line of work."

"Yeah. Especially if she loses at trial," he joked.

"Where does she practice shooting?"

"There's a gun shop in the next town, you probably know it. Stokes?"

"I know all about it," she said, watching him wipe the gravy from his chin.

CHAPTER THIRTY-NINE

"Ah, Detective Alvarez." Marie wiped her sweaty palm on her workout pants and shook hands.

Don't let him in.

"Won't you come in?" She led him and Detective Copley into her living room.

Get rid of them.

"Would you like some coffee?"

"No, thank you. We won't be staying long. Attorney Yates, this is my partner, Elizabeth Copley."

"Please, sit down. What can I do for you?"

Alvarez and Copley sat on two expensive-looking armchairs as he started: "First, I'd like to thank you for your patience during the past few weeks, and for dropping your complaint against Officer Frost. We've all felt the frustration recently, especially Kate. I know you understand how badly she wants to get this guy."

Grab your purse and tell him you're running late for an appointment.

"It's perfectly understandable," she said, taking a seat on the couch. Her stomach churned. Alvarez's passing gaze made her uncomfortable and she made a hasty apology. "Pardon my appearance." She tucked an unruly strand of hair behind her ear. "I've been working out."

He gave her a strange look, and continued. "Like I said, I'm sorry to intrude. I'm following up on our last visit, wondering if

223

you have any ideas."

"I heard the official ruling. And you agree?"

"Yes. I hate to keep asking, but I'm looking for your help, anything that you might have heard recently."

"It's perfectly understandable to approach me about possible leads. After all, I deal with criminals on such a personal level that it's possible I might have heard something from one of them. I think you know in that situation that the attorney-client privilege prevents me from speaking out. I wish I could help, Detective, but I'm afraid I have nothing to tell you. You feel it's at a standstill?"

"Unfortunately, yes."

"My heart truly goes out to her parents. I lost my Chandler a few years ago; I can't tell you how devastating it is to lose a child. You have children, am I correct?"

"Yes. Two boys."

Get rid of him now!

"Then you can only imagine." She gave a shudder.

"Well, thank you for your time." Alvarez moved toward the door. "Again, we're sorry to bother you at home. If you think of anything, please call me or Detective Copley." They headed for the door, with Marie following close behind.

"I certainly will."

She closed the door, leaning against it.

"You disobeyed me!" the commander thundered.

"I had no choice," she said nervously.

"We have miles to go, before our work is complete."

Marie headed into the kitchen and grabbed her headache medicine.

When Alvarez had confronted her the first time for help to prove his suspicions, she'd written it off as denial of a grieving partner. She knew from experience how difficult it was to accept suicide. It had taken years for her to realize it was just another way to die.

Looking back, it appeared the detective's visit might have been more than a plea for her to keep her ears open. In his mind, everyone was a suspect. But why her? Everyone knew she and Detective Frost hadn't seen eye to eye, but their rivalry certainly didn't warrant violence. Now he'd returned with his suspicions still intact.

Although she took pity on poor Lindsay's parents, Marie couldn't feel any true remorse over the detective's demise. Through the years, she'd butted heads with Lindsay on everything from loopholes to incriminating evidence, but Marie could magically pull a technicality out of thin air better than Johnny Cochran, sending some of the strongest investigations back to square one. It held as a cold fact in Marie's world that a criminal lawyer is never appreciated by law enforcement; instead, they're viewed as the bad guy trying to undo police work. Someone had to do it, or innocent people would rot in prison. It was her job and she never made apologies for it.

She shook out two migraine tablets, downing them without water. The headaches had become an everyday occurrence, forcing her to reschedule court appearances and cancel appointments. She vowed to see a doctor when her schedule cleared, but she knew it wouldn't happen because her time was never her own. The growing concern over memory lapses nudged her guilty conscience. They too had become more frequent, costing her an important case last week, causing added stress when she considered she might have Alzheimer's.

Her hands shook at the most recent development. That voice. It echoed so loud that she wondered why no one else seemed to hear it. *The commander,* it called itself, always barking orders and hovering close by. Her thoughts weren't her own any longer, and she feared to conjure a plan for help. Perhaps more headache medicine would ease the incessant commands.

"Put down that bottle. You've had enough," the command came.

Knowing better than to disobey, she returned it to the shelf.

Grateful that Alvarez hadn't actually pinned her down about her whereabouts the night of Lindsay's attack, she leafed through her kitchen calendar and found Friday the thirteenth challenging her. Panic seared another layer through her stomach ulcer, when she realized she had no idea what she'd done that evening. Her memory washed a complete blank.

The commander's roar pounded in her brain, chasing her thoughts.

"Get started!"

Obeying, she went to the basement and picked up where she'd left off when the doorbell had rung. The commander had assured her that her reward would come soon. But not until they completed their task. If only she knew what that was.

"I'm afraid your friend's visit has forced our plans into premature action. His suspicion is dangerous. Work faster."

"I've done all that you've asked. Make good on your promise."

"I can't do that. The battle isn't over."

She spied the 45mm. "I still don't understand the need for that thing. Weapons are easily traced."

"I happen to be somewhat of a weapons expert, Marie. Don't underestimate my intelligence. The time will come for its use. Trust me."

"You haven't forgotten your promise, have you?"

Marie knew she couldn't bear to lose the chance to make things right with her daughter. Her captor had promised to reunite them, even though Chandler had passed away. She wondered if her own mind was playing the cruelest of tricks on her, and whether she'd become delusional in believing the voice and the promises it made. Still, she couldn't deny that the commander had made good on all its threats so far. She didn't like the power it had over her, but hoped it had the ability to bring her to Chandler.

If only she'd been a better mother and friend to her daughter. If she'd listened to the pain in her child all those years, she might have saved her life. She hadn't even known Chandler had been diagnosed as bipolar, until the end.

The chance to say the things she should have said and make things right was an opportunity she couldn't pass up, even if it meant she'd lose her mind in the process. The guilt ate at her, leaving nothing but a hollow shell performing the mundane activities of daily living. But she wasn't living, not anymore. The best she could hope for was to gain her daughter's forgiveness and move on from there.

She began assembling the hardware items before her on the workbench, with the commander ringing in her ears.

"The reward will be yours if you earn it. I suggest you make it your incentive to work faster."

"What if they find out? What if your plan falls through?"

"Don't invite defeat! Victory will be ours when we complete the final task—our duty to finally serve punishment."

Marie grabbed a piece of plastic tubing and waited for instructions. Swiping tears from her face, she thought about the glorious day when she'd be reunited with her daughter, and free of her captor.

CHAPTER FORTY

In my parent's kitchen, I watched Kate tick off the reasons she liked Marie Yates as the prime suspect. Looking past the frilly lace curtains above the sink I saw Mom and Dad sitting at the patio table sipping lemonade. All things considered, they looked well. I missed them.

My sister poured herself a diet soda, and added an ice cube for each reason.

"First of all Marie was the one who suggested to Janice Stokes that she talk to the newspaper. It was a subtle way to plant the story, without directly linking it to herself.

"Second, she has a black sedan like the one described by your neighbor."

"Yes, but Janice Stokes has already admitted she was there," I cut in.

"Right, but that doesn't mean Marie didn't come afterward. Janice said she didn't see anything unusual at your place, including another car or any movement. She said it looked deserted and that's why she left. When you came home you turned on lights, didn't you?"

"Yes."

"Well, then Janice had to have left before you came home."

"You're pushing."

"Hold on and listen. Third, on the day of my near miss at the airfield, the mechanic said he saw an expensive-looking black sedan, but he never said Beemer, which is what Janice drives.

The car could have easily been Marie's Mercedes."

I was as frustrated as Kate, but all of her reasons proved circumstantial and weren't enough to gain a warrant to search Marie's house.

"Kate?" Dad called out from the patio. "What are you doing in there?"

"I spilled my drink," Kate lied through the screen. "I'll be right out."

I saw my mother shaking her head and knew what she was thinking. As a child, Kate had earned the nickname of Ferdinand because she was as clumsy as a bull in a china shop. It was a trait that eventually earned her relief from kitchen duty, because my mother was running out of dishes. If there'd been an Olympic event in spilling, Kate would have taken the gold.

"Kate," I said, watching her plop one last cube into the already full glass. "You said the floor in my bathroom was dry. No water, no blood, right?"

"Right." She mopped the overflowing soda with a paper towel. "No muss, no fuss. Except the perpetrator had gone to *a lot* of fuss to take the evidence with him or her."

"Alvarez had the officers do a search of neighborhood garbage cans that night, right?" I was sure he had.

"Yup. Came up clean, so to speak."

"And they didn't find traces of blood on the tiles?"

"Nope. But there had to be water. If you didn't kill yourself, there would have been spillage." She caught a soda drip before it landed on her halter top.

I immediately thought of Marie the day Kate and I had visited her in her office. She'd spilled a glass of water, nearly tripping over herself to clean it up before it could do damage to her designer suit. My memory caught on a detail I hadn't considered important until now. When she'd closed the desk drawer, something had caught and it hadn't shut all the way. The item had been white, but too flimsy to be paper and it had been thick enough to keep the drawer from closing properly. Revelation.

"Kate, we need a warrant for Marie's office," I blurted.

She rolled her eyes and shrugged. "Sure. I'll run to the drive-through at Warrants-R-Us. Would you like a subpoena with that?"

I explained my idea, knowing it would be impossible to get the warrant without something more substantial and hoping for her input. Suddenly she grabbed her car keys.

"Where are you going?" I asked.

"I need to get something on her, anything. I'm going to the station to look up recent cases she's tried. Check out the who's-who in her life. There has to be a lead there."

"What are you going to tell Mom and Dad?" I asked.

"They're out of paper towels."

At the station, I watched Kate bring up a search on the computer, looking for Marie's name as defense attorney. I agreed that if we landed on the right track, eventually something would lead us to her.

An hour later, Kate slumped back in the chair looking defeated.

"Nothing."

I had a hunch. "Look up juvie cases, from 1996. Specifically, those Marie Yates handled."

After several minutes, we both scanned the logs and I found that my hunch had paid off.

"Look," I pointed. "Marie represented Tanner Jean Hoyt on a shoplifting charge back in '96. That's our link. I bet Tanner and Marie are working together."

Kate started to say something, but an officer walked through the office, causing her to pause. After he left, I followed her once again to our familiar meeting place in the ladies' room.

She relayed what she'd learned about Marie from her cafeteria lunch with Jake Tucker.

"I don't know what it means, but it looks like Marie could have been quite familiar with Calvin's gun supply if she was spending time at his range. It might have been easy for her to make plans to steal a gun. If we can find the gun—"

"That's a big *if.* It's probably wrapped in my towels."

I watched the sparkle die in her eyes along with the hungry look of victory on her face. She was feeling the adrenaline drain, since this major breakthrough wasn't going to lead anywhere.

CHAPTER FORTY-ONE

Marie wrapped the towel around her wet body after showering. Her skin tingled pink after standing under the hot spray until the water had grown cold.

Shivering, she hurried to dress before making herself something for dinner. The migraines had finally ceased, but only after she'd downed nearly the entire bottle of Excedrin she'd purchased yesterday. When would this nightmare end, she wondered? She didn't know how much more she could take of the headaches and memory loss; recently she'd found several hardware store receipts for items she didn't recall buying. She searched her mind to recall where the nearest hardware shop might be. Her schedule, as well as her weekly nail appointment, demanded she hire work done around the house. She came up blank over the purchased items, wondering what was happening to her.

Thinking about it sent the panic she'd washed away in the shower creeping up her spine, and sent *her* for the phone. If she didn't call her doctor right now, she knew she would talk herself out of it.

"What are you doing?" the question boomed in her head.

"I . . . I'm calling someone," Marie stammered.

"Put down the phone! Now! That's an order," the commander said.

"I need help. I'm sick," she muttered, more to herself than to her captor.

"Go to the basement and retrieve your weapon. It is time."

"No! I won't do it."

Suddenly Marie tore at her ears. A deafening sound screeched through her brain, forcing her to her knees. "Stop it! Please stop!"

The roaring ceased and she slowly pulled her hands away to find them covered with blood. The right side of her head burned like fire and she ran to the front hall mirror. She gasped when she saw that her right ear had been partially torn from her head. Blood oozed down her neck, soaking her shirt collar.

"What do you want from me!" she screamed.

"Obey my orders. Go get the gun," the commander stated calmly.

She did as told, fighting back pain and fright. Picking up the gun, her hands shook so badly she dropped it.

"It isn't loaded, yet," the commander assured her. "Go find the bullets in the kitchen drawer beside the refrigerator."

"What are you going to do?" she asked, stalling.

"Not me. Us. We're going to finalize the punishment of Detective Frost."

"Her life is over. Isn't that enough?"

"Do you really think that's enough for her? Think about it, all the pain she has caused you."

"Who *are* you?"

"You defended me so well on that shoplifting charge, I figured you'd never forget me. But *I* remember everything from that day. The look on your face when we left the courtroom and you saw Detective Frost. The way she breezed past like you were nothing. I saw the hatred burning in your eyes.

"Later, when I read about Chandler's suicide, I knew that Frost bitch had to be responsible. And I think you know it, too."

Marie suddenly recognized the dark voice in her head. It still held the same ominous tone it had years ago when she'd represented Tanner Jean Hoyt in court. She'd won the trial and escorted her young delinquent out of the courtroom, nearly colliding with then-Officer Frost as she hurried inside for a court appearance.

Tanner interrupted her thoughts. "You couldn't hide your contempt for Frost. You knew she was evil even before she caused your daughter's death. That's why you and I are the perfect team. We're both entitled to revenge. I want her to lose everything, like I have. Then we'll be even. And you have the chance to take something of hers and balance the debt of injustice between the two of you."

Marie knew her history with Detective Frost didn't end outside the scope of work. Lindsay had gone to high school with her daughter, Chandler, and had become a household word during those painful years when the perky blonde had beaten her daughter out of everything she'd tried out for. It hadn't been until after Chandler's passing that Marie learned of her daughter's silent battle with bipolar disease.

"But Chandler was ill," Marie argued. "She didn't know what she was doing."

"She was desperate to end the pain. There was no way to change the past."

Marie still blamed Lindsay for Chandler's painful end, although her daughter's therapist assured her Chandler had become unstable after refusing to take her medication. It rang too coincidental to Marie that the suicide came shortly after her daughter's ten-year high school reunion, where she relived all of her painful memories when Lindsay walked in, no longer gangly and too tall, but instead beautiful, trim, and a respected detective. Chandler had revealed to her mother that she'd felt inadequate as a struggling journalist with a local newspaper, telling Marie, "Lindsay makes headlines; I only get to write them." A week later, Marie buried her daughter.

With the help of Janice Stokes, it had been easy to convince her daughter's reporter friend at the newspaper to print the story on Lindsay. It had soothed her anger, knowing the perfect image of Detective Frost had been permanently tarnished, and her daughter's paper had been the one to run the story. That would have been enough for Marie. But other incidents had followed, things she barely remembered doing, like driving away from the airfield on the day of Kate's accident. That morning she'd finished up a client meeting and the next thing she knew, she found herself leaving the parking lot at the small airport.

Marie decided to stall her captor and maybe find a bargaining chip in the deal.

"What happened to you, Tanner? I held high hopes for your future when I last saw you."

Tanner hesitated and Marie knew she'd hit a nerve.

"I helped you once, Tanner. Let me try again."

"You will help by doing as I say."

"That's not what I mean. It's not too late to stop—"

"You're out of line! We have a mission to complete, only then will we stop."

Marie winced at Tanner's skull-cracking roar inside her head. Years of dealing with irrational, high-strung criminals cautioned her to revise her approach. Tanner had to feel she could trust her.

"Your command of military tactics and strategy is impressive, but I don't recall you ever having enlisted."

"I was raised to be a soldier. It was my father's greatest gift to me."

"Yes, I know he was a Vietnam vet. He wanted you to join the ranks?"

Frightened by the sudden silence, Marie steeled herself to keep going, knowing she risked another outburst that might cost her more pain. "Tanner? Won't you tell me about it? It must get lonesome without someone to talk to. I suppose, right now, I'm your only friend."

"Civilians seek friendship, soldiers learn camaraderie."

"True. We have become comrades, and as such, I'd like to know your background." Marie waited for a response, then asked, "Your father encouraged your love for the military?"

"Too many questions! I can't think with all your chatter."

Marie gasped as a fragmented scene filled her mind. She saw Tanner as a child of about nine, tears washing her pale cheeks as she held a large pair of scissors.

A dark-haired woman, washing apples at the kitchen sink, jerked around in surprise.

"What in the world are you doing with those?" she asked the young girl.

"I'm cutting my hair like a boy's." Tanner snipped off a chunk and let it drop to the floor.

"Tanner! What's gotten into you?" Her mother tried to pry the scissors away.

"No! I want my hair cut!" She wriggled away and cut her bangs across in one snip. "Why doesn't Daddy like me, Mama? Is it because I'm a girl?"

"Put down the scissors and we'll talk." The woman's lips curled into a frown as she thought a moment. "Daddy loves you, he just doesn't understand you. He's had a rough time of it since the war ended, but he's doing his best. Try and be patient with him. Can you do that?" She tried to finger brush what was left of Tanner's hair into shape.

"Why does the war make *me* hard to understand?" the child wanted to know.

"It doesn't." Her mother smiled. "You're too smart for your own good."

"I heard you talking to Aunt Betty on the phone last week,

and you said Daddy always wanted a son. Is that why he doesn't like me?"

"You were listening in on my phone conversation?"

"I didn't try, I just heard, that's all."

Her mother rested her hands on Tanner's bony shoulders. "Listen to me. While it's true your father always wanted a son to follow in his footsteps, he loves you just the same."

A tall shadow filled the doorway and Tanner moved behind her mother, as the room seemed to shrink.

"Where's Tanner?" The man limped hard across the yellowed linoleum. His buzz cut glistened with sweat in the humidity of the cramped kitchen and he wiped his forehead with a paper towel. Dark eyes zeroed in on the scrawny bare legs peeking out from behind his wife's.

He pointed to her with a snarl. "Git out from behind your mama and face me."

Tanner peeled herself away and he bent to meet her eye to eye, his prosthetic leg standing askew from the rest of him.

"I heard what you said about me."

Tanner stared at her dirty bare feet.

"Look at me," he commanded.

She obeyed with fear in her eyes.

"I don't love you any less 'cause you're a girl. You're a Hoyt, and that makes you soldier material.

"If you're to survive this world, you've got to have the proper training and that's my job as your father. Up until now I didn't think you were ready, but with you asking all these questions, I think it's time. So, buck up little soldier. No more tears. We have a mission, and the first order of the day is to get you a decent haircut."

Following her father out of the kitchen, Tanner turned back to offer her mother a smile. "I'm going to be like Daddy."

The vision ended abruptly, leading Marie to believe that was all Tanner wanted her to see. She heard Tanner cut through her thoughts.

"And now it is time to fulfill *our* mission as comrades and, as you say, *friends.*"

Marie stuffed the loaded gun, which she suspected was the gun Perry Frost had been accused of stealing, into her purse. She couldn't remember taking it and wondered how she'd gotten away with a robbery like that. Marie thought about Tanner's promised reward for her hard work, and focused on getting the chance she'd prayed for since Chandler died.

"All right," Marie seethed. "Let's get this over with. I want to see my daughter tonight."

"Your reward will follow our victory," Tanner said.

Marie got into her car and headed for Perry and Carla Frost's house.

CHAPTER FORTY-TWO

I watched Kate stare at the computer screen before her. The hour had grown late at the precinct, with only a skeleton crew hanging around doing paperwork and taking calls.

"Sorry, Linz." She rubbed her eyes, looking tired and defeated.

"It's not your fault. Not all the answers come right away. This isn't a TV crime show."

"But I know we're so close. It's something seemingly insignificant, something we've never considered. And I know it's Marie."

"No, you don't. You have a gut feeling, but you don't know. That's one thing you need to get used to if you're going to be a detective. Play your hunches carefully or you could blow it."

"Right," Kate said, standing to stretch. "I think right now I'll play the hunch that it's time to get home. Care to join me?"

"Sure," said a voice from the doorway.

Kate's cheeks burned red when she saw Alvarez staring at her.

"You caught me off guard." She grabbed her car keys from the desk.

"I guessed that. Rough day?" he asked with a smirk.

"Every day is a rough day until we solve this."

"Want a cup of coffee?"

"Sure. Why not?" Kate followed him to his office and I couldn't resist joining them. It had been ages since I'd sat in on a late-night pow-wow at the station.

In his office, Alvarez poured two cups and took a seat. His pale blue dress shirt was unbuttoned at the top, sleeves rolled up to the elbows. He looked beat.

Kate sat on the edge of the desk, sipping her mug. "Don't you ever go home?"

"The kids are with their mom tonight."

"Oh? I thought she was out of the picture."

He winced as if her words cut. "She's off and on. It's sending the wrong message to the boys. But I have to let her work things out or she might bolt for good. I guess it's better they have a part-time mom instead of none at all."

"I'm sorry," Kate apologized. "I didn't mean to sound judgmental. The late hour is getting to me." She turned to go.

"No harm, Kate. Really." He shoved a small stack of photos aside.

"Thanks for the coffee." She set the cup down, but her hand caught the handle, overturning the mug. 'Coffee snaked across the desk like a narrow river. Luckily there hadn't been much left.

"Oh, I'm so sorry. I'm such a klutz. Here let me wipe that up," she said, grabbing a handful of paper towels.

As Kate sopped up the liquid, she stopped to stare at the photos that had blessedly avoided the caffeine pool. Her hand grabbed the top picture.

"Where did this come from?" she asked.

"One of Lindsay's neighbors, Mrs. . . . uh." Alvarez reached for the file. "Mrs. Jenkins brought them in this morning. Said her grandson is an amateur photographer and had taken these pictures the day Lindsay died. She hoped they might be helpful. I don't see much of anything in them. They were taken before the crime, and don't show any of the crowd. But the crime team has that covered."

"Look, here's the black sedan. I'm sure of it." She held the photo for him to see. I rounded the desk for a peek. Kate was right.

"The car belonging to Janice Stokes," Alvarez nodded. "All that proves is that she's telling the truth about being there that night."

Kate squinted closer. "Does Janice have a vanity plate?"

"I don't think so." He rifled quickly through the file. "No. Stokes' last two numbers are 25."

"This is a vanity plate. The last two letters are AW."

Alvarez shook his head. "I know what you're thinking."

"Damn right. And I don't need to run the plates to know that Marie Yates' tag reads, CRIM LAW."

"Kate—" Alvarez's smile was genuine "—we've got our probable cause."

I wasn't surprised to see the fast pace at which the warrants came through to search Marie's home, car, and office. Judge Parker had been more than happy to provide some well-deserved annoyance to the defense attorney who'd made some of his time on the bench a living hell.

Kate's cheeks flushed in excitement as she prepared to serve a healthy portion of justice to Marie Yates. I tried to give her last-minute instructions as she put on her Kevlar vest.

"Now let Alvarez and the team take the lead," I cautioned.

"Linz, don't start. I've been trained, remember?"

"Yes, but this is personal with you. I have to say I'm surprised Alvarez is letting you in on this."

"He trusts my judgment and knows I'm a good cop. That's why I'm going."

"I know that. But . . ."

"But what? You think it's because there's something between us? I don't believe you. Give us both more credit than that."

I'd screwed up. If I wanted Kate's trust, I'd have to earn it and keep earning until it solidified. So far, we'd made a good team and I didn't want to jeopardize that. "Sorry. It was a stupid thing to say."

She waved me on with a grin as we passed Alvarez's empty office. His phone rang for the third time, and she rushed to answer it.

"Detective Alvarez's office. Can I help you?"

I watched my sister's blue eyes widen slightly, then glaze over with tears, jotting down a message.

"Pick you up for dinner at seven instead of six. What's that?" she asked. "Oh, thank him for the flowers. Right. I'll be sure he gets this, Mrs. Alvarez."

She disconnected, staring at the phone like an enemy.

"Kate, wait," I started. "Are you sure it wasn't his mother?"

"I doubt it. She sounded young. Forget it, Linz. It's over. I should have known better. He has kids to think about. They need a mother, and if she's finally ready to be one, I can't stand in the way. Wouldn't want to." She secured her gun in its holster and headed for the door.

CHAPTER FORTY-THREE

Marie wasn't home when we served the warrant, which meant we couldn't search the car. I doubted that she'd be dumb enough to put the towels in her car anyway; still, I'd seen stranger things happen. For all we knew, she'd discarded the towels completely, which would take us right back to square one.

Kate kept her composure and maintained a professional attitude, managing to avoid Alvarez throughout most of the search. When we finished, I rode with Kate in the squad, heading to Marie's office in town.

"You did good," I offered.

"Not good enough. We still have dick."

"I meant Alvarez."

"Me too." She grimaced.

Marie's office lay dark at the late hour. Alvarez had contacted the building's landlord to meet us there with a key. The warrant covered the entire building, including the shoe repair shop below the defense attorney's office. We were only interested in all things Marie.

With everyone in position, we entered the stuffy blackness and trudged up the stairs to the second floor. We made sure the reception area and office were clear, then proceeded with our search. As Alvarez, Copley, and several officers made their way about the rooms, I told Kate to check the desk drawers where

I'd seen something sticking out on our last visit.

"I'll check the desk," she told Alvarez.

"Go ahead," he said, opening the closet.

Kate's hand tugged at the drawer.

"Got a locked drawer here," she informed him.

"Open it," he instructed.

It took her less than thirty seconds to jimmy the lock. She yanked open the bottom drawer, searching inside for the towels. A stack of folders, several bottles of Wite-Out, and a stapler rested neatly inside. No towels.

"Damn, she's moved them," I said, frustrated.

Kate nodded in agreement, quickly riffling through the remaining drawers. A typical array of desk junk lay inside. Tampons, expensive lipstick, Post-it notes, and a pack of gum were among her prized possessions. Nothing we could arrest her for, unless the god-awful lipstick color could be considered a crime.

"Where could they be?" I said to Kate, who was down on her knees searching under the desk.

Suddenly she stopped, her head popping up from behind. *C'mon,* she nodded toward the door.

I followed her outside and behind the building to the alley and a Dumpster. It was a long shot. Chances are, if Marie had gotten rid of them there, they were long gone. Recalling my latest faux pas with Kate, I decided to keep my mouth shut and trust her instincts. After all, it looked like she'd been right about Marie.

Gravel crunched under her shoes, causing a stray cat to startle away from the large waste container. She hoisted the lid back and brushed off her hands.

"Well? What are you waiting for?" she asked me.

"Me?"

"Yeah, you. You won't get dirty, remember?"

"Oh. Right." I stalled. Everyone has his or her weakness. Mine is the rancid stench of rotting food or unsightly mold. I can steel myself against the bloodiest, dismembered corpse, but show me refrigerator leftovers wearing a fur coat and I'll gag every time.

"I'm going to check with the paranormal union to see if this is considered discrimination. Just because I'm a ghost doesn't mean I should get all the dirty work."

Her merciless look prompted me to climb inside. Luckily I couldn't smell anything, and I quickly discovered the trash consisted mostly of shredded paper, a few food wrappers, and a couple of old shoes. Not surprising with a shoe repair shop nearby.

"Anything?" Kate called.

"No." I made my way out.

"Hey! What are you doing back here?" a man with an Italian accent asked.

I saw Antonio Barilla, the shoe repair shop owner.

Tony had been a friend to local law enforcement, offering free repairs to the Southfield Heights officers. He'd been in business as long as I could remember.

"Good evening, Tony," Kate said. "No need for alarm, I'm here on police business."

"Oh, is you, Missy Kate. Anything wrong?"

"We're just looking for something."

"Mebe I kenna help you."

"Thanks, Tony, but I think I'm almost through here. What brings you here so late?" she said, closing the Dumpster's lid.

"I had to come back for the sausage I left in the basement icebox. My wife, she kill me if I don't bring it home."

"What else is in the basement?" Kate fished.

"Oh the usual stuff, you know, tenant storage closets, unused office furniture. And of course, an icebox."

"Storage." Kate snapped her fingers. "Thanks, Tony. I owe you."

I saw the short man's dark clipped mustache twitch into a smile.

In the basement, the building's landlord unlocked Marie Yates' storage compartment with Alvarez, Copley, and Kate standing by. The three-by-six space held a file cabinet, a faded artificial plant, and an old gym bag stuffed into the corner.

Alvarez stepped aside to allow for evidence photos, then donned his gloves. He held up a muddy pair of combat boots. "Maybe Mrs. Jenkins was right about someone sneaking into her backyard."

Copley started for the gym bag, but Alvarez stopped her. "I'd like to let Kate have the honors." He tossed her a pair of latex gloves.

Kate stretched them on, yanked open the bag, and mulled over its contents, which looked more like equipment for a science project than workout gear. The bag held pieces of cut wire, plastic tubing, hemostats, and, finally, two white towels.

"Towels. And they look stiffened." She opened the bag's mouth wider. "What the hell is all this stuff for?"

Even in the dim light of the basement, I could make out the monogrammed L on one of the towels. They were mine. Then something scraped along the inside nylon and Kate prodded out a lock pick. Now we knew how she'd gotten into my house, and probably Calvin's, without much trouble.

Alvarez stripped off his gloves. "Looks like we have a suspect."

Suspect, hell. It was official. Marie Yates had taken my life. I turned away as Kate beamed at the find. I barely heard Alvarez radio in to have Marie Yates picked up. My emotions spilled into overload. There was joy and relief in finally knowing who my killer was, mixed with anger and a slow bubbling hatred for the bitch who'd stolen my future and broken my family's heart.

I felt frustration in knowing I wouldn't be the one to take her down.

I followed Kate numbly to the squad. Her face glowed in anticipation of seeing justice served and somehow finding closure in this sick, twisted scenario. I felt happy for her, for my parents, for everyone involved. For everyone but me. I remained deceased, and no matter what happened to Marie that would never change. In my mind, there would never be any true closure in this.

"I wonder if she knows something's up?" Kate broke my thoughts. "She's not home or at her office, and I'm pretty sure she doesn't have a social life, unless you count meetings with the criminals she represents. Where could she be?"

I thought about this a moment, trying to pull my head out of my own problems long enough to think like a detective. There'd been many times I'd had to force myself to leave my personal baggage outside the precinct door and get on with the job. Tonight, I decided, would be no different.

I realized I didn't know much about Marie. Our paths never crossed outside of the job, except for her daughter Chandler. That's when it hit me. I had to find Chandler and ask her for help. For that I knew I'd need help.

"Listen, Kate. I have to leave for a while. I have a hunch about Marie."

"You know where to find me."

CHAPTER FORTY-FOUR

Sally O'Shannon rounded the building of her old job site. I suspected I'd find her here, based on what she'd told me about the deceased returning to their last scene. I waved her over.

Her distorted grin was welcoming. In a twisted way I'd become more at ease in this realm than in the land of the living. Here, things were supposed to be weird and unexplainable and those around me understood my frustrations.

"Sally, I need your help," I said.

"Of course, you do. What's up?"

I explained that I needed to locate Chandler Yates and didn't have a clue how to go about it.

Her scarred lip twitched into a snarling frown. "That's not always so easy. You need to know where she died to even begin a search. No yellow pages here." She snorted at her own joke.

"I know where she died," I said.

I'd heard through the grapevine that Chandler's end had been a horrific scene. Only twenty-eight at the time, she had stopped taking the medication for her bipolar disorder. One night in a manic state, she'd rented a hotel room, taken a pair of sewing shears, and ripped open the veins up and down her arms. They'd found her on blood-soaked newspapers of the local rag she worked for, clutching a photo of herself and Marie during happier times. No one understood how she'd endured the pain of slashing her arms, but in her manic state, she'd probably been so pumped that self-mutilation won out.

Marie had nearly collapsed at the scene, cradling her daughter, covering herself in Chandler's blood. In her shock and grief, she'd vowed to get the person responsible for causing her daughter's final act, unable to accept the possibility that no one caused it or could have prevented it.

Looking back, I figured my attack could have been part of her pledge, but I couldn't understand it completely. Everyone in high school knew Chandler Yates and her mom were as distant as fifth cousins. It didn't take a Freudian mind to consider perhaps Marie herself had been part of Chandler's pain. Back in high school, no one thought much about their strained relationship because most teenage girls worked to lengthen the apron strings. But in Chandler's case, it had been Marie who'd cut the ties in order to build her name in the legal system. When Chandler started acting out with truancy and minor acts of vandalism, everyone guessed it was the only way to get a private audience with her attorney mother. Unfortunately, her final act cost her more than a night in lockup.

Sally waved a hand before my face. "Are you with me?"

I nodded.

"Good. Now in order to get to her scene, all you need to do is picture it in great detail and will yourself there."

"Thanks, Sally," I said, closing my eyes.

Although I hadn't been there the night of Chandler's death, I knew the place. I saw the seedy motel on Fourth Street perched at the edge of town like a dirty spider waiting for its next victim. The location was ideal for catching incoming tourists from other states because of its close proximity to the Interstate.

Faded brick the color of dog shit held the place together under a beat-up sign that boasted the best rates in town. It should. No one in their right *or* wrong mind would pay more than they had to. Unfortunately, Chandler Yates had been in a manic state of mind and the threadbare sheets and stained toilets didn't matter.

I recalled the room number like an old friend's birthday. Disturbing memories tend to stick and it had been an emotional time for everyone on the department. As much as Marie and I didn't see eye to eye, I really felt for her and wept at her daughter's funeral.

Room 112 stood only inches away and I easily passed through its paint-chipped door. Inside, I imagined the scene as it might have looked that night, with police tape and bloodied newspapers. Instead, I saw a full-size bed dressed in a faded flower print bedspread.

Chandler's form sat motionless near the bedside table.

"I see the playing field has finally been leveled," she said to me.

"I don't know what you mean."

She came forward carrying a framed photo of her and Marie, her tag. I saw the open slits along her inner forearms. "We're both here. Now maybe we can start over."

"Chandler, look. I really don't know what you're talking about. I need—"

"To listen," she finished.

I knew she had it coming. If I'd been responsible for her pain or passing in any way, I owed her that much. "Tell me," I said.

The tension in her face eased as she started. "Throughout our whole high school career you took every chance I had to make it and be someone. Cheerleading, the school play, first chair in band, for Christ's sake! You couldn't leave one thing for me to call my own. You had to have it all."

I tried to think back to our high school days, to a time when I might have hurt her. Nothing came to mind. Could I have really been so self-absorbed and callous that I hadn't even noticed her pain?

"I'm sorry if I hurt you," I replied sincerely. "It wasn't intentional. You know how high school is. Every man for himself. I didn't know you were hurting. You should have said something."

"Right. And you would have listened?"

"Probably not, but you could have tried. That's what life is about, Chandler. There are no guarantees or gimmes, unless you're Paris Hilton. Along the way we have to stick up for ourselves and go after the things we want. I'm finding out it's not much different on this side."

I followed her to the window, where she stared out into the parking lot. "Can you forgive me?"

She eyed me carefully. "You're still going after what you want, aren't you? Only this time it's more than a spot on the cheerleading squad; it's my mother."

"Sorry, you won't get any sympathy here. She took my life."

"No, she didn't. Tanner Jean Hoyt is responsible."

"She's a ghost."

"I know. That's precisely how she got away with it. She's taken possession of my mother's mind, holding her hostage until she does Tanner's bidding. Part of the deal was killing you, but there's more. Tanner isn't finished yet."

"If you knew this, why didn't you try and stop her?"

"I don't have that kind of power. Suicide creates a weaker spirit." Her laugh sounded bitter. "Once again I'm the loser, with no hope of becoming any more than I am right now. But *you* can do it." She turned to me with what looked like real tears. "Lindsay, please stop Tanner, for my mother's sake."

"What do you mean, Tanner isn't through? Other than stalking me and sending me to the next level, what more can she do?"

"It's not you she's after."

Chapter Forty-Five

Marie clamped the shackles around Perry Frost's wrists where he sat on the floor. The restraints linked to heavy chains bolted into the bomb shelter's cinder-block walls. The dampness smelled of worms and her own sweat, causing her to work faster.

Perry sat in silence, watching her set up the IV tubing beside him. She followed his gaze to the skeleton not two feet away, which was dressed in military fatigues and cradling an M16. The soldier's left-leg prosthesis stuck out from the pant leg, the silver gleaming under the shelter lights.

"Try not to think about that," Marie told him. The sight had unnerved her at first, but as she'd been forced to spend time in the shelter in preparation for this moment, she'd grown used to seeing the remains.

Tanner explained the mystery of the soldier's identity to her the first day.

"I believe you never had the privilege of meeting Private First Class John J. Hoyt." Tanner's voice oozed pride.

Marie stared at the hollow eye sockets staring out from under his helmet.

"Your father abandoned you and your mother years ago. Is this where he ended up?" Marie refrained from using an accusatory tone.

"My father would have never abandoned his duties. That was a cruel lie told by the nosey neighbors in this silly little town."

"Tell me what happened, Tanner." Marie wanted to know.

"At seventeen, I came home from school one day to find him dead

on the couch. Gone. I never had the chance to say goodbye, never knew what happened. Heroes deserve a better death. It angered me to know he'd never see me achieve all we'd worked for.

"*My mother had gone to her sister's for a few days, so I cleaned him up and dressed him in full uniform before carrying him to the shelter after dark.*

"*My father and I built this shelter together and I felt it was the best place to honor his memory, until I could make him proud.*"

Marie fought down nausea when she wondered if he'd truly been dead yet. Perhaps he'd had a seizure or a stroke and could have been saved if only Tanner had taken action. The man had been left to rot in his own bomb shelter, with no one the wiser. His own wife thought he'd abandoned them.

"*Why didn't you tell someone? He could have received a proper military burial and your mother would have had closure.*"

"*My mother didn't need closure. She'd found other activities to occupy her time by then. A crippled vet no longer interested her.*

"*I have yet to achieve my mission and make him proud. I failed at everything I ever tried, until I righted the wrongs that our legal system couldn't.*"

"*But you took lives . . .*"

"*My life was taken as well! Is mine less important?*"

"*Not at all. But surely you could have found another way.*"

"*My time has come, after all these years. Then my father will be proud and able to rest in peace.*"

The memory faded when Tanner exploded in Marie's head. "You're taking too long. We've practiced this a hundred times. You should have it down by now."

Marie's hands shook as she strapped the tourniquet around Perry's arm. She felt his dark stare penetrating and forced herself to keep her mind on the task. Soon she would gain her reward. It would all be worth it.

"Why are you doing this, Attorney Yates?" Perry asked.

Taking him hostage had gone easier than she'd thought. His wife, Carla, had opened the door wide, even offering to make coffee.

"That's not necessary. I won't be staying that long," she'd assured Carla.

When Perry came into the living room and shook hands, his smile dropped at the sight of the 45mm pointed at his chest. His wife had stepped timidly behind her husband, clutching his arm.

"What's all this about?" he asked, looking brave.

"I need you to come quietly with me, Mr. Frost. We have some unfinished business."

"What kind of business?"

"We'll attend to that later." Marie tossed him a hefty roll of duct tape and motioned with the gun for Carla to sit in a nearby chair.

"Secure her," she ordered at Tanner's prompting.

"I want to come with you, Perry." Mrs. Frost's eyes brimmed.

"Just sit quietly, Carla. Everything's going to be all right. I promise." He began taping her to the chair.

He'd been more cooperative after that, getting into her car without any attempts at escape, and they'd arrived at the bomb shelter five minutes ahead of schedule.

Now, she slapped the veins of his left arm, causing them to stand at attention. He flinched when she slid the needle into his vein.

Tanner forced Marie to say, "*You're* almost done."

Marie watched in horrified silence, entombed, and forced to watch someone else moving in her body. She'd become Tanner's marionette.

If only she could stop this sick turn of events and get out. Surely it wasn't too late to stop the madness. That's what had happened. She'd gone insane. No one would blame her for her actions.

She watched her hands working to start the drip of saline solution into Perry's arm, while she contemplated her defense and mentally scanned attorney names suitable for representation. Soon it would all be over and she would receive her reward.

Marie thought about Chandler, and the moment she'd be able to see and speak to her beloved daughter again. The dark veil would be torn open and they'd move on from there, to heal their wounded relationship. Everything would be made right.

"Are you familiar with Dr. Kevorkian's Thanatron, Mr. Frost?" Tanner made Marie say.

When he didn't answer, she continued, "You're looking at a reasonable facsimile. I've had to make a few adjustments for my personal needs, but it works on the same premise. Allow me to demonstrate."

Marie watched her finger point to two plastic IV bags rigged onto a short metal pole with hooks. She pointed to the first one. "Sodium chloride, or saline. However," she said, tracing the tubing of the second bag with her finger, "this tubing hasn't been purged of air.

"For now, harmless saline is running into your system. Enough to keep the vein open for later. At just the right moment, I'll stop the flow of the first bag and begin the second. The air inside the tubing will enter your vein and cause an embolism. You'll die in minutes, right in front of your daughter."

"Leave Katie out of this." He struggled against the shackles.

"I'm talking about Lindsay."

Perry shook his head. "You're a sick woman. You need help. Why are you doing this?"

"I want your daughter to lose everything that I have. So far, she's lost her good name in the community, and she's lost her life. There's just one more thing that will make us even."

She nodded to the skeleton in the corner. "Lindsay needs to suffer the loss of her father."

Perry rose up as much as possible. "You still haven't answered my question. Why is all this necessary?"

"My father was a military man, a Marine, serving his country with pride and honor. He came home a wounded man, in many ways. As a female, I was just one more disappointment to him, but he did the best he could with me. I lost him before getting the chance to make him proud.

"You want to know why, Mr. Frost? My father would have wanted justice served and I intend to make him proud."

Marie watched the confusion on Perry Frost's face from behind her inner wall of silence. He couldn't possibly understand the situation and she had no way to break through to him. Even if she wanted to.

CHAPTER FORTY-SIX

I caught up with Kate patrolling Marie's neighborhood in the squad. This time I did a better job of warning her of my impending appearance, causing several bursts of radio static.

She nodded and grinned. "Okay, Linz. Gotcha."

I formed in the passenger seat. "Any sign of Marie?"

"Nope. She's simply disappeared. She must be on to us."

"Don't be too sure. This might end up being a mission to save, as well as arrest her." I explained my meeting with Chandler.

"Oh, my God. If she's not after you it must be someone you care about."

Kate turned on the squad lights and siren, pressed the accelerator, and headed toward our parents' house.

Our first clue that something bad had happened was the locked front door. Some suburbs allow such luxuries as unsecured houses and the absence of watchdogs, and my parents' was one of them. Dad's car sat in the drive, telling us they should be home. When no one answered, I went in.

I saw my mother duct-taped to a dining room chair in the middle of the living room, set far enough away from anything that might attract attention. Tears stained her cheeks, and I watched as she helplessly tried to scoot the chair across the thick carpet toward the door.

Back outside, Kate pounded the screen door with her fist.

"Break it down, now," I ordered.

In seconds, Kate was inside, calling for backup.

She carefully removed the tape, stroking my mother's gray-streaked hair from her wet cheeks.

"She took your father! She took him! You've got to find him!" my mother cried.

"Who Mom? Who took him?" Kate removed the last of the tape and started rubbing Mom's wrists where they'd turned red.

"Marie Yates! That evil bitch!"

My mother never swore unless she'd been pushed to her absolute limits. As far as I remember, the only thing that ever brought her close was our old rickety vacuum cleaner.

A brief knock at the door, and Alvarez stepped inside with Copley close behind.

"Marie's kidnapped my father," Kate told him.

He bent beside my mother, still trembling in the chair. "Mrs. Frost, can you tell me what happened?"

"She came in here with a gun and forced him to tie me up. Then they left and oh, I just don't know what's going to happen." She began to cry.

"Did she say anything that might lead us to where she took him?" Alvarez asked gently.

"Let me think. Uh, she said something about unfinished business. But that's all."

"Okay, we'll find her, I promise. Do you feel you need to go to the hospital?"

"No. I want to stay here and wait for Perry. I can't lose another person . . . I won't!"

An officer helped her into the kitchen for a cup of tea.

"I'll call you as soon as we find him, Mom," Kate called on her way out the front door.

Outside, she caught up with Alvarez in the darkness. "What's the plan?"

"We keep looking. Every available officer is searching, but so far it's like she's disappeared."

I thought of Tanner inside Marie's head, commanding her own private war. If Chandler was right, it wasn't a matter of finding Marie; we needed to find Tanner. Sally's words jumped into my mind about returning to a spirit's place of death.

I knew where Tanner had taken my father.

"Kate! C'mon, get in the squad. Tell Alvarez to meet us at 409 Birch. If he asks why, tell him you're following a hunch."

"What's on Birch Street?"

"Tanner Jean Hoyt's childhood home."

It took less than five minutes to arrive, with Alvarez and Copley joining us there seconds later. Kate met him at his car, explaining she felt Marie might be inside. I took the opportunity to explore the grounds.

"Tell me again why we're here?" He looked skeptical.

"Something Marie said earlier. I'll explain later," she lied, and took off before he could press her further.

I spotted Marie's Mercedes parked between the garage and a thick row of tall hedges. In the dark, the black car was nearly invisible.

Coming around the front of the house, I heard Alvarez talking to Kate as she headed up the drive.

"Even though it's abandoned, we can't just go busting in there without probable cause."

From behind him, I motioned toward the garage, miming a steering wheel.

"Is that enough probable cause for you?" She pointed to the thick hedges.

Squinting, he spied the familiar vanity plate partially hidden in the brush.

"Let's go," he said, calling for backup into his radio.

It felt as if I was reliving a nightmare. The inside of Tanner's home hadn't changed much since that night with Joe, but it all came back quickly. The crossbow's drywall damage showed the split, gaping wound.

I went ahead of Kate and Alvarez to look for booby traps, but the house was clean. The homemade hospital setup that had served Tanner's mom remained in the living room. Cobwebs hung from an unused IV pole beside a plastic commode. Dingy bedsheets lay wadded on the couch as if someone had recently gotten up, planning to return. I knew no one had been here in years.

By the time backup arrived, we'd covered the entire house, including the basement, where the cinder blocks lay stacked and dusty.

"Clear," Alvarez called into his radio, letting everyone know the house was safe—but, unfortunately, empty.

"Damn!" Kate cursed. "Where could she be? Is the car here to throw us off?"

"I don't think so," I said. "She wouldn't get far with Dad in tow without a ride. Something tells me they're here, somewhere."

The team determined the garage lay empty, leaving us with nowhere to search except the spacious backyard.

"Wait," I said. "Remember those cinder blocks in the basement?"

Kate merely nodded, seeing an officer close by.

"They weren't mortared together like a wall or anything. It almost looked like they were leftovers."

"From what?" Kate whispered.

"Think about it. Tanner's dad was ex-military, and if Tanner is any indication of his fanaticism, it wouldn't be a stretch to think he might have built some sort of shelter."

"A bomb shelter." Kate scanned the yard slowly, heading

toward the far edge near the garage. "Here!" she called, alerting the others to a metal door that was flush with the ground.

She yanked it open, announcing, "Police!" then disappeared inside, with me leading the way down the narrow wooden steps.

I felt naked without my gun; I guess being a spirit has its advantages. My only danger was a crazed ghost.

Suddenly the door above slammed closed and I heard Alvarez shouting for Kate to open it up. Tanner knew we were here.

I went ahead of Kate as she quietly snaked her way down the steps with her gun drawn.

A halogen lamp burned bright in a room about sixteen by eight. I froze at the sight of Tanner in the flesh, dressed in military fatigues. Her buzz cut looked freshly cropped and she wore her usual facial camo. My mind raced to understand how she'd defeated death and returned to life. Now I'd have to find a way to kill her again.

She crouched beside my poor father on the floor. For a brief moment, I panicked. I couldn't see him breathing. His skin bleached pale against the halogen, his body unmoving. Then he flinched when she yanked a piece of surgical tape from his arm. With his wrists shackled to the wall, I saw IV tubing slowly delivering a clear solution into an arm vein.

A dark mound of clothing lay crumpled in the corner, the remains of a skeleton's hand poking out from underneath. I saw a military helmet propped askew over a smiling skull, its other hand still clutching an M16. A dog-eared Polaroid stuck out of the fatigue-shirt pocket and I knew it was the photo of Linh taken so many years ago.

Kate stopped on the bottom step, weapon pointed. Her eyes narrowed briefly and I suspected she was as confused as I was.

She surprised me, saying, "Hands up, Marie. It's over."

When the woman stood, I saw it was, indeed, Marie Yates, staring coldly past my sister at me. Gone were the Katie Couric coiffure, designer duds, and, most noticeably, her soul. Tanner had completely taken over. I watched her face morph in and out of a blend of Tanner and Marie. It was like watching Jekyll and Hyde.

Tanner's gruff mannerisms took over Marie's body as she stood with arms at her sides in defiance. It was the criminal attorney's voice that echoed across the small room.

Her eyes glared through me. Hate etched into their core. "I see you made it, Detective."

"Wouldn't miss it. I always like putting a case to bed, Tanner. I'll even sing you a lullaby." I inched toward my father, wondering what I could do to stop her.

She showed no fear, pointing to the skeleton. "I'd like everyone to meet my father, Private First Class John J. Hoyt." I watched Marie's finger open the IV line to the second hanging bottle.

"That isn't your father, Marie," Kate said.

"I'm *not* Marie! My name is Tanner Jean Hoyt and you are trespassing!"

Following the trail of IV tubing, I saw it held no fluid. "Kate! She's killing Dad. You've got to pull that IV now!"

Marie aimed the 45mm pistol at my father's head.

Kate froze, staring helplessly with her gun drawn.

Marie pressed the barrel to his temple. "Drop your weapon, Officer Frost."

"You first, counselor."

I saw my sister steady the gun ready to fire.

"We can stand here all day, but your father doesn't have that luxury. He'll be dead in minutes."

Suddenly a tall figure stepped from the shadows and aimed a Glock at the back of Marie's head. It fired. She never flinched, but I saw Tanner jump and roll from Marie's body.

Joe Sumner offered me his familiar off-centered grin, and a

mock salute. "Go get 'em, Linz," was all he said.

I saluted back in honor of our last time together. Our eyes met briefly and I didn't have to speak the words I'd longed to say for so many years. It became suddenly clear that I'd been wrong to think I'd failed him and needed his forgiveness. It was a risk that came with the job that we both loved so well, and the chips could have fallen the other way too easily. As it turned out, he'd taken his loss with dignity. I saw that now. It wasn't my fault.

With that, the Glock faded from his hands, and his form followed shortly, the smile never leaving his face.

Marie had become dazed, dropping the gun to cradle her head. Dried blood caked her neck and I saw one of her ears had been badly torn.

It was the diversion Kate needed. She tackled Marie, and hit her hard in the face. Relief filled me when she yanked the IV needle from my father's arm.

Then a piercing scream signaled Tanner's attack. "You ruined everything! I'll give you a personal escort to hell, Frost!"

Her head butted mine and we both went down. I left my shield wide open for her reach while I yanked hard at her AR15, tearing it from her fingers. When she came at me I landed a thrust kick into her face, knocking her back hard.

Without her tag, her strength waned, and I watched her form fade as she attempted to come at me again. Suddenly she stopped, crawling on all fours to her father's skeleton.

"I'm sorry, Daddy." She sounded like a wounded child. "I never made you proud. Forgive me . . ."

What happened next surpassed every horror flick I'd ever seen, turning my ghostly knees to pudding.

The skeleton's lower jaw began to move, making a grating sound. The yellowed teeth clacked together like loose dentures and I heard John Hoyt speak one last time to his daughter.

"The tour has ended for both of us. Time to put down our weapons and leave this place for good."

Tanner's eyes widened. She crawled to his side, laying her head against his sunken chest.

I saw Sally O'Shannon in the corner, offering a thumbs-up and I knew she'd used her mimic skills to lure Tanner to eternity.

As Tanner wept beside her father's bones, she began to fade. I clutched her weapon tight, watching her form lose its definition and vanish completely. It was finally over.

A sudden gunshot blast filled the small space within the shelter and I saw Kate fall back.

Marie straddled Kate's body, gun shaking in her pale hands. "I won't get my reward now. You took away my reward!"

I heard the shelter door open and a series of frantic footsteps descending the stairs.

Seeing several guns pointed in her direction, Marie dropped her weapon and curled into fetal position.

Copley cuffed her, as Alvarez dropped down beside Kate.

"Officer down!" he yelled into his shoulder radio. "Get a bus here quick!"

The surreal scene moved in slow motion. First, Alvarez felt for a pulse, and started CPR. No one spoke as he worked his hardest to bring her back.

I watched the most beautiful light shoot upward from my sister's body and I recognized her spirit.

Her form became clearer with each passing second, and I knew Alvarez was too late.

"Kate?" I spoke softly beside her. "Can you see me?"

"Yeah. Why?"

"Uh, listen, there's something you should know."

She turned to see Alvarez bent over her body, attempting to force the life back into her.

"Linz?" Her eyes questioned me.

I wanted to hug her and tell her it would be okay, but the anger in her expression told me to back off.

"That bitch killed me? After all we went through, she wins?"

"You're not alone," I said, trying to comfort her.

"That's unacceptable. I'm going back." She headed toward her body.

If it were only that simple.

Alvarez stopped his efforts briefly, cradling her blonde head in his lap. His face had lost all expression. He looked old and tired, stroking her cheek.

"Come back to me, Kate. Please come back."

Kate's spirit began to fade before me, a brief look of panic etched on her face. "What's happening?" she wanted to know.

Not seeing a tag, I feared she might be going on to the next level. Suddenly her spirit vanished completely, and I saw her body give a sudden jerk in Alvarez's arms.

He felt her neck, yelling, "Get the medic down here now! She has a pulse!"

Chapter Forty-Seven

A couple of weeks later, Kate seemed to have recovered nicely after her near-death experience, although we both knew it had been closer than *near*. She didn't seem ready to talk about it, but I had plenty of time to wait. An eternity.

I met Kate at the softball park to watch Richard play. She still moved a bit slow from the surgery to remove the bullet, but her enthusiasm had stayed intact. She couldn't wait to get back on the job and on with life.

I finally relaxed, knowing Tanner's AR15 was secured with Mike. Sally confirmed my suspicions that as long as Tanner's tag stayed out of her reach, she had no chance of coming back.

Kate sat beside Alvarez on the bleachers, waiting for Richard's turn at bat. They made a nice couple, but I stopped myself when I started picturing their children. Patience is a virtue I don't have, so I reminded myself that for now it would have to be enough to know that they looked truly happy. The rest would fall into place.

As for me, I guess I'm destined to remain a hopeless romantic—meaning, my chances of romance seem hopeless. Mike makes an occasional appearance, but I don't get the initial vibe I used to get from him. Truthfully, I'm not ready. Maybe I never will be.

When Alvarez made his way toward the concession stand, I caught Kate's attention from near the batter's box. Waiting for her, I watched the teams play to the best of their abilities, thinking they aren't any different from the general population, with the exception of their attitudes. These special kids had dreams, goals, and struggles, and somehow managed to rise above their challenges with a positive, happy outlook. I thought of Tanner Jean Hoyt, and how she never had the challenges these kids had, yet she'd still had no chance at all. Her father had snuffed out any hope of a normal, happy childhood—instead creating a machine-like warrior unable to feel anything but hate.

"Hey, Linz." Kate stayed hidden by the batter's box.

"How'd everything turn out with Marie?" I asked.

"She's shaken, but will probably recover enough to enter an insanity plea."

"That's no stretch, although it rarely works."

"You'll be glad to hear that the newspaper is retracting its statement. It'll help heal some of the wounds Marie caused."

"Don't forget she had help."

"You don't feel sorry for her, do you?"

"In a way," I said honestly. "She was just as much a victim as I was. Without Tanner, I don't think her feelings for me would have come to all this."

We both glanced over at Alvarez, who was placing his order at the stand, and I changed the subject. "So?"

She raised a blonde eyebrow. "So, what?"

"Alvarez. What happened with his wife?"

"Oh, that." Her freckles blended into a blush. "It seems I got the signals crossed, and the dinner and flowers had nothing to do with love rekindled. The dinner turned out to be a get-together with the kids for her birthday, and the flowers were from the boys. Harmless. I feel like such an ass."

"It had me fooled, too, Kate."

"We've decided to take things slow. He still has a lot of things to hash out with her over the boys. Of course, Mom wants to meet him. I swear I saw a banquet hall list on her kitchen bulletin board the other day."

"She'll be busy for a while taking care of Dad."

My father had been released from the hospital the day after Marie's capture. He'd suffered minor cuts and bruising but nothing permanent.

Kate chuckled. "Yeah, he's already asking about his Purple Heart."

"So what are your plans now?" I asked as a foul ball hit the fence.

"What would you say to me keeping your house?" she asked.

"I'd like that very much," I grinned. As much as I hated to part with it, I had no choice. With Kate living there, I wouldn't feel like I'd lost everything.

She started to say something, then hesitated, brushing dirt from her grubby tennis shoes.

I saved her the trouble. "And?"

"I'm wondering what you thought about my performance? You never came out and said anything."

Now *I* felt like an ass. In all the excitement, I'd never even bothered to thank her. Kate's determination, perseverance, and gut instincts had been the reason we'd solved it at all. And so I told her that.

Her cheeks flushed with new excitement. "I'm glad you feel that way, because I'm applying for the detective position they posted."

A pang of remorse filled me when I realized it was my old position.

I quickly pushed past it, saying, "You've earned it. I'm really proud of you."

Her smile warmed me. "Yeah, me, too."

"We made a good team, don't you think?"

"I had my doubts at first, but we did fine." She watched the game a moment, then asked, "Remember when you told me about your tag and moving on to the next level?"

I did. I also knew what her next question would be. "Yes I do. And no I don't."

She wrinkled her blonde brows, annoyed that I'd jumped ahead. Guess our competition would never die completely. "What the hell does that mean?"

"I remember the conversation, but I don't plan to give up my tag and move on. I'm not ready."

"Do you have a choice now that your issue has been resolved?"

"Which one? I'm a complicated girl. Ask my therapist."

"Your murder," she said.

"I'm not so sure that was my real concern. After all, I'm still here, so to speak."

"Maybe it's not about resolving past problems at all. Could be you've just been called to another job."

"You mean my passing was a conspiracy by fate to get me to work on the other side? Why me?"

"The master plan. You know, the one that no one seems to understand except God?"

"Thanks for believing I'm so special, but I don't agree. What I *do* know for certain is that we make a hellluva team, and since I don't appear to be going anywhere I think we should consider making it permanent."

"Just what the department needs, two Detective Frosts." She grinned. "Poor Gerard."

I nodded toward the bleachers, seeing Alvarez headed that way juggling two sodas and a large container of popcorn. "You'd better get back before he sees you talking to yourself behind the batter's box. It might be a relationship killer."

"Oh look," she said, pointing, "Richard is up to bat." She clutched the fence and called out like a softball mom, "Go get 'em Richard! Outta the park!"

Richard squinted in the bright sun to see her, then saluted and grinned.

The pitch came fast and low. Richard waited.

My ethereal stomach twisted into knots as the pitcher wound up again.

Richard swung this time, missing by centimeters.

"Strike one!" called the umpire.

Kate called out, "Hit it for Lindsay, Richard!"

He pounded the bat a couple of times on the plate at his feet, then raised his chin high. "This one's for Yinsay!"

He swung hard and I heard the loud crack of bat kissing ball. It sailed high over the center outfielder's reach, landing a few feet behind him.

Richard rounded the bases heading for home as both sides of the crowded bleachers jumped up cheering. His teammates tore at the batter's fence in a wild display of encouragement. I couldn't help running to home plate to meet him, even though he'd never see me. It was a moment I promised I'd never miss.

As Richard neared home, I saw the exhilaration on his face, the fierce determination in his eyes, and I knew he and I had accomplished the wonderful dream of beating the odds.

ABOUT THE AUTHOR

Scarlett Dean has been a true horror and mystery fan since childhood, always creating her own dark worlds and characters for fun. As a full-time author, she has three published novels and has published her own quarterly fiction magazine. She enjoys motivational speaking to promote the gift of writing. Scarlett lives in Northwest Indiana and is currently at work on her next novel.

For more, see www.scarlettdean.com.